RUGRATS™

VOLUME ONE

kaboom!™

COVER BY
JORGE CORONA

DESIGNER
JILLIAN CRAB

ASSOCIATE EDITOR
MATTHEW LEVINE

EDITOR
WHITNEY LEOPARD

SPECIAL THANKS TO **JOAN HILTY, LINDA LEE, JAMES SALERNO, ALEXANDRA MAURER** AND THE WONDERFUL TEAM AT **NICKELODEON**

kaboom!™ **nickelodeon**™

RUGRATS Volume One, May 2018. Published by KaBOOM!, a division of Boom Entertainment, Inc. © 2018 Viacom International Inc. All Rights Reserved. Nickelodeon, Rugrats and all related titles, logos, and characters are trademarks of Viacom International Inc. Originally published in single magazine form as RUGRATS No. 1-4. © 2017, 2018 Viacom International Inc. Created by Klasky Csupo. KaBOOM! and the KaBOOM! logo are trademarks of Boom Entertainment, Inc., registered in various countries and categories. All characters, events, and institutions depicted herein are fictional. Any similarity between any of the names, characters, persons, events, and/or institutions in this publication to actual names, characters, and persons, whether living or dead, events, and/or institutions is unintended and purely coincidental. KaBOOM! does not read or accept unsolicited submissions of ideas, stories, or artwork.

For information regarding the CPSIA on this printed material, call: (203) 595-3636 and provide reference #RICH – 779494.

BOOM! Studios, 5670 Wilshire Boulevard, Suite 400, Los Angeles, CA 90036-5679. Printed in USA. First Printing.

ISBN: 978-1-68415-176-9, eISBN: 978-1-61398-991-3

WRITTEN BY
BOX BROWN

ILLUSTRATED BY
LISA DuBOIS

CHAPTER THREE INKS BY
CAROLYN NOWAK

**"DESPERATELY
SEEKING CYNTHIA"**

WRITTEN BY
PRANAS T. NAUJOKAITIS

ILLUSTRATED BY
JORGE MONLONGO

COLORS BY
ELEONORA BRUNI

LETTERS BY
JIM CAMPBELL

CHAPTER ONE

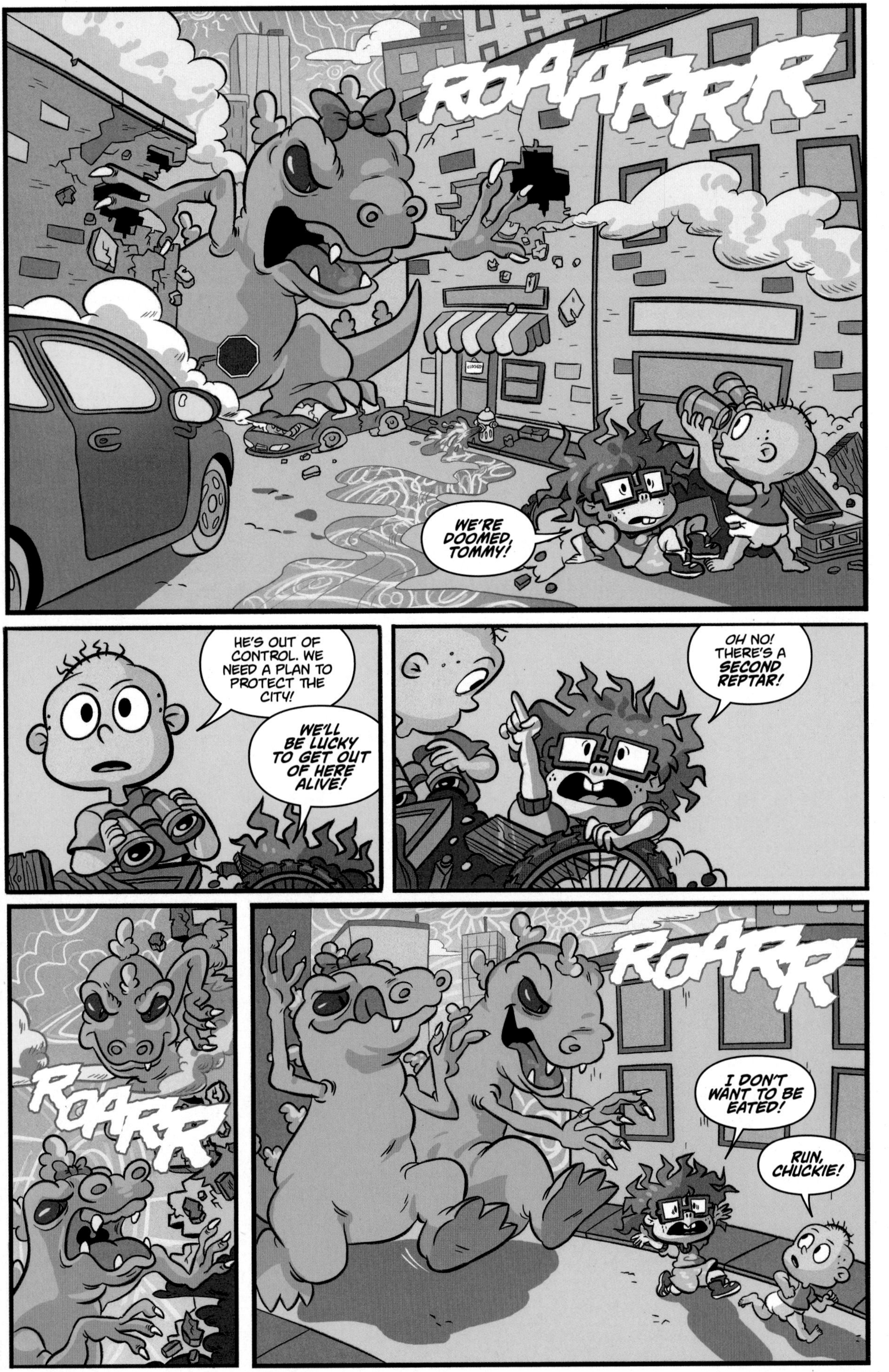
ROAAARRR
WE'RE DOOMED, TOMMY!
HE'S OUT OF CONTROL. WE NEED A PLAN TO PROTECT THE CITY!
WE'LL BE LUCKY TO GET OUT OF HERE ALIVE!
OH NO! THERE'S A SECOND REPTAR!
ROARR
ROARR
I DON'T WANT TO BE EATED!
RUN, CHUCKIE!

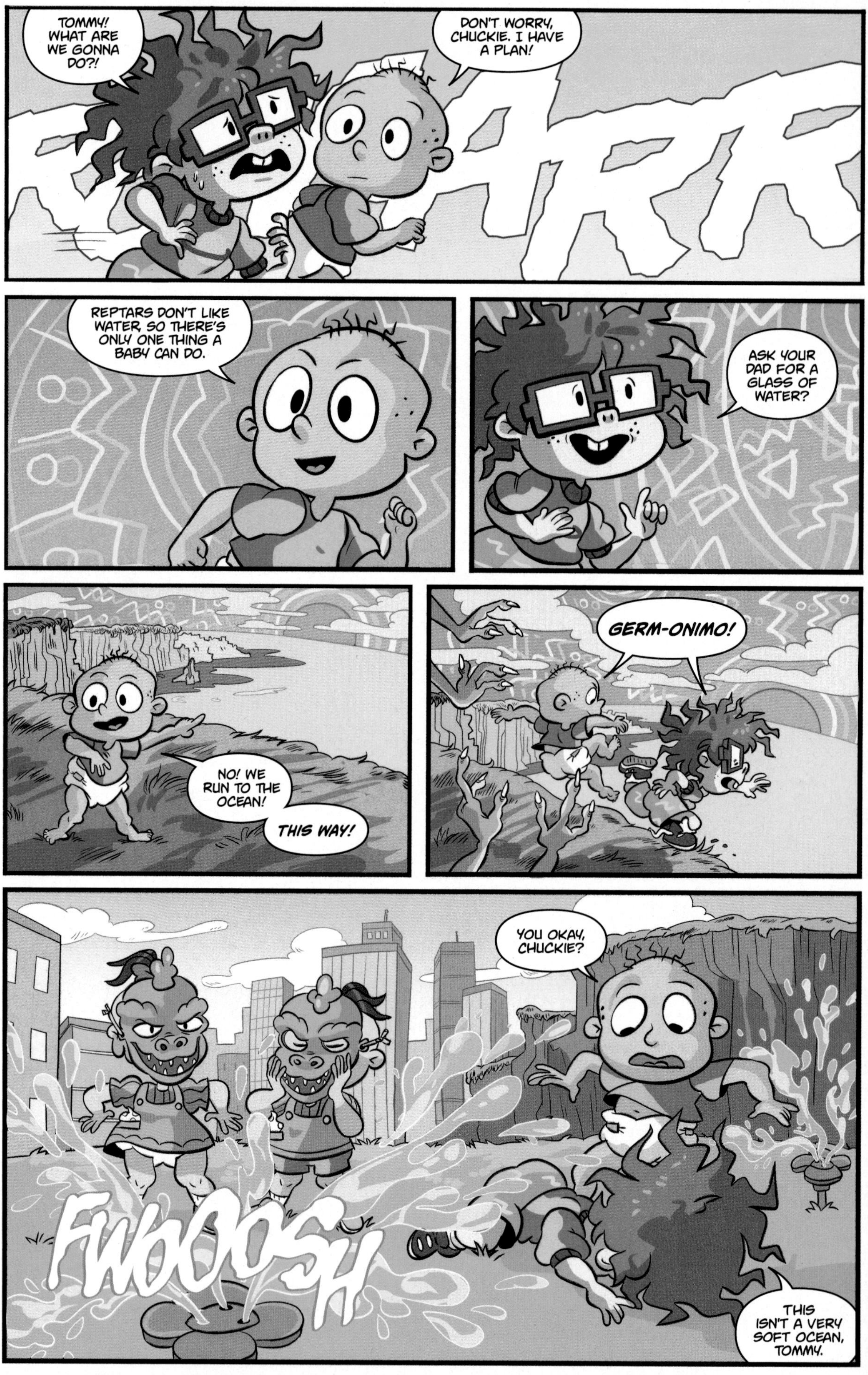

TOMMY! WHAT ARE WE GONNA DO?!
DON'T WORRY, CHUCKIE. I HAVE A PLAN!
RRR
REPTARS DON'T LIKE WATER, SO THERE'S ONLY ONE THING A BABY CAN DO.
ASK YOUR DAD FOR A GLASS OF WATER?
NO! WE RUN TO THE OCEAN!
THIS WAY!
GERM-ONIMO!
YOU OKAY, CHUCKIE?
FWOOOSH
THIS ISN'T A VERY SOFT OCEAN, TOMMY.

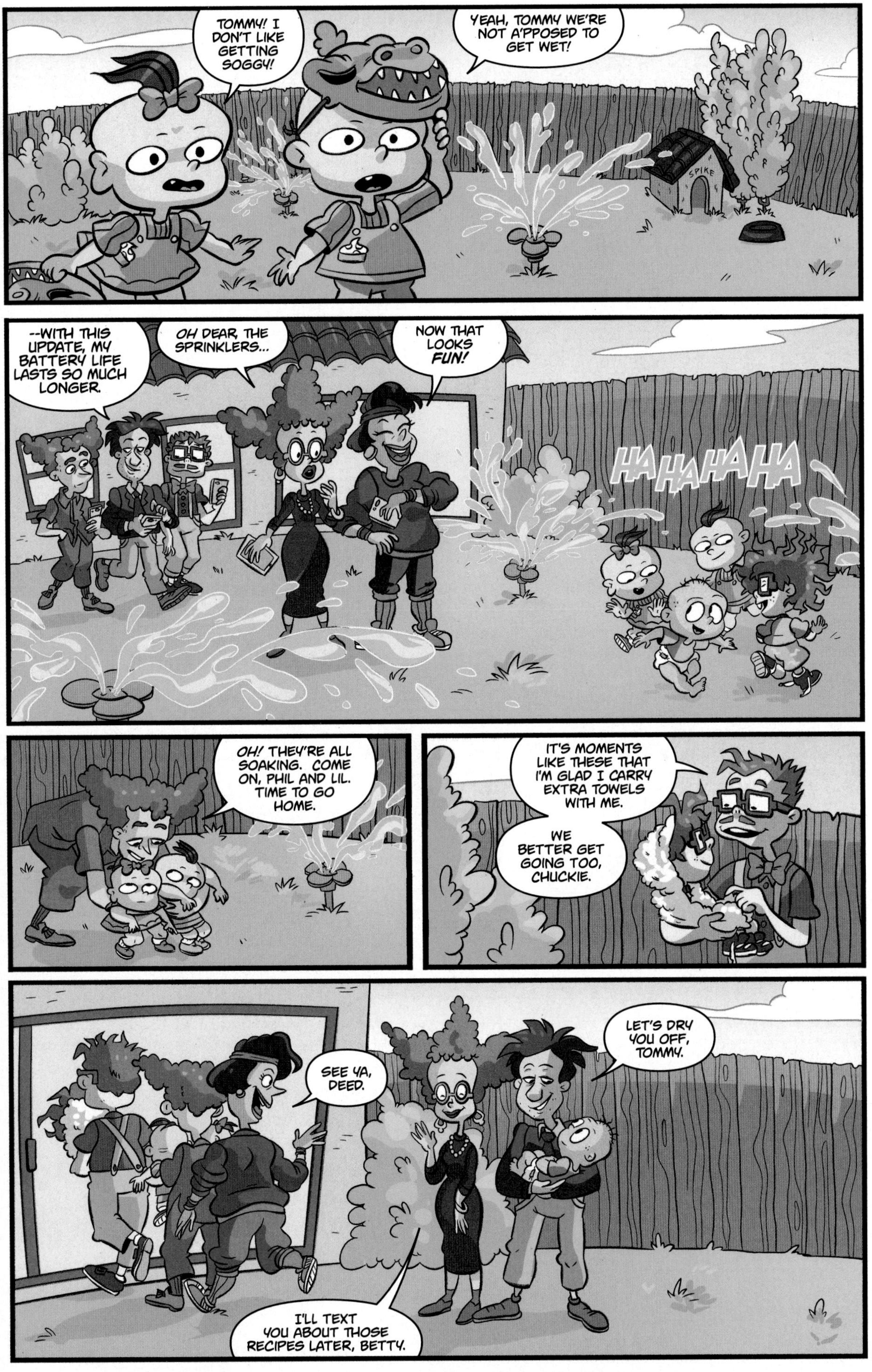
TOMMY! I DON'T LIKE GETTING SOGGY!
YEAH, TOMMY WE'RE NOT A'PPOSED TO GET WET!
SPIKE
--WITH THIS UPDATE, MY BATTERY LIFE LASTS SO MUCH LONGER.
OH DEAR, THE SPRINKLERS...
NOW THAT LOOKS FUN!
HAHAHAHA
OH! THEY'RE ALL SOAKING. COME ON, PHIL AND LIL. TIME TO GO HOME.
IT'S MOMENTS LIKE THESE THAT I'M GLAD I CARRY EXTRA TOWELS WITH ME.
WE BETTER GET GOING TOO, CHUCKIE.
SEE YA, DEED.
LET'S DRY YOU OFF, TOMMY.
I'LL TEXT YOU ABOUT THOSE RECIPES LATER, BETTY.

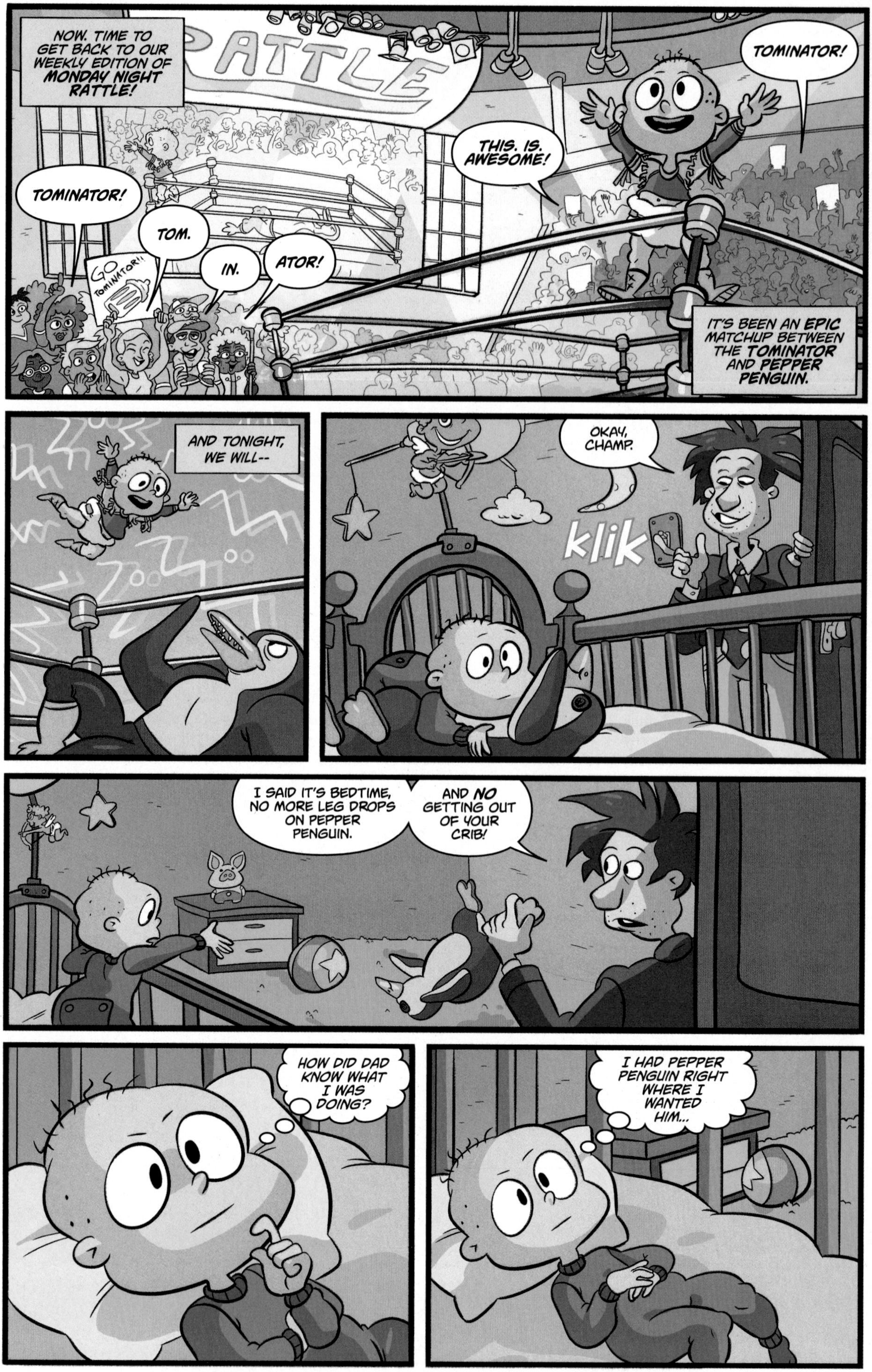
NOW. TIME TO GET BACK TO OUR WEEKLY EDITION OF MONDAY NIGHT RATTLE!
RATTLE
TOMINATOR!
THIS. IS. AWESOME!
TOMINATOR!
TOM.
IN.
ATOR!
GO TOMINATOR!!
IT'S BEEN AN EPIC MATCHUP BETWEEN THE TOMINATOR AND PEPPER PENGUIN.
AND TONIGHT, WE WILL--
OKAY, CHAMP.
klik
I SAID IT'S BEDTIME, NO MORE LEG DROPS ON PEPPER PENGUIN.
AND NO GETTING OUT OF YOUR CRIB!
HOW DID DAD KNOW WHAT I WAS DOING?
I HAD PEPPER PENGUIN RIGHT WHERE I WANTED HIM...

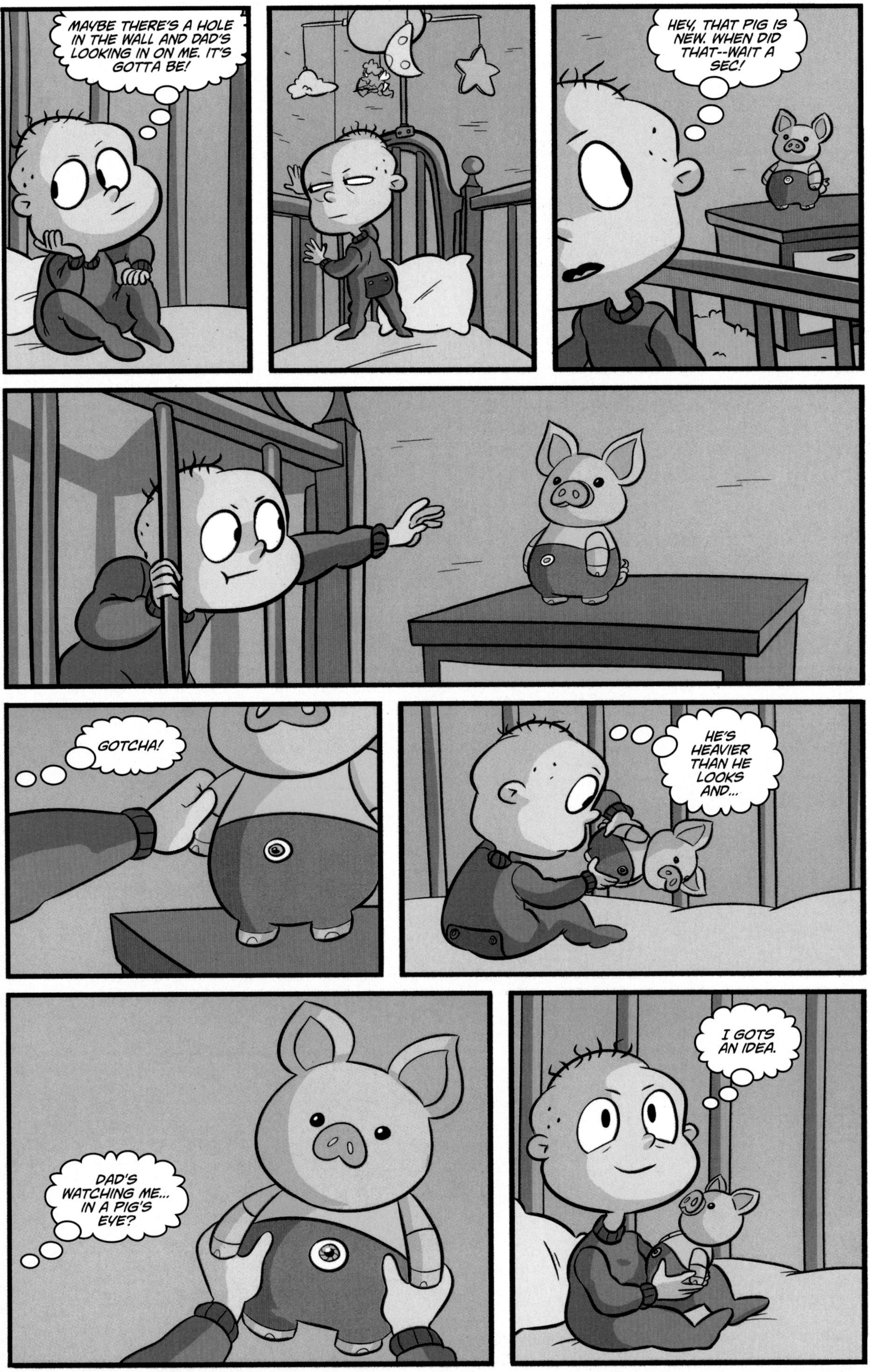
MAYBE THERE'S A HOLE IN THE WALL AND DAD'S LOOKING IN ON ME. IT'S GOTTA BE!
HEY, THAT PIG IS NEW. WHEN DID THAT--WAIT A SEC!
GOTCHA!
HE'S HEAVIER THAN HE LOOKS AND...
DAD'S WATCHING ME... IN A PIG'S EYE?
I GOTS AN IDEA.

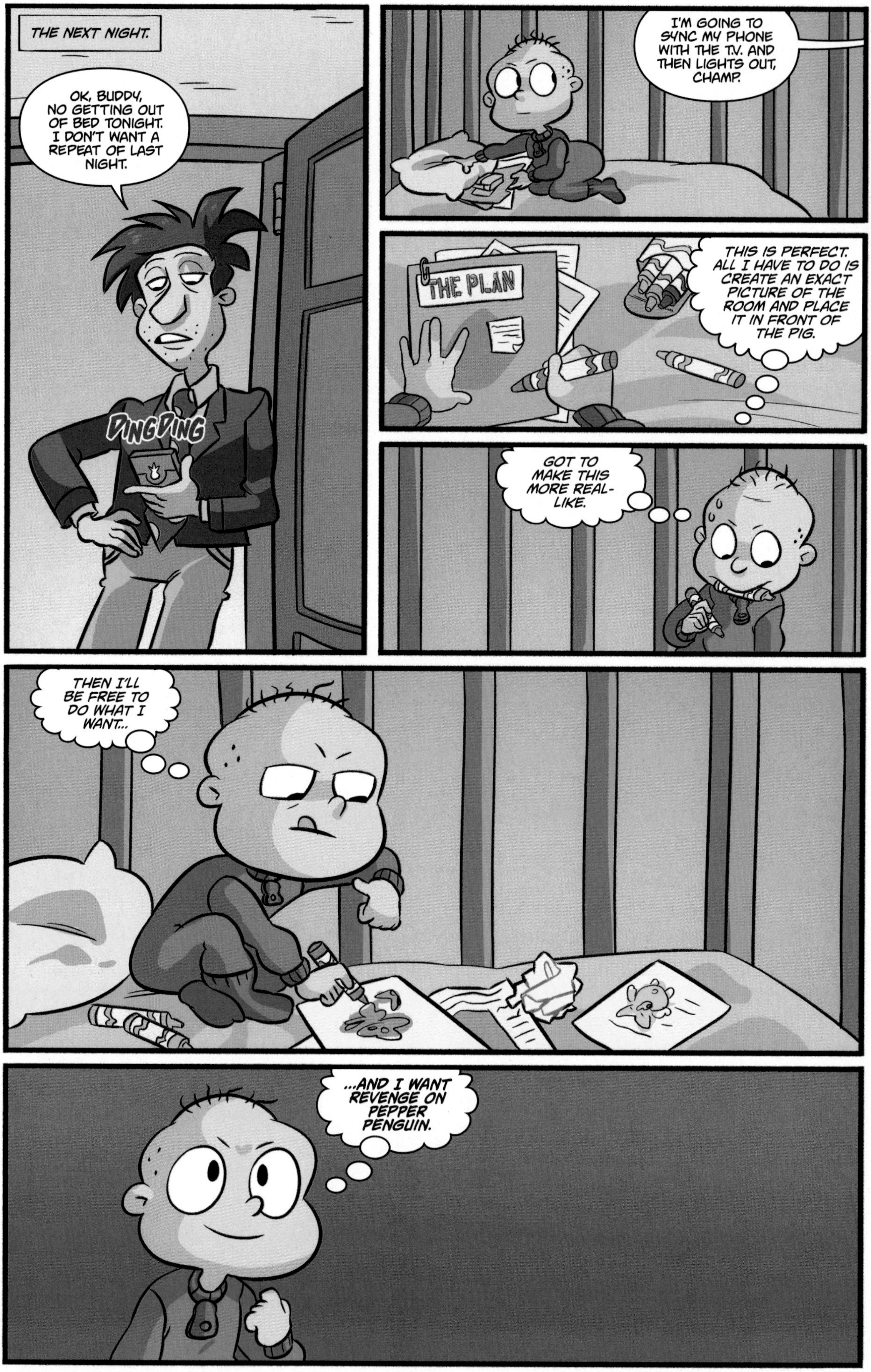
THE NEXT NIGHT.
OK, BUDDY, NO GETTING OUT OF BED TONIGHT. I DON'T WANT A REPEAT OF LAST NIGHT.
DING DING
I'M GOING TO SYNC MY PHONE WITH THE T.V. AND THEN LIGHTS OUT, CHAMP.
THE PLAN
THIS IS PERFECT. ALL I HAVE TO DO IS CREATE AN EXACT PICTURE OF THE ROOM AND PLACE IT IN FRONT OF THE PIG.
GOT TO MAKE THIS MORE REAL-LIKE.
THEN I'LL BE FREE TO DO WHAT I WANT...
...AND I WANT REVENGE ON PEPPER PENGUIN.

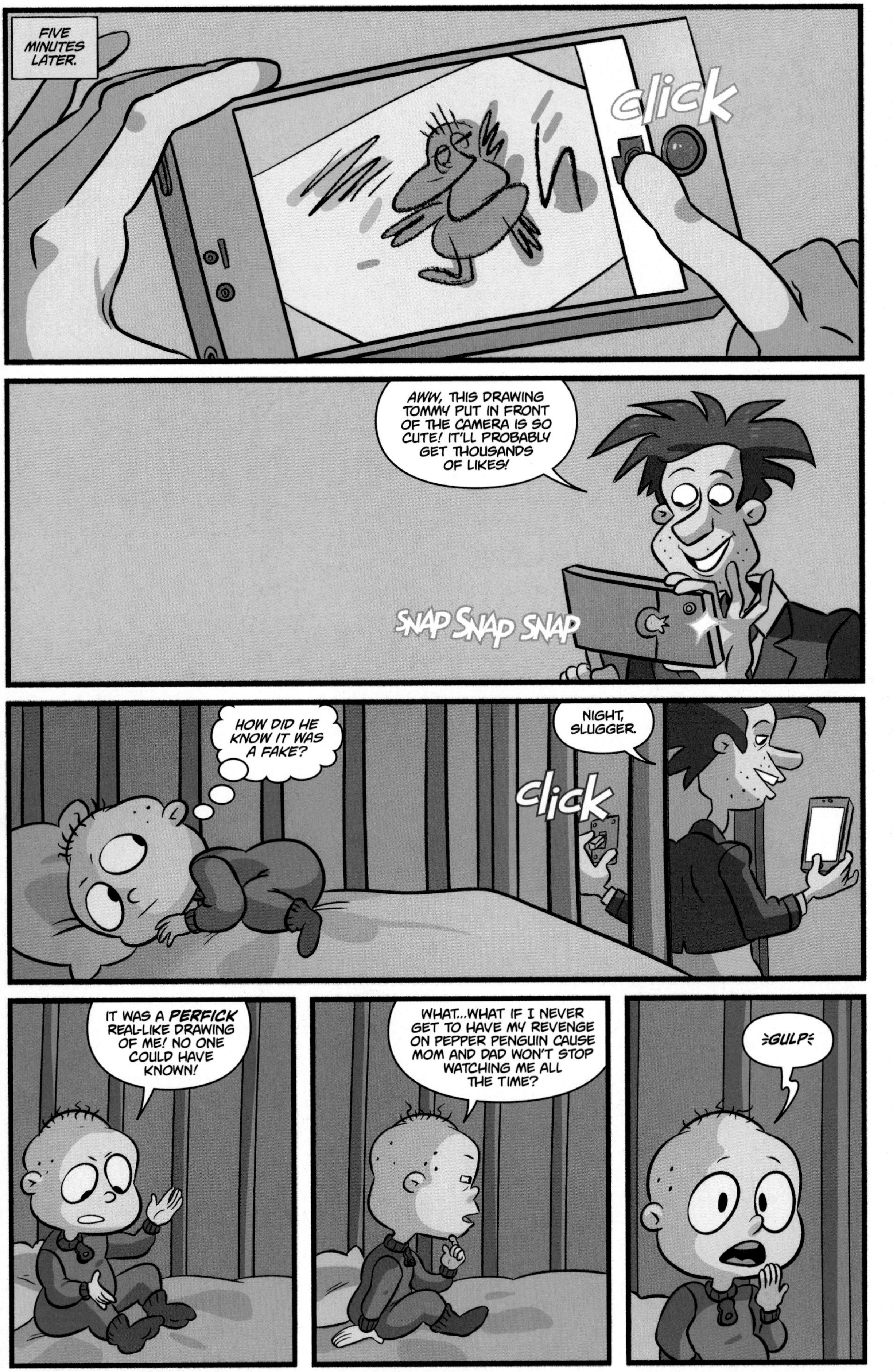
FIVE MINUTES LATER.
click
AWW, THIS DRAWING TOMMY PUT IN FRONT OF THE CAMERA IS SO CUTE! IT'LL PROBABLY GET THOUSANDS OF LIKES!
SNAP SNAP SNAP
HOW DID HE KNOW IT WAS A FAKE?
NIGHT, SLUGGER.
click
IT WAS A PERFICK REAL-LIKE DRAWING OF ME! NO ONE COULD HAVE KNOWN!
WHAT...WHAT IF I NEVER GET TO HAVE MY REVENGE ON PEPPER PENGUIN CAUSE MOM AND DAD WON'T STOP WATCHING ME ALL THE TIME?
GULP

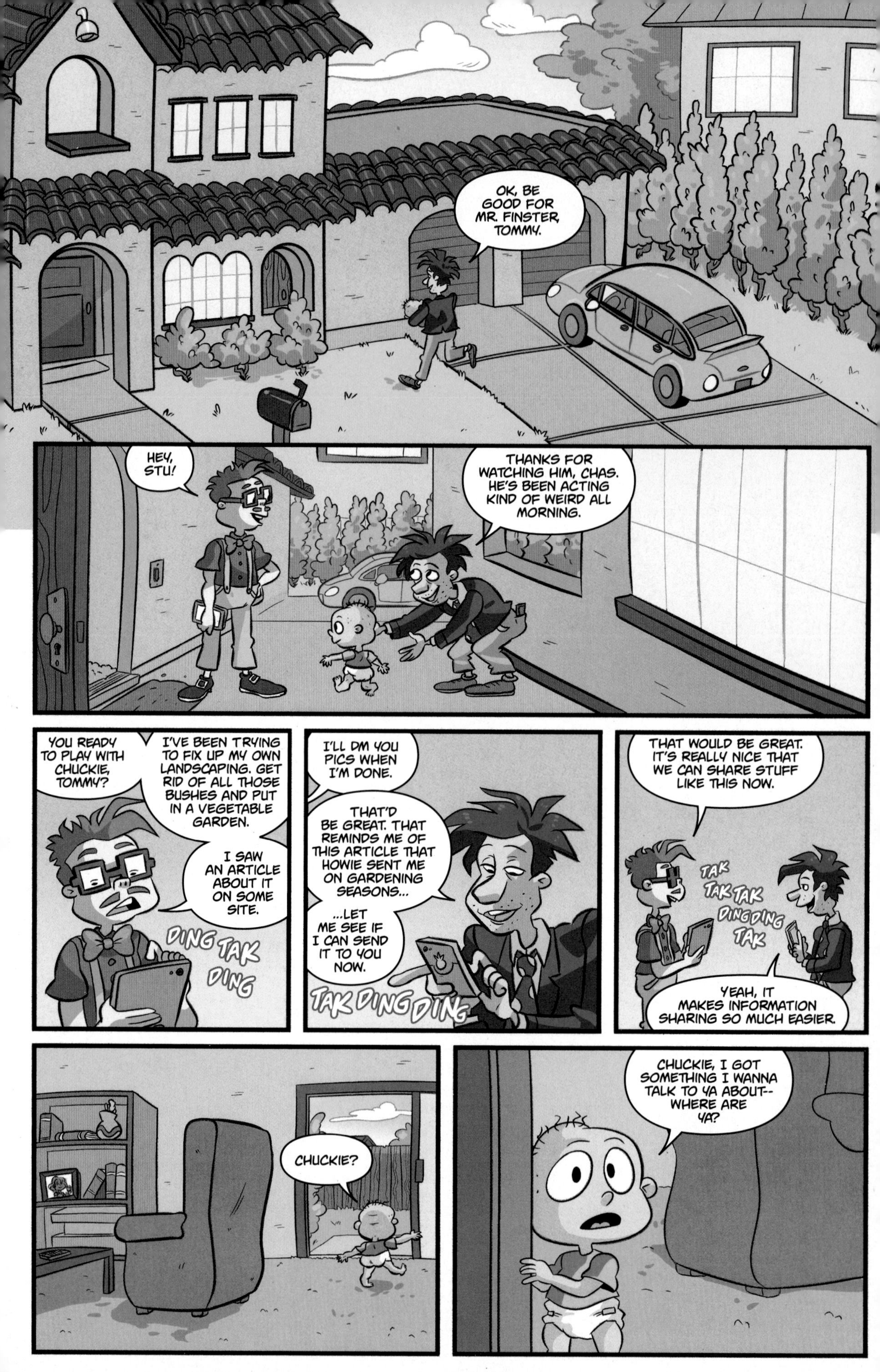
OK, BE GOOD FOR MR. FINSTER, TOMMY.
HEY, STU!
THANKS FOR WATCHING HIM, CHAS. HE'S BEEN ACTING KIND OF WEIRD ALL MORNING.
YOU READY TO PLAY WITH CHUCKIE, TOMMY?
I'VE BEEN TRYING TO FIX UP MY OWN LANDSCAPING. GET RID OF ALL THOSE BUSHES AND PUT IN A VEGETABLE GARDEN.
I SAW AN ARTICLE ABOUT IT ON SOME SITE.
DING TAK DING
I'LL DM YOU PICS WHEN I'M DONE.
THAT'D BE GREAT. THAT REMINDS ME OF THIS ARTICLE THAT HOWIE SENT ME ON GARDENING SEASONS...
...LET ME SEE IF I CAN SEND IT TO YOU NOW.
TAK DING DING
THAT WOULD BE GREAT. IT'S REALLY NICE THAT WE CAN SHARE STUFF LIKE THIS NOW.
TAK TAK TAK DING DING TAK
YEAH, IT MAKES INFORMATION SHARING SO MUCH EASIER.
CHUCKIE?
CHUCKIE, I GOT SOMETHING I WANNA TALK TO YA ABOUT-- WHERE ARE YA?

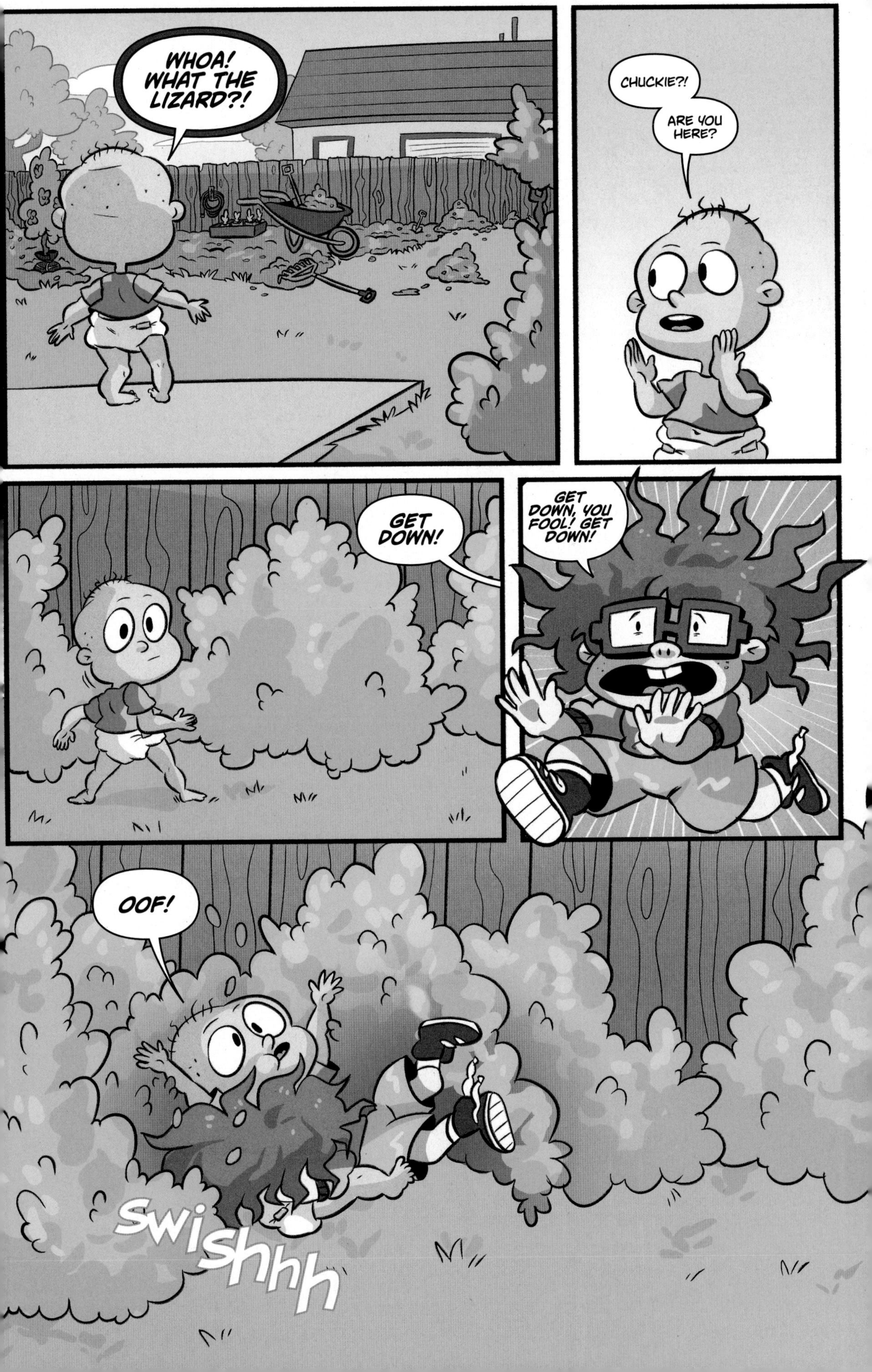
WHOA! WHAT THE LIZARD?!
CHUCKIE?!
ARE YOU HERE?
GET DOWN!
GET DOWN, YOU FOOL! GET DOWN!
OOF!
SWISHHH

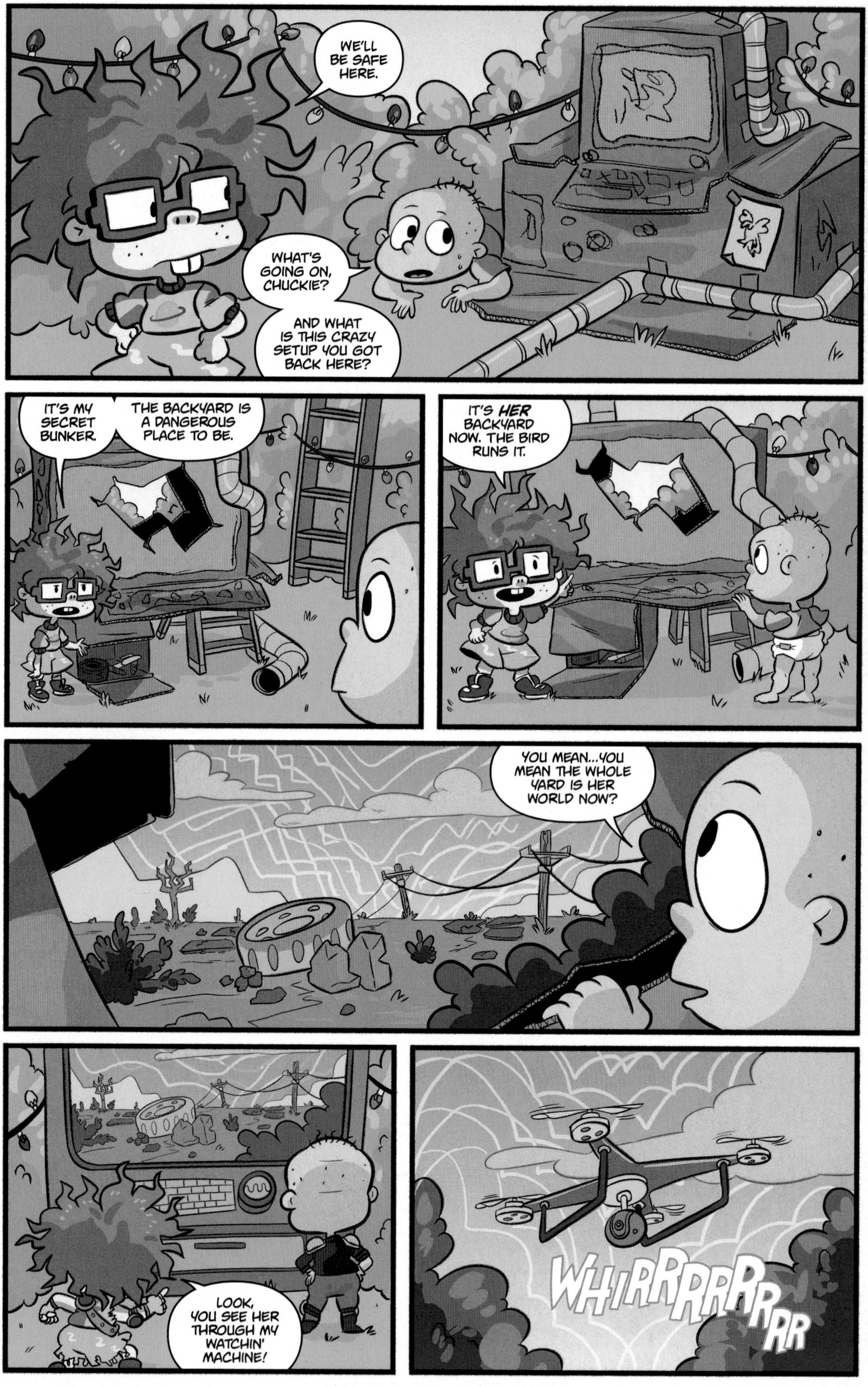
WE'LL BE SAFE HERE.
WHAT'S GOING ON, CHUCKIE?
AND WHAT IS THIS CRAZY SETUP YOU GOT BACK HERE?
IT'S MY SECRET BUNKER.
THE BACKYARD IS A DANGEROUS PLACE TO BE.
IT'S HER BACKYARD NOW. THE BIRD RUNS IT.
YOU MEAN...YOU MEAN THE WHOLE YARD IS HER WORLD NOW?
LOOK, YOU SEE HER THROUGH MY WATCHIN' MACHINE!
WHIRRRRRRRRR

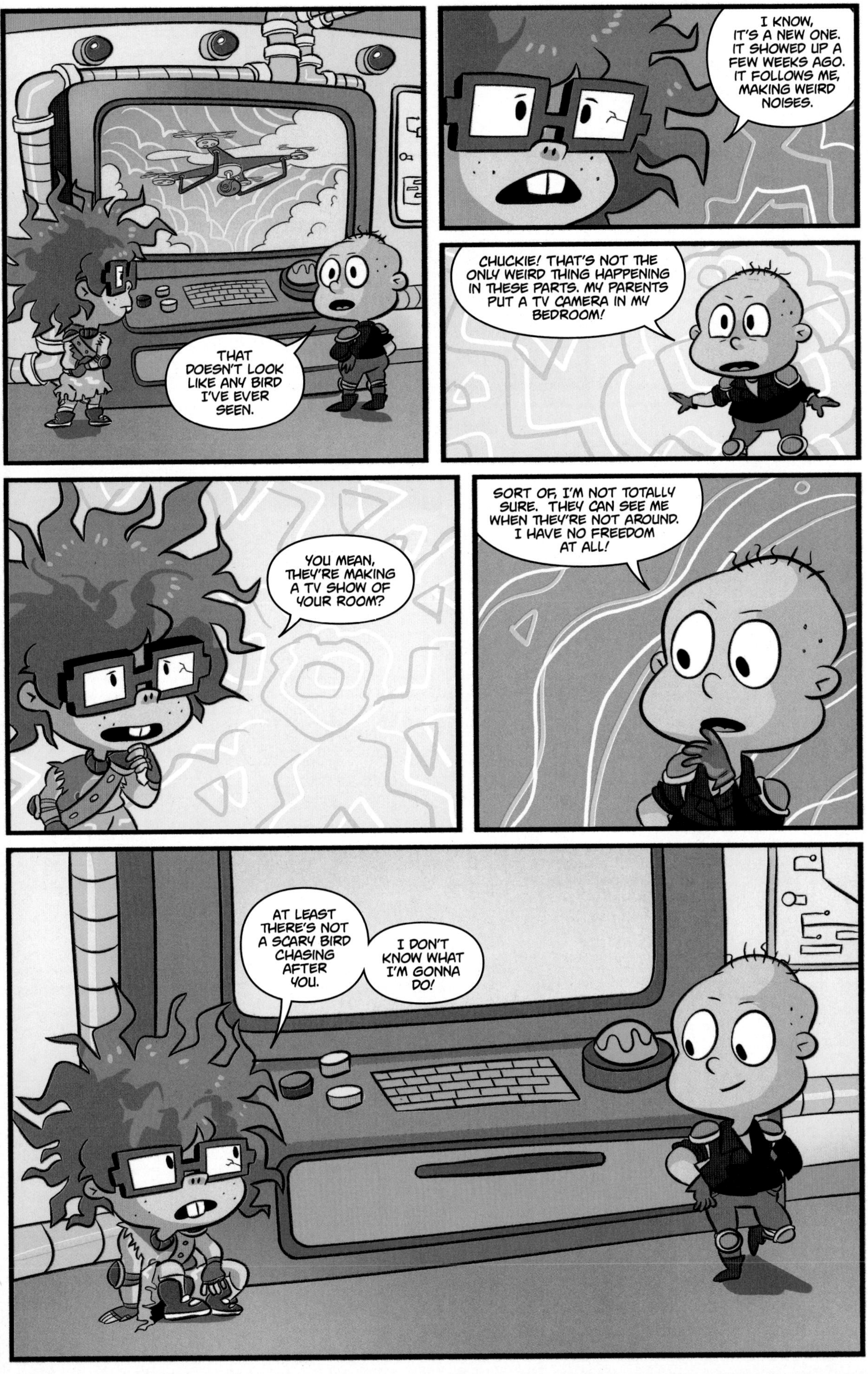
THAT DOESN'T LOOK LIKE ANY BIRD I'VE EVER SEEN.
I KNOW, IT'S A NEW ONE. IT SHOWED UP A FEW WEEKS AGO. IT FOLLOWS ME, MAKING WEIRD NOISES.
CHUCKIE! THAT'S NOT THE ONLY WEIRD THING HAPPENING IN THESE PARTS. MY PARENTS PUT A TV CAMERA IN MY BEDROOM!
YOU MEAN, THEY'RE MAKING A TV SHOW OF YOUR ROOM?
SORT OF, I'M NOT TOTALLY SURE. THEY CAN SEE ME WHEN THEY'RE NOT AROUND. I HAVE NO FREEDOM AT ALL!
AT LEAST THERE'S NOT A SCARY BIRD CHASING AFTER YOU.
I DON'T KNOW WHAT I'M GONNA DO!

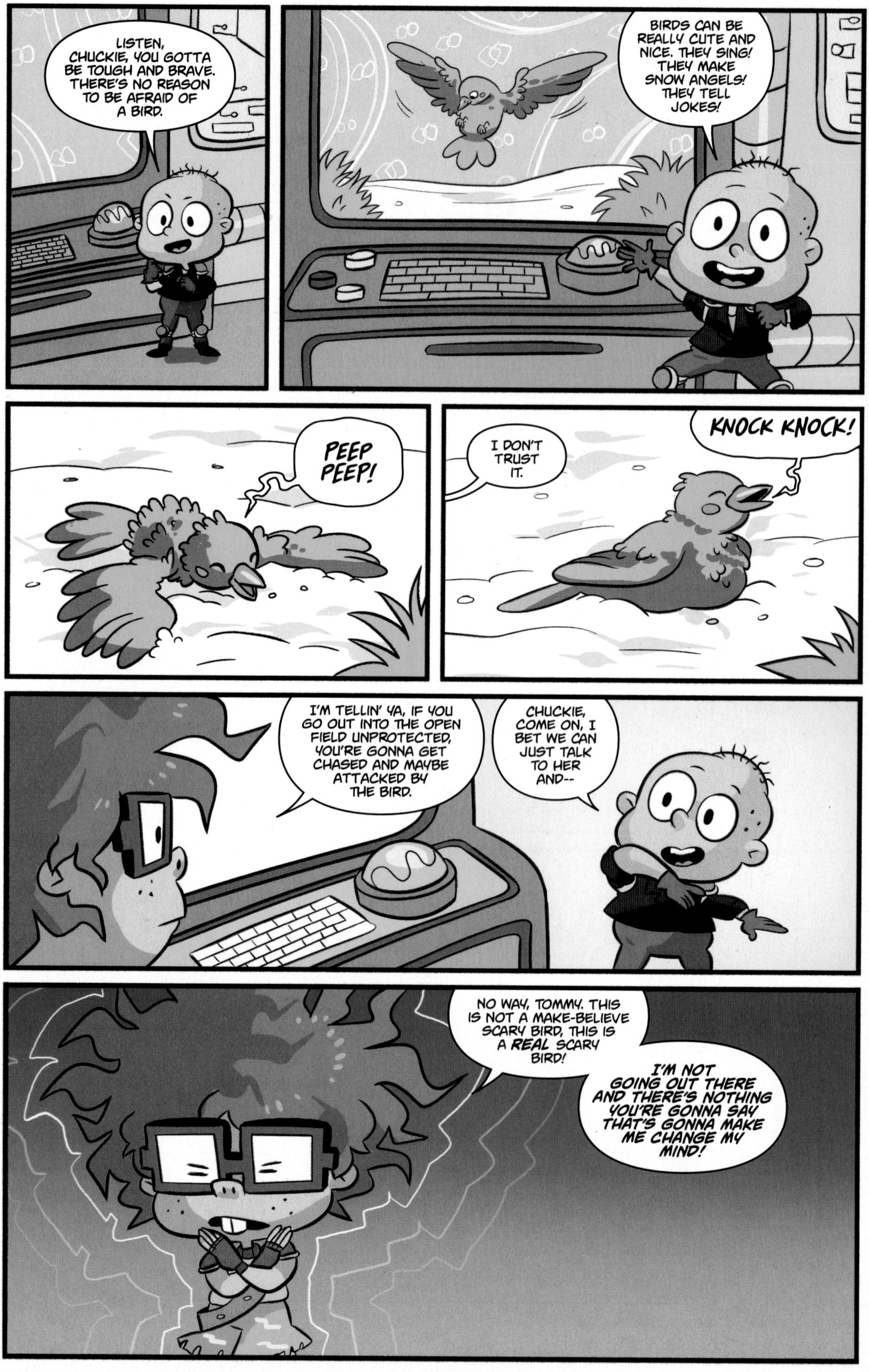
LISTEN, CHUCKIE, YOU GOTTA BE TOUGH AND BRAVE. THERE'S NO REASON TO BE AFRAID OF A BIRD.
BIRDS CAN BE REALLY CUTE AND NICE. THEY SING! THEY MAKE SNOW ANGELS! THEY TELL JOKES!
PEEP PEEP!
I DON'T TRUST IT.
KNOCK KNOCK!
I'M TELLIN' YA, IF YOU GO OUT INTO THE OPEN FIELD UNPROTECTED, YOU'RE GONNA GET CHASED AND MAYBE ATTACKED BY THE BIRD.
CHUCKIE, COME ON, I BET WE CAN JUST TALK TO HER AND--
NO WAY, TOMMY. THIS IS NOT A MAKE-BELIEVE SCARY BIRD, THIS IS A REAL SCARY BIRD!
I'M NOT GOING OUT THERE AND THERE'S NOTHING YOU'RE GONNA SAY THAT'S GONNA MAKE ME CHANGE MY MIND!

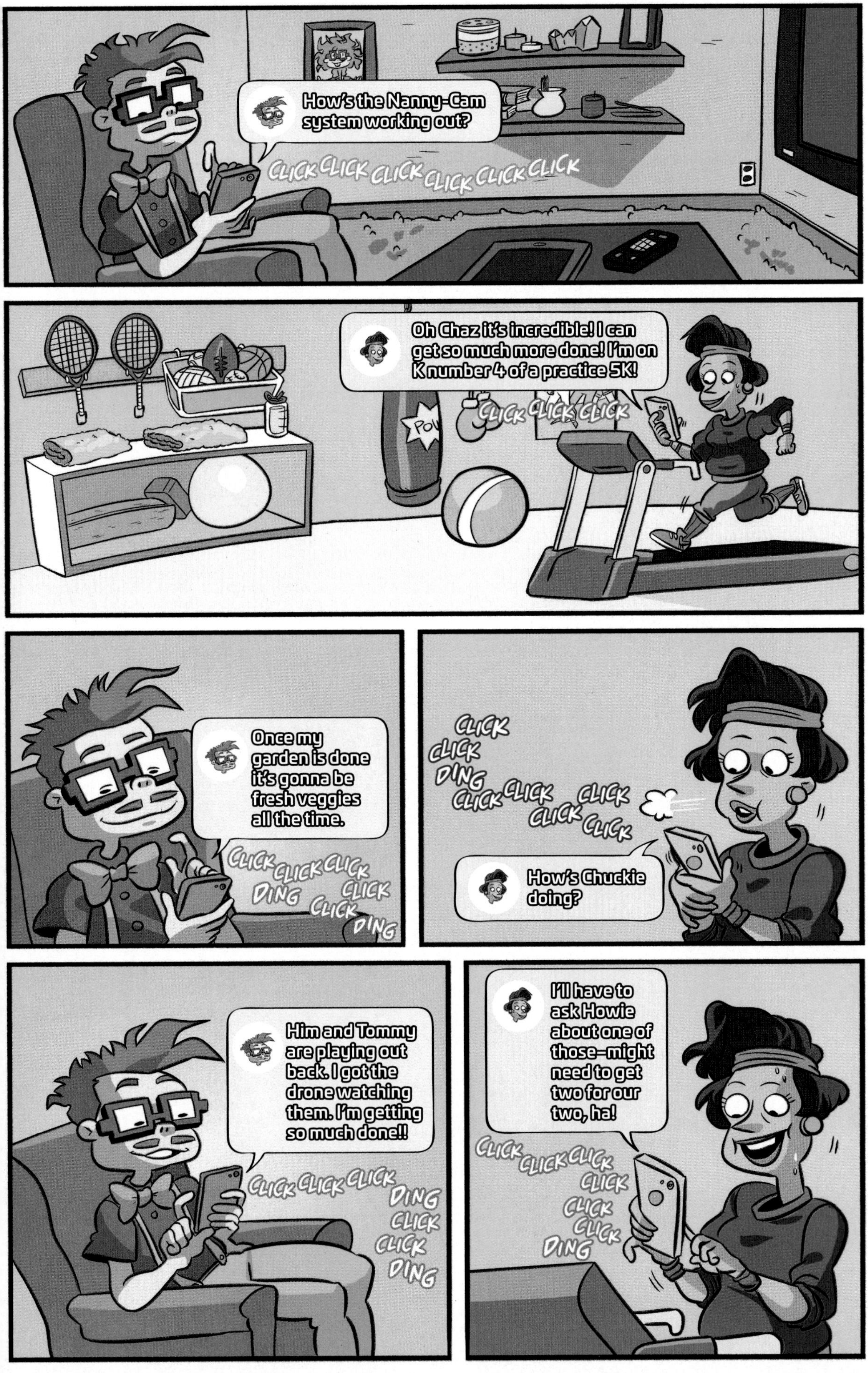
How's the Nanny-Cam system working out?
CLICK CLICK CLICK CLICK CLICK CLICK
Oh Chaz it's incredible! I can get so much more done! I'm on K number 4 of a practice 5K!
CLICK CLICK CLICK
POW
Once my garden is done it's gonna be fresh veggies all the time.
CLICK CLICK CLICK DING CLICK CLICK DING
CLICK CLICK DING CLICK CLICK CLICK CLICK CLICK
How's Chuckie doing?
Him and Tommy are playing out back. I got the drone watching them. I'm getting so much done!!
CLICK CLICK CLICK DING CLICK CLICK DING
I'll have to ask Howie about one of those—might need to get two for our two, ha!
CLICK CLICK CLICK CLICK CLICK CLICK DING

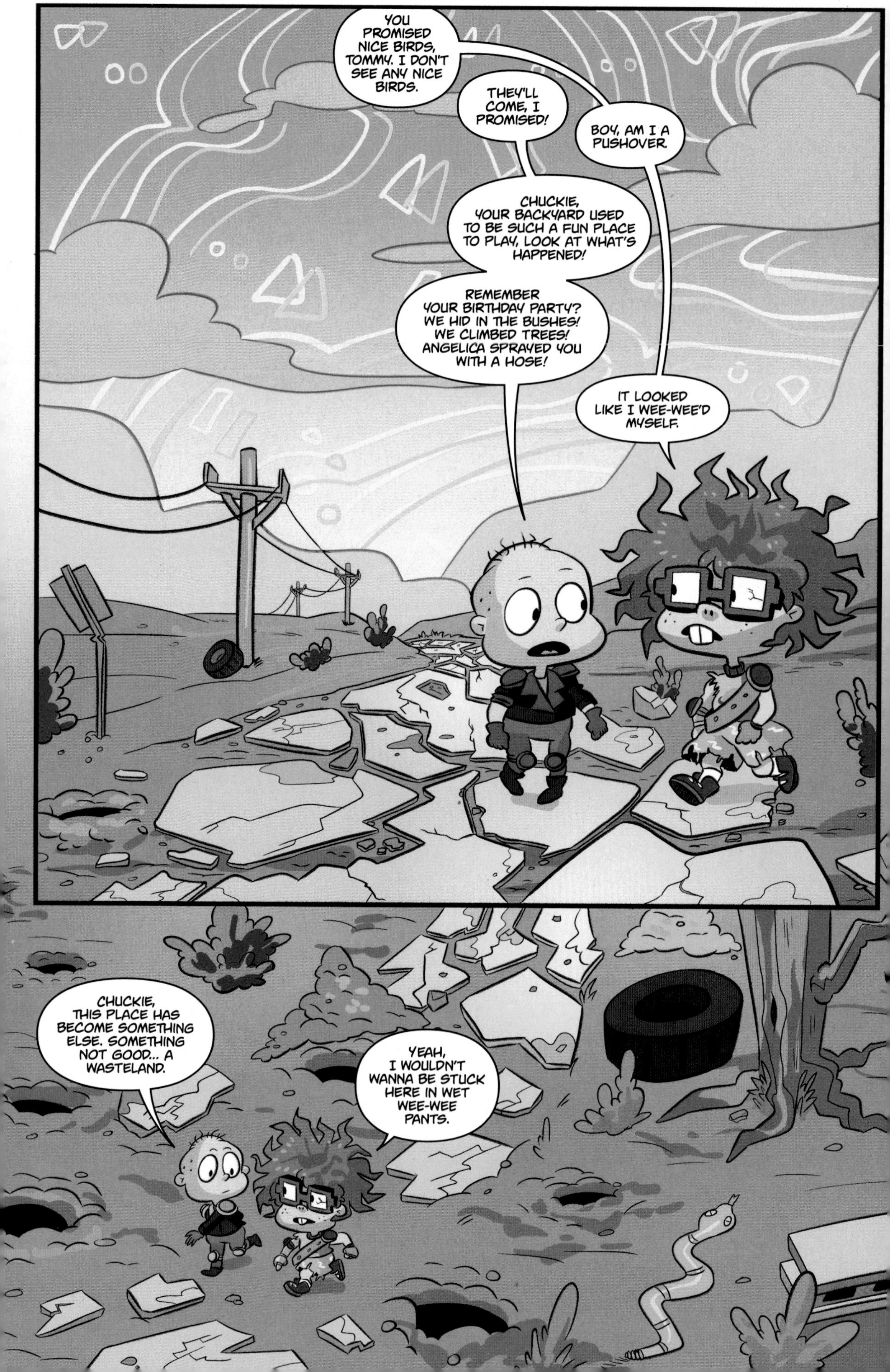
YOU PROMISED NICE BIRDS, TOMMY. I DON'T SEE ANY NICE BIRDS.
THEY'LL COME, I PROMISED!
BOY, AM I A PUSHOVER.
CHUCKIE, YOUR BACKYARD USED TO BE SUCH A FUN PLACE TO PLAY, LOOK AT WHAT'S HAPPENED!
REMEMBER YOUR BIRTHDAY PARTY? WE HID IN THE BUSHES! WE CLIMBED TREES! ANGELICA SPRAYED YOU WITH A HOSE!
IT LOOKED LIKE I WEE-WEE'D MYSELF.
CHUCKIE, THIS PLACE HAS BECOME SOMETHING ELSE. SOMETHING NOT GOOD... A WASTELAND.
YEAH, I WOULDN'T WANNA BE STUCK HERE IN WET WEE-WEE PANTS.

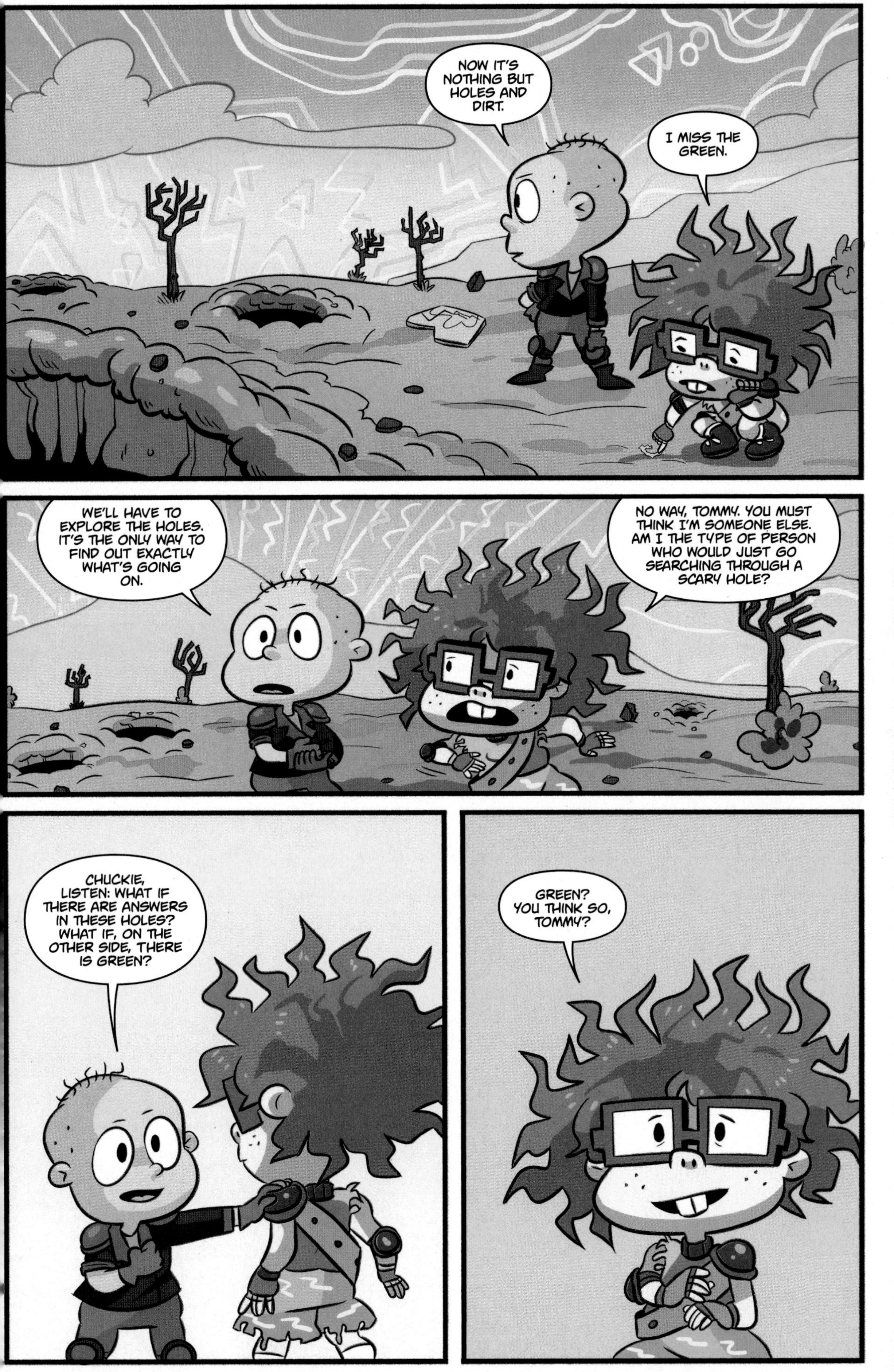
NOW IT'S NOTHING BUT HOLES AND DIRT.
I MISS THE GREEN.
WE'LL HAVE TO EXPLORE THE HOLES. IT'S THE ONLY WAY TO FIND OUT EXACTLY WHAT'S GOING ON.
NO WAY, TOMMY. YOU MUST THINK I'M SOMEONE ELSE. AM I THE TYPE OF PERSON WHO WOULD JUST GO SEARCHING THROUGH A SCARY HOLE?
CHUCKIE, LISTEN: WHAT IF THERE ARE ANSWERS IN THESE HOLES? WHAT IF, ON THE OTHER SIDE, THERE IS GREEN?
GREEN? YOU THINK SO, TOMMY?

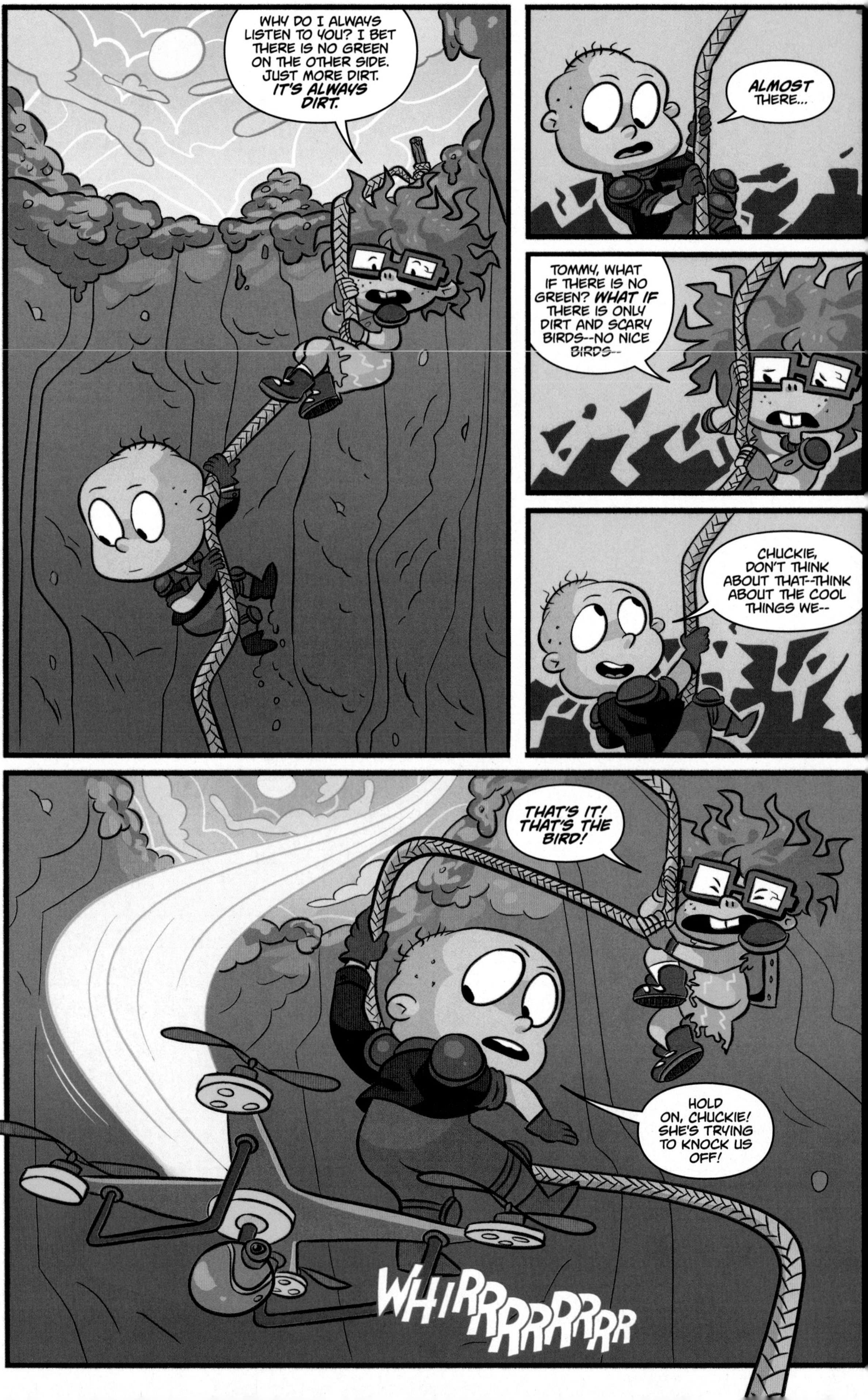
WHY DO I ALWAYS LISTEN TO YOU? I BET THERE IS NO GREEN ON THE OTHER SIDE. JUST MORE DIRT. *IT'S ALWAYS DIRT.*
ALMOST THERE...
TOMMY, WHAT IF THERE IS NO GREEN? *WHAT IF* THERE IS ONLY DIRT AND SCARY BIRDS--NO NICE BIRDS--
CHUCKIE, DON'T THINK ABOUT THAT--THINK ABOUT THE COOL THINGS WE--
THAT'S IT! THAT'S THE BIRD!
HOLD ON, CHUCKIE! SHE'S TRYING TO KNOCK US OFF!
WHIRRRRRRRR

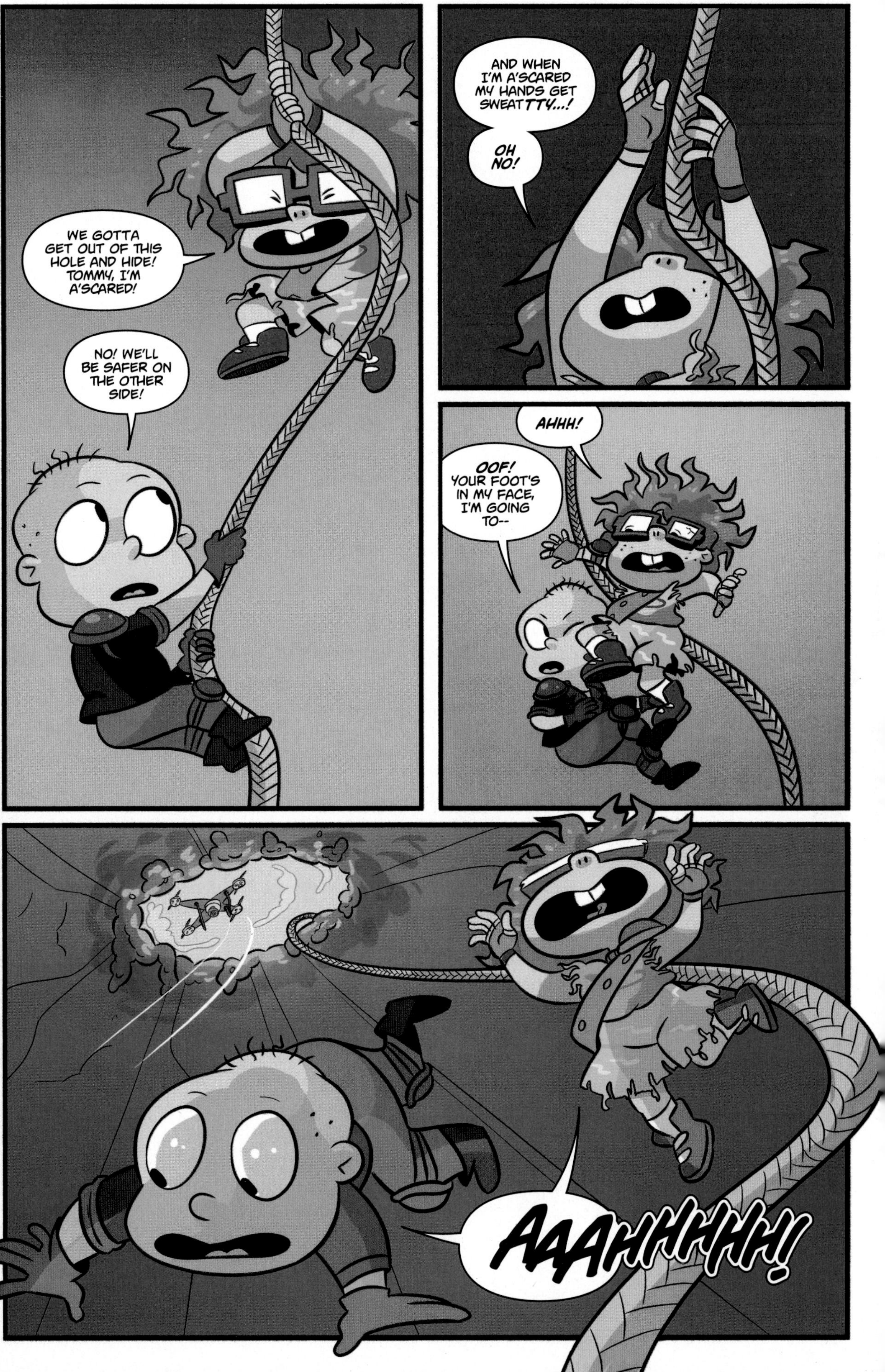
WE GOTTA GET OUT OF THIS HOLE AND HIDE! TOMMY, I'M A'SCARED!
NO! WE'LL BE SAFER ON THE OTHER SIDE!
AND WHEN I'M A'SCARED MY HANDS GET SWEATTTY...!
OH NO!
AHHH!
OOF! YOUR FOOT'S IN MY FACE, I'M GOING TO--
AAAHHHHH!

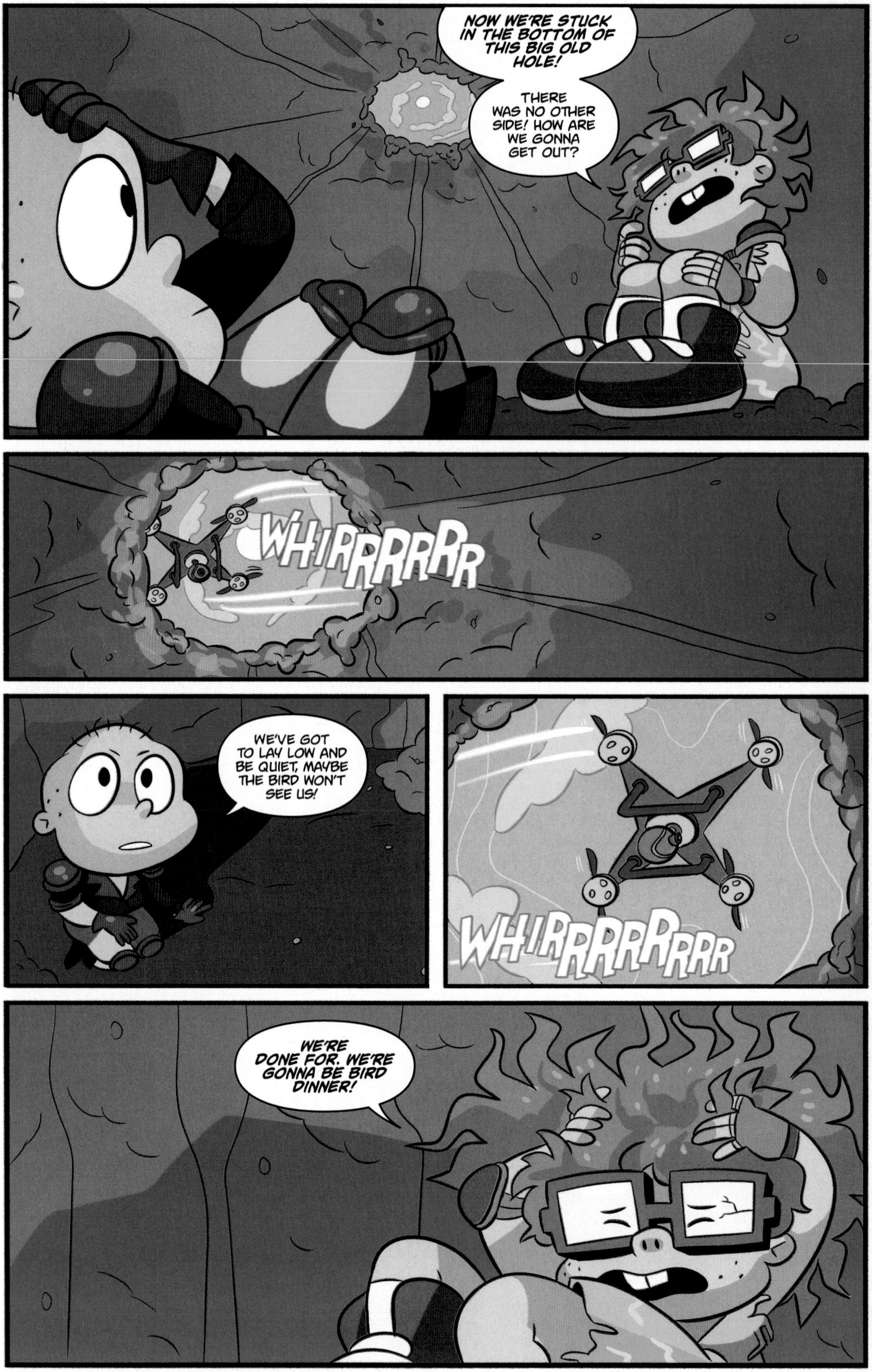
NOW WE'RE STUCK IN THE BOTTOM OF THIS BIG OLD HOLE!
THERE WAS NO OTHER SIDE! HOW ARE WE GONNA GET OUT?
WHIRRRRRR
WE'VE GOT TO LAY LOW AND BE QUIET, MAYBE THE BIRD WON'T SEE US!
WHIRRRRRRR
WE'RE DONE FOR. WE'RE GONNA BE BIRD DINNER!

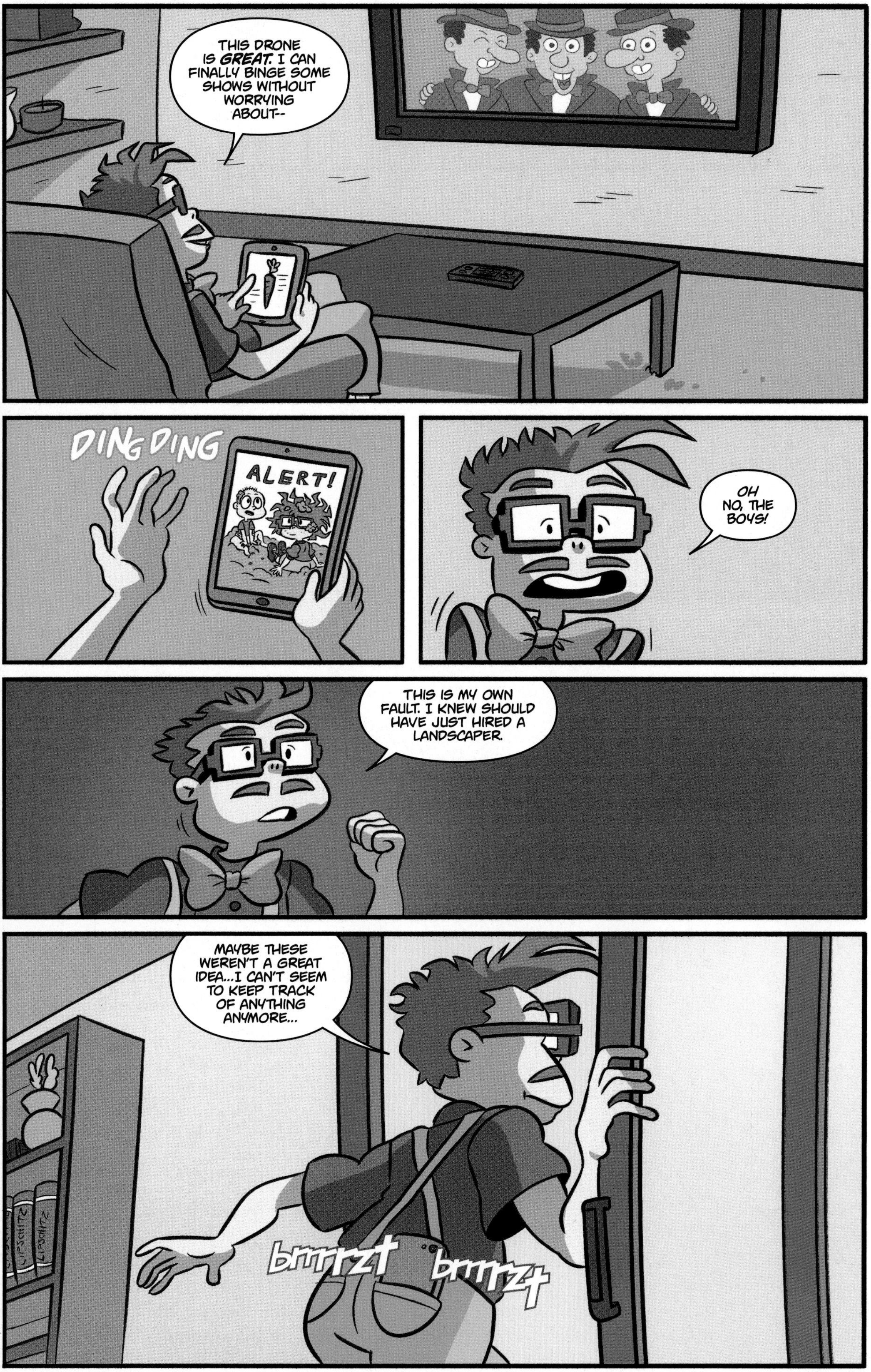
THIS DRONE IS GREAT. I CAN FINALLY BINGE SOME SHOWS WITHOUT WORRYING ABOUT--
DING DING
ALERT!
OH NO, THE BOYS!
THIS IS MY OWN FAULT. I KNEW SHOULD HAVE JUST HIRED A LANDSCAPER.
MAYBE THESE WEREN'T A GREAT IDEA...I CAN'T SEEM TO KEEP TRACK OF ANYTHING ANYMORE...
LIPSCHITZ
LIPSCHITZ
brrrrzt
brrrrzt

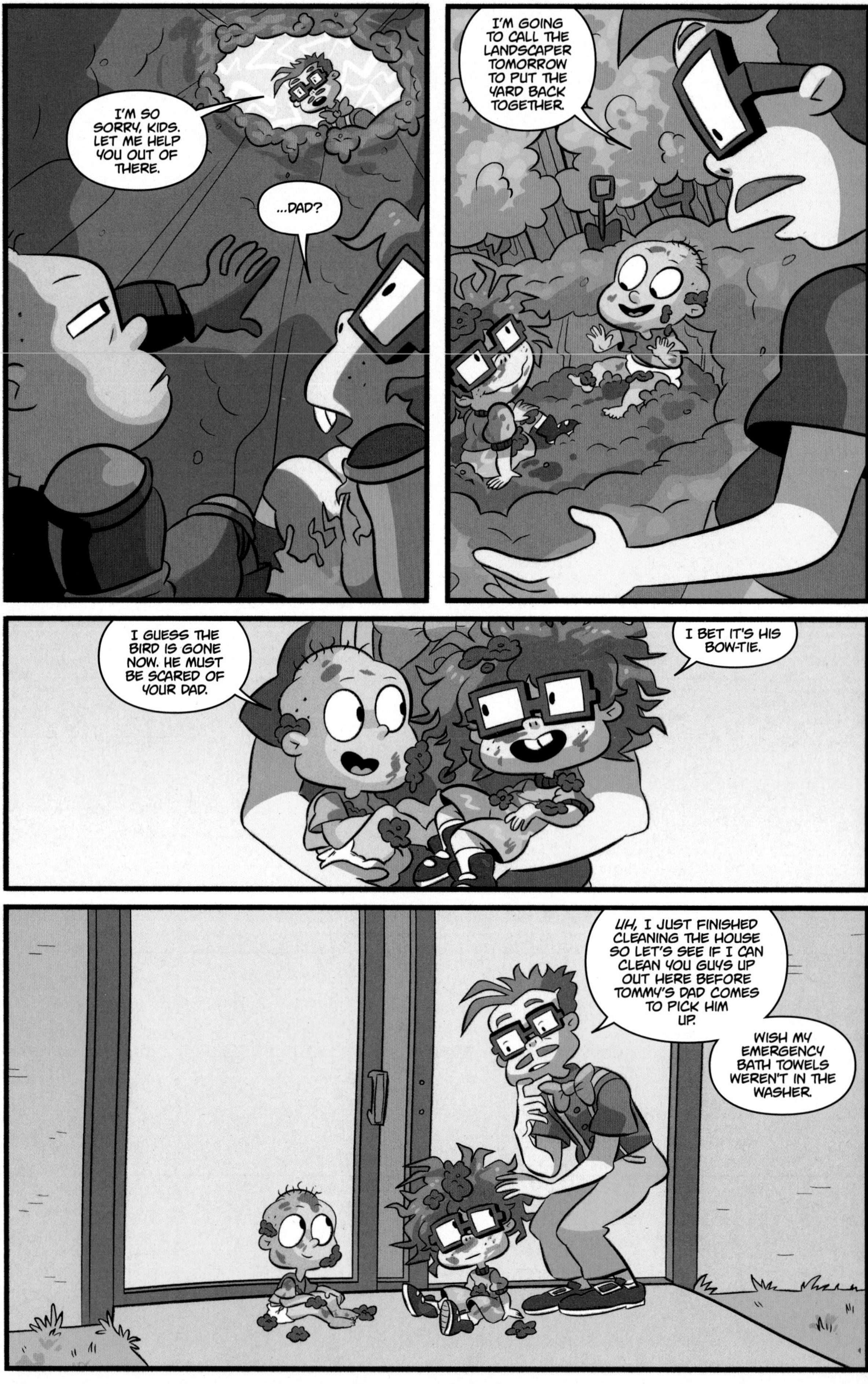
I'M SO SORRY, KIDS. LET ME HELP YOU OUT OF THERE.
...DAD?
I'M GOING TO CALL THE LANDSCAPER TOMORROW TO PUT THE YARD BACK TOGETHER.
I GUESS THE BIRD IS GONE NOW. HE MUST BE SCARED OF YOUR DAD.
I BET IT'S HIS BOW-TIE.
UH, I JUST FINISHED CLEANING THE HOUSE SO LET'S SEE IF I CAN CLEAN YOU GUYS UP OUT HERE BEFORE TOMMY'S DAD COMES TO PICK HIM UP.
WISH MY EMERGENCY BATH TOWELS WEREN'T IN THE WASHER.

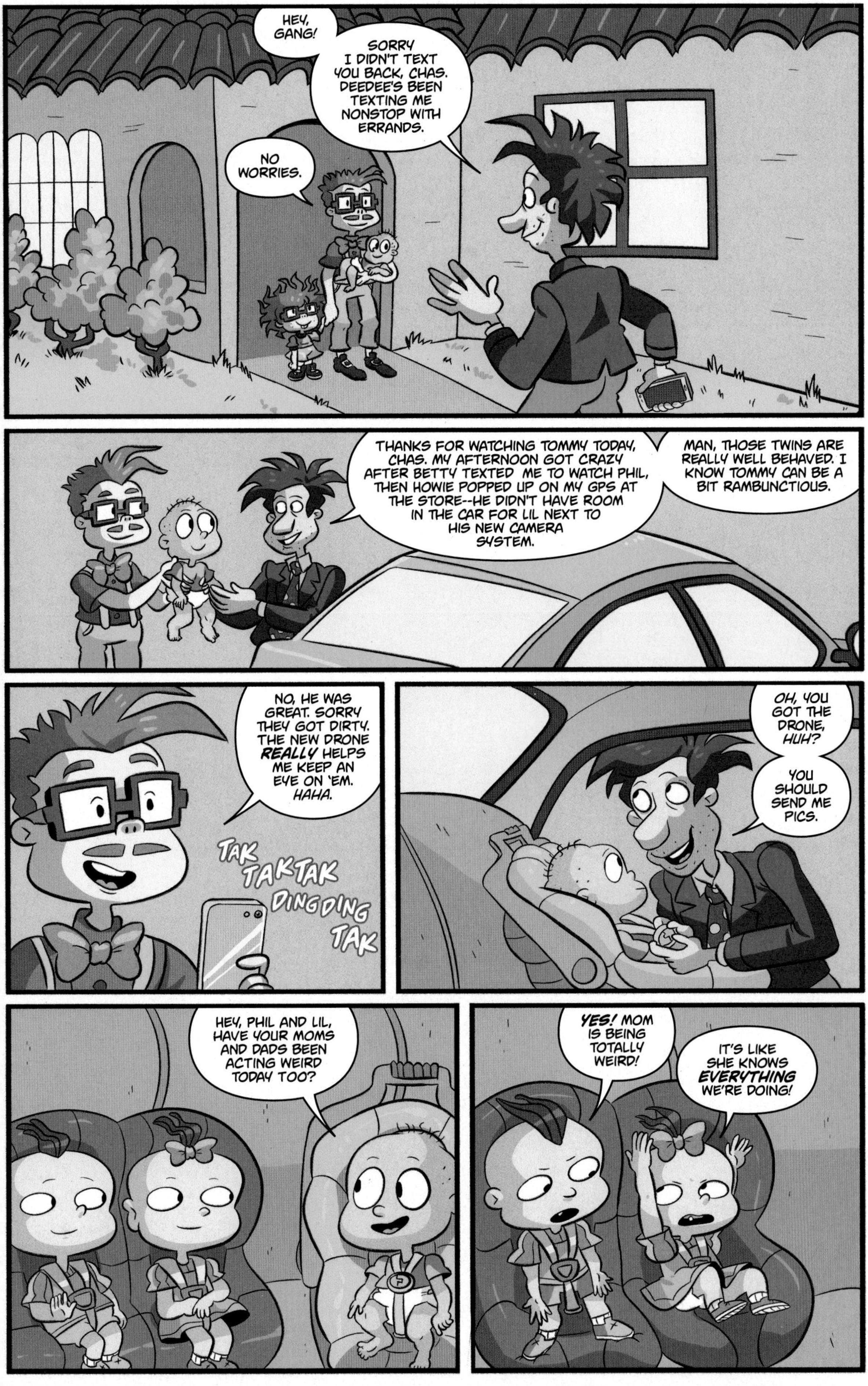
HEY, GANG!
SORRY I DIDN'T TEXT YOU BACK, CHAS. DEEDEE'S BEEN TEXTING ME NONSTOP WITH ERRANDS.
NO WORRIES.
THANKS FOR WATCHING TOMMY TODAY, CHAS. MY AFTERNOON GOT CRAZY AFTER BETTY TEXTED ME TO WATCH PHIL, THEN HOWIE POPPED UP ON MY GPS AT THE STORE--HE DIDN'T HAVE ROOM IN THE CAR FOR LIL NEXT TO HIS NEW CAMERA SYSTEM.
MAN, THOSE TWINS ARE REALLY WELL BEHAVED. I KNOW TOMMY CAN BE A BIT RAMBUNCTIOUS.
NO, HE WAS GREAT. SORRY THEY GOT DIRTY. THE NEW DRONE *REALLY* HELPS ME KEEP AN EYE ON 'EM. *HAHA.*
TAK TAKTAK DINGDING TAK
OH, YOU GOT THE DRONE, HUH?
YOU SHOULD SEND ME PICS.
HEY, PHIL AND LIL, HAVE YOUR MOMS AND DADS BEEN ACTING WEIRD TODAY TOO?
YES! MOM IS BEING TOTALLY WEIRD!
IT'S LIKE SHE KNOWS *EVERYTHING* WE'RE DOING!

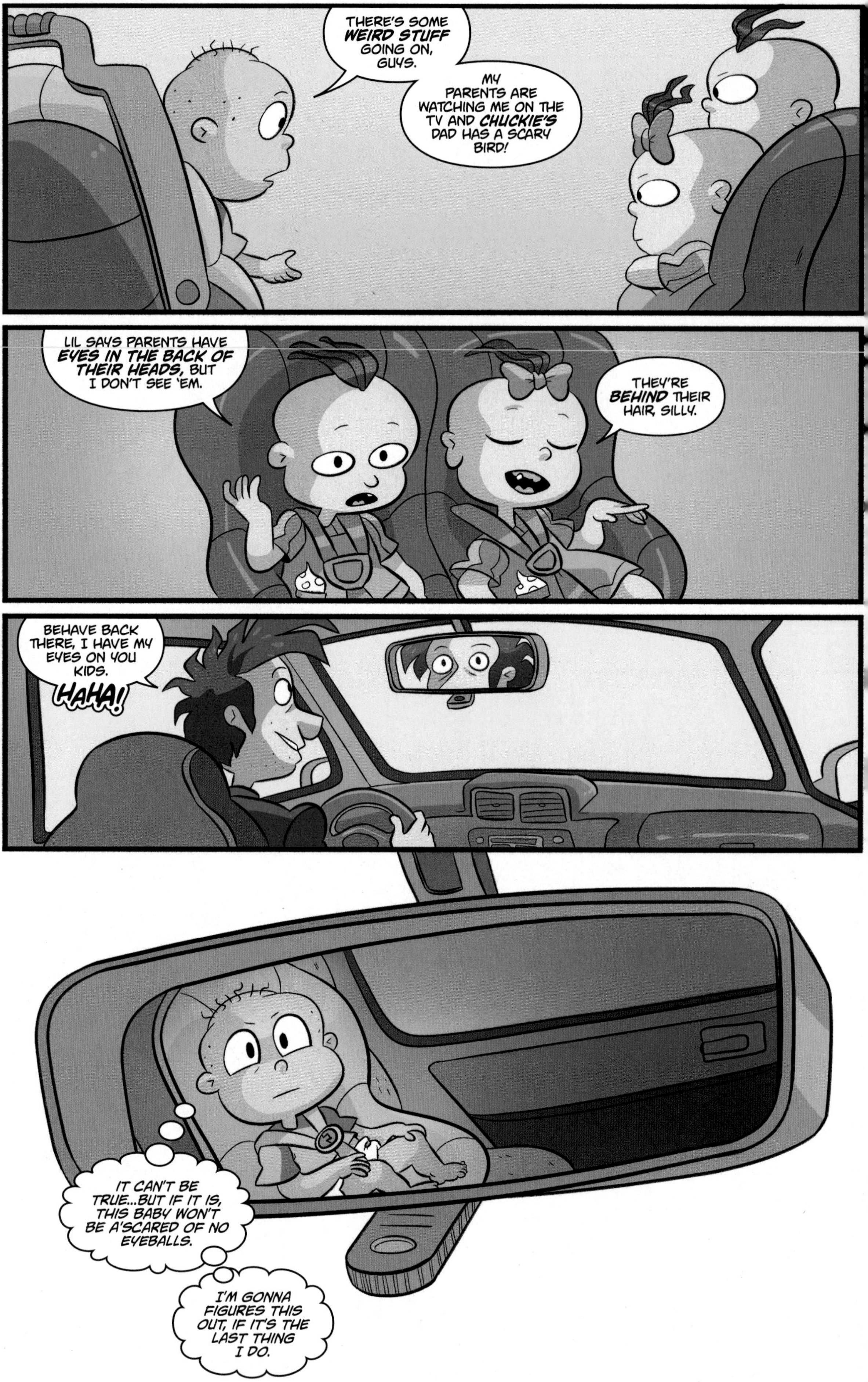

THERE'S SOME WEIRD STUFF GOING ON, GUYS.
MY PARENTS ARE WATCHING ME ON THE TV AND CHUCKIE'S DAD HAS A SCARY BIRD!
LIL SAYS PARENTS HAVE EYES IN THE BACK OF THEIR HEADS, BUT I DON'T SEE 'EM.
THEY'RE BEHIND THEIR HAIR, SILLY.
BEHAVE BACK THERE, I HAVE MY EYES ON YOU KIDS.
HAHA!
IT CAN'T BE TRUE...BUT IF IT IS, THIS BABY WON'T BE A'SCARED OF NO EYEBALLS.
I'M GONNA FIGURES THIS OUT, IF IT'S THE LAST THING I DO.

LISTEN, CHUCKIE, YOU GOTTA BE BRAVE. THERE'S NO REASON TO BE AFRAID OF A BIRD.

CHAPTER
TWO

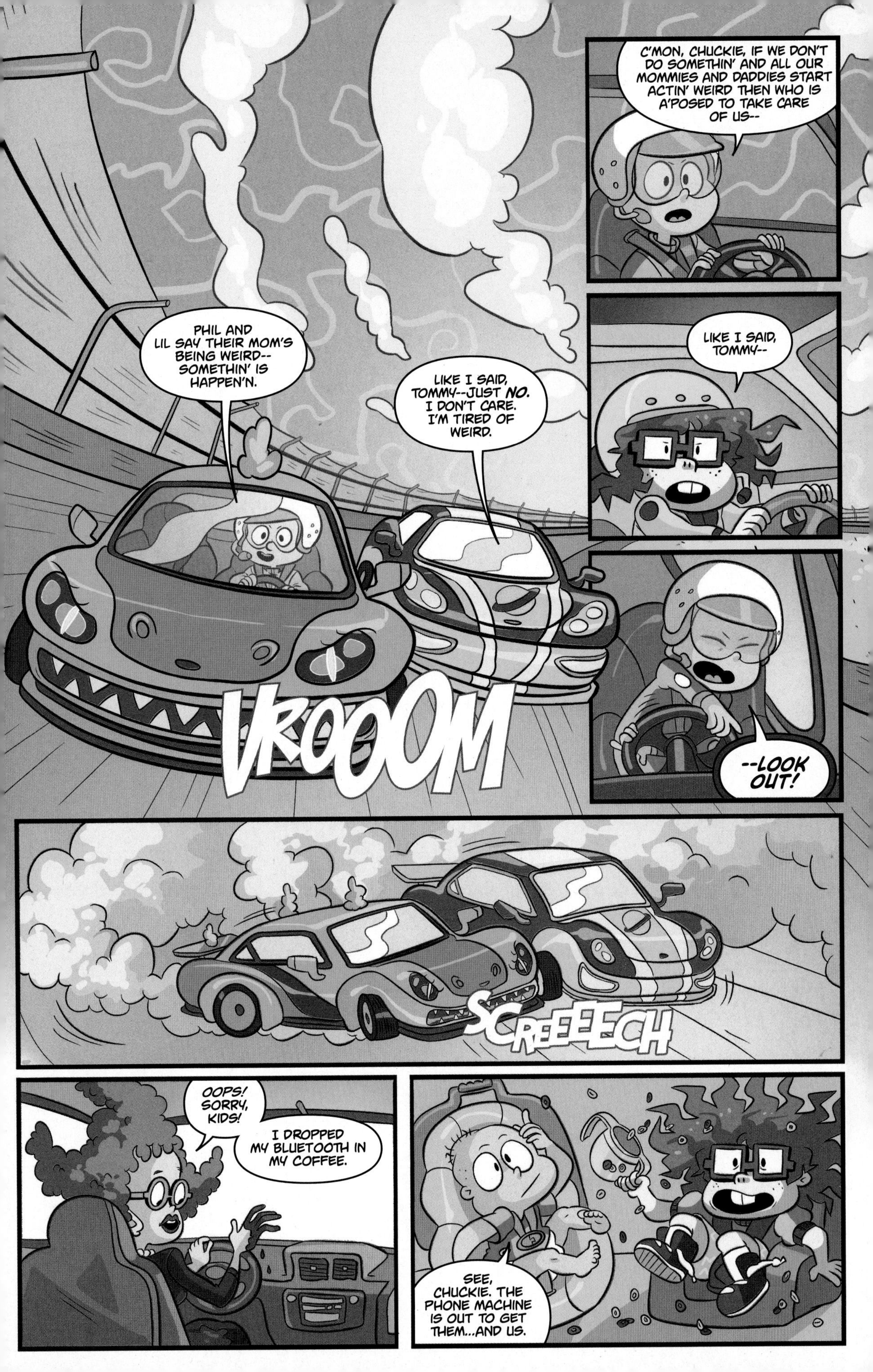
PHIL AND LIL SAY THEIR MOM'S BEING WEIRD-- SOMETHIN' IS HAPPEN'N.
LIKE I SAID, TOMMY--JUST NO. I DON'T CARE. I'M TIRED OF WEIRD.
VROOOM
C'MON, CHUCKIE, IF WE DON'T DO SOMETHIN' AND ALL OUR MOMMIES AND DADDIES START ACTIN' WEIRD THEN WHO IS A'POSED TO TAKE CARE OF US--
LIKE I SAID, TOMMY--
--LOOK OUT!
SCREEEECH
OOPS! SORRY, KIDS!
I DROPPED MY BLUETOOTH IN MY COFFEE.
SEE, CHUCKIE. THE PHONE MACHINE IS OUT TO GET THEM...AND US.

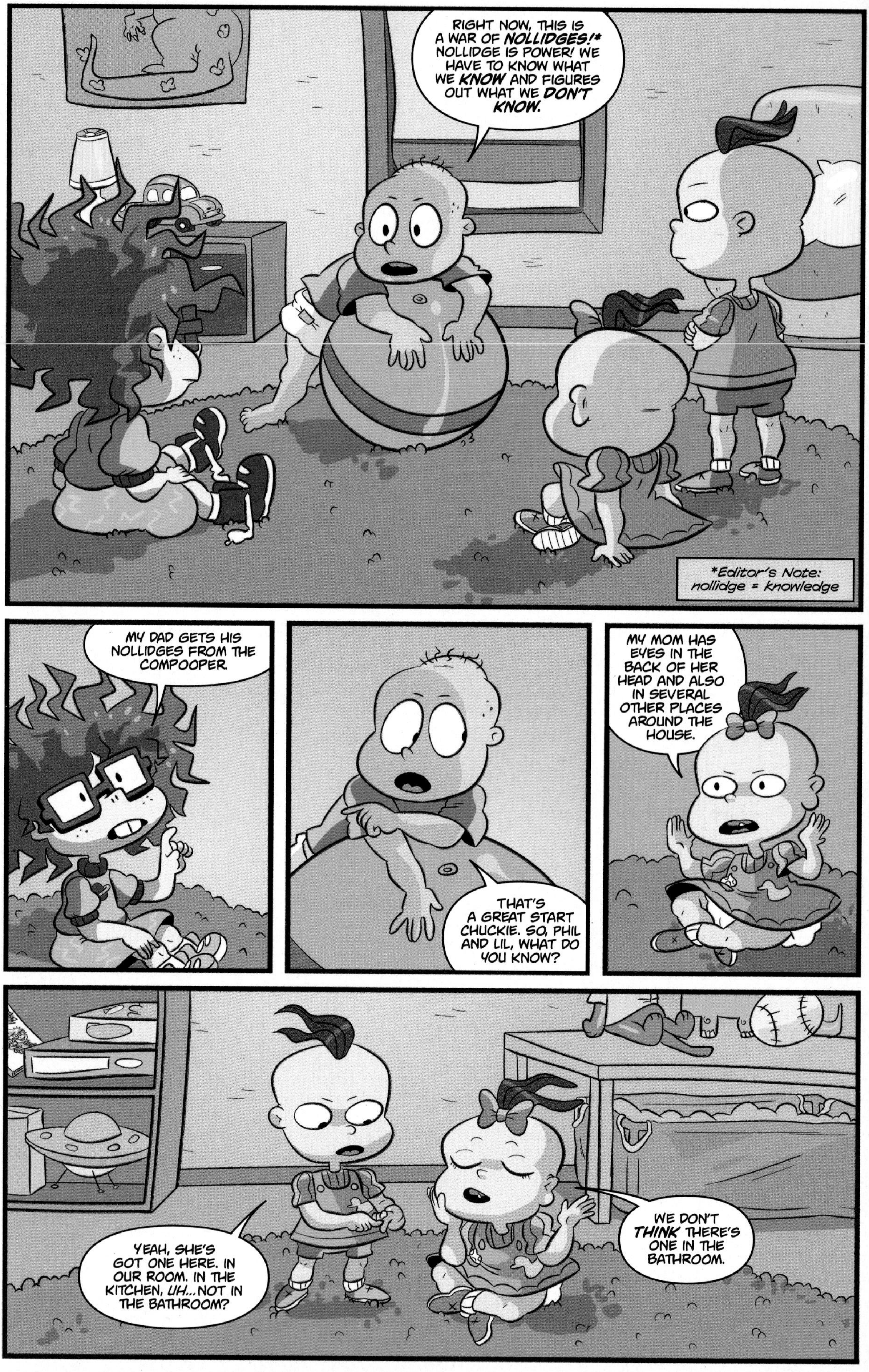
RIGHT NOW, THIS IS A WAR OF NOLLIDGES!* NOLLIDGE IS POWER! WE HAVE TO KNOW WHAT WE KNOW AND FIGURES OUT WHAT WE DON'T KNOW.
*Editor's Note: nollidge = knowledge
MY DAD GETS HIS NOLLIDGES FROM THE COMPOOPER.
THAT'S A GREAT START CHUCKIE. SO, PHIL AND LIL, WHAT DO YOU KNOW?
MY MOM HAS EYES IN THE BACK OF HER HEAD AND ALSO IN SEVERAL OTHER PLACES AROUND THE HOUSE.
YEAH, SHE'S GOT ONE HERE. IN OUR ROOM. IN THE KITCHEN, UH...NOT IN THE BATHROOM?
WE DON'T THINK THERE'S ONE IN THE BATHROOM.

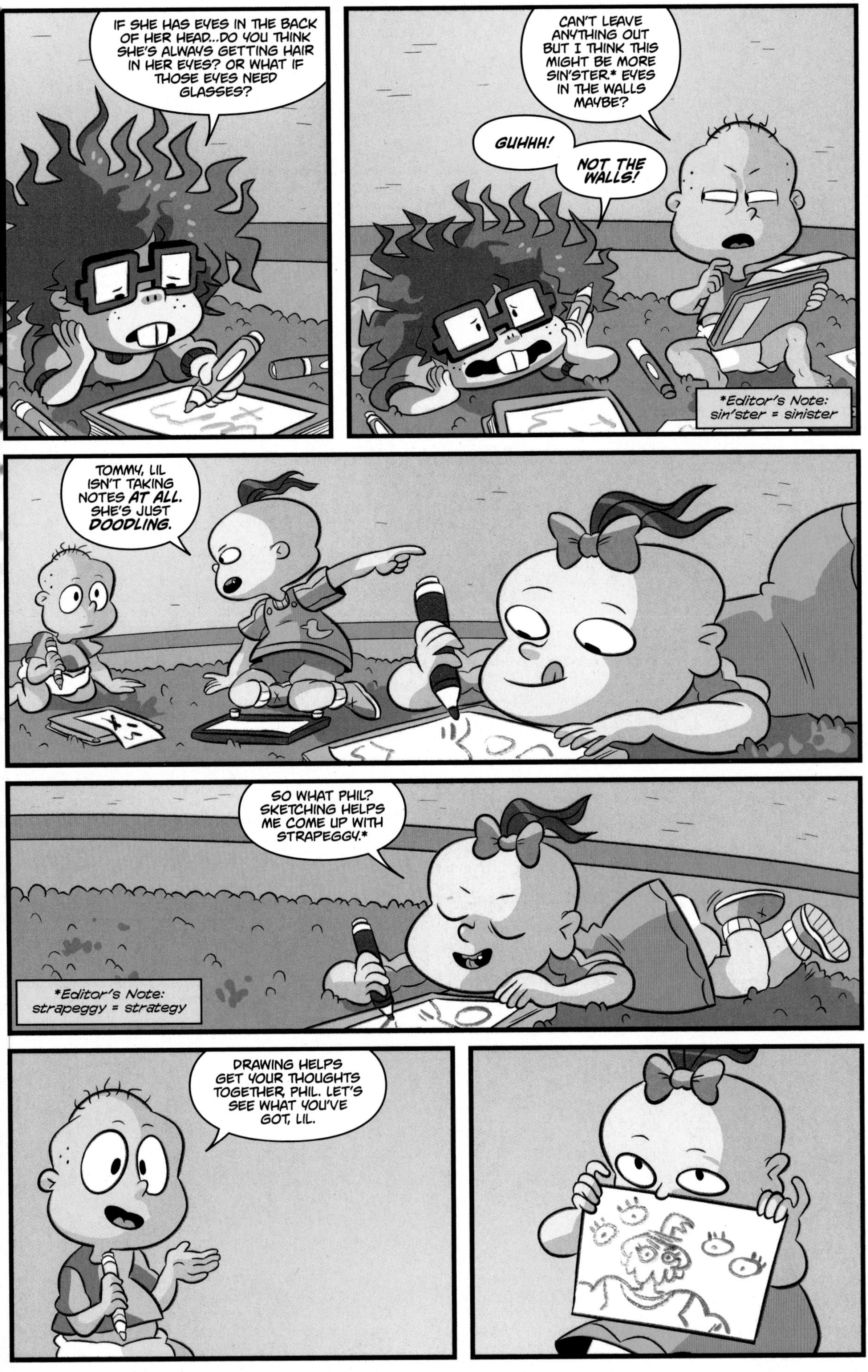
IF SHE HAS EYES IN THE BACK OF HER HEAD...DO YOU THINK SHE'S ALWAYS GETTING HAIR IN HER EYES? OR WHAT IF THOSE EYES NEED GLASSES?
CAN'T LEAVE ANYTHING OUT BUT I THINK THIS MIGHT BE MORE SIN'STER.* EYES IN THE WALLS MAYBE?
GUHHH!
NOT THE WALLS!
*Editor's Note: sin'ster = sinister
TOMMY, LIL ISN'T TAKING NOTES AT ALL. SHE'S JUST DOODLING.
SO WHAT PHIL? SKETCHING HELPS ME COME UP WITH STRAPEGGY.*
*Editor's Note: strapeggy = strategy
DRAWING HELPS GET YOUR THOUGHTS TOGETHER, PHIL. LET'S SEE WHAT YOU'VE GOT, LIL.

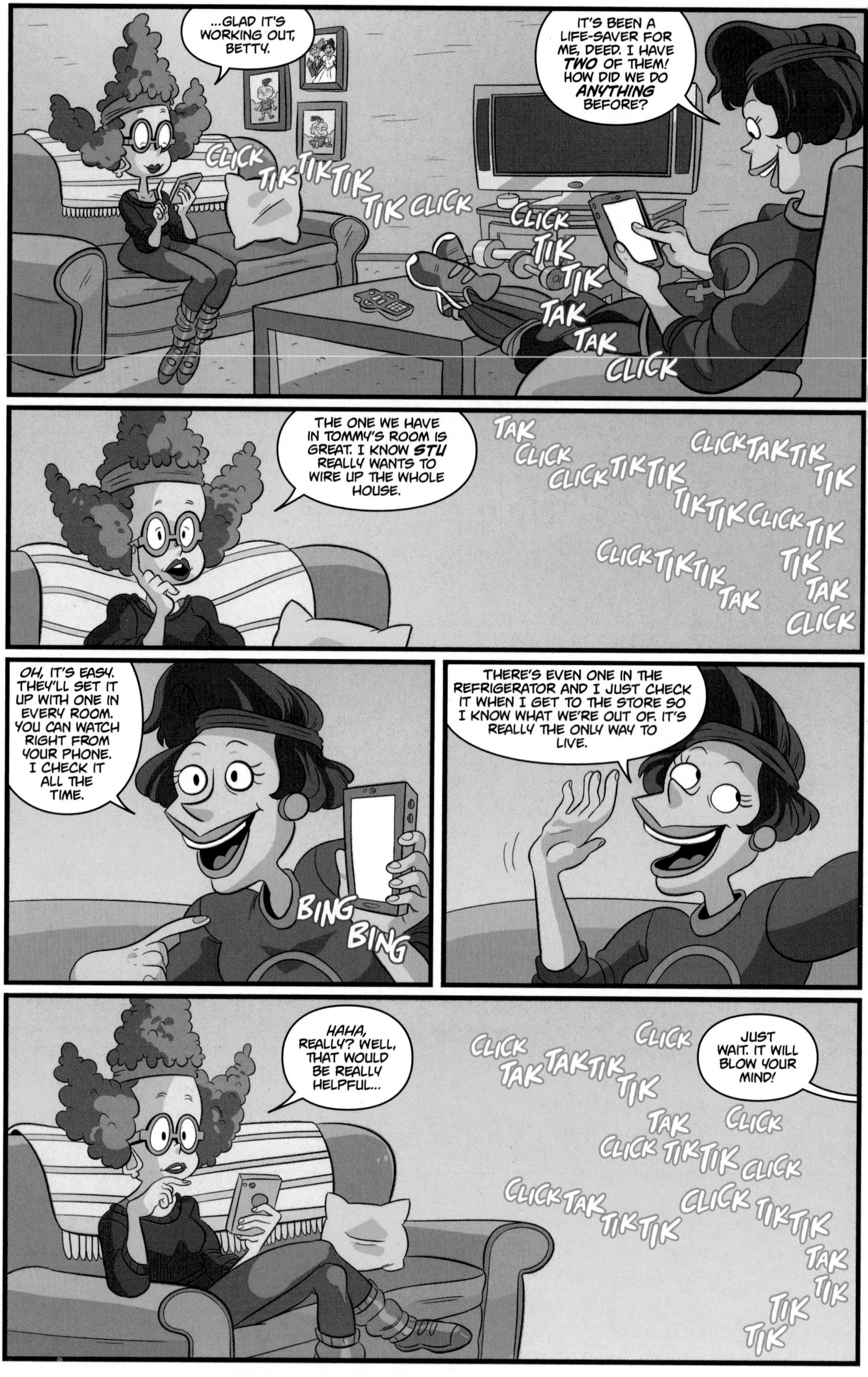
...GLAD IT'S WORKING OUT, BETTY.
IT'S BEEN A LIFE-SAVER FOR ME, DEED. I HAVE TWO OF THEM! HOW DID WE DO ANYTHING BEFORE?
CLICK TIK TIK TIK TIK CLICK
CLICK TIK TIK TAK TAK CLICK
THE ONE WE HAVE IN TOMMY'S ROOM IS GREAT. I KNOW STU REALLY WANTS TO WIRE UP THE WHOLE HOUSE.
TAK CLICK CLICK TIK TIK CLICK TAK TIK TIK TIK TIK CLICK TIK CLICK TIK TIK TAK TIK TAK CLICK
OH, IT'S EASY. THEY'LL SET IT UP WITH ONE IN EVERY ROOM. YOU CAN WATCH RIGHT FROM YOUR PHONE. I CHECK IT ALL THE TIME.
BING BING
THERE'S EVEN ONE IN THE REFRIGERATOR AND I JUST CHECK IT WHEN I GET TO THE STORE SO I KNOW WHAT WE'RE OUT OF. IT'S REALLY THE ONLY WAY TO LIVE.
HAHA, REALLY? WELL, THAT WOULD BE REALLY HELPFUL...
JUST WAIT. IT WILL BLOW YOUR MIND!
CLICK TAK TAK TIK TIK CLICK TAK CLICK CLICK TIK TIK CLICK CLICK TAK TIK TIK CLICK TIK TIK TAK TIK TIK TIK

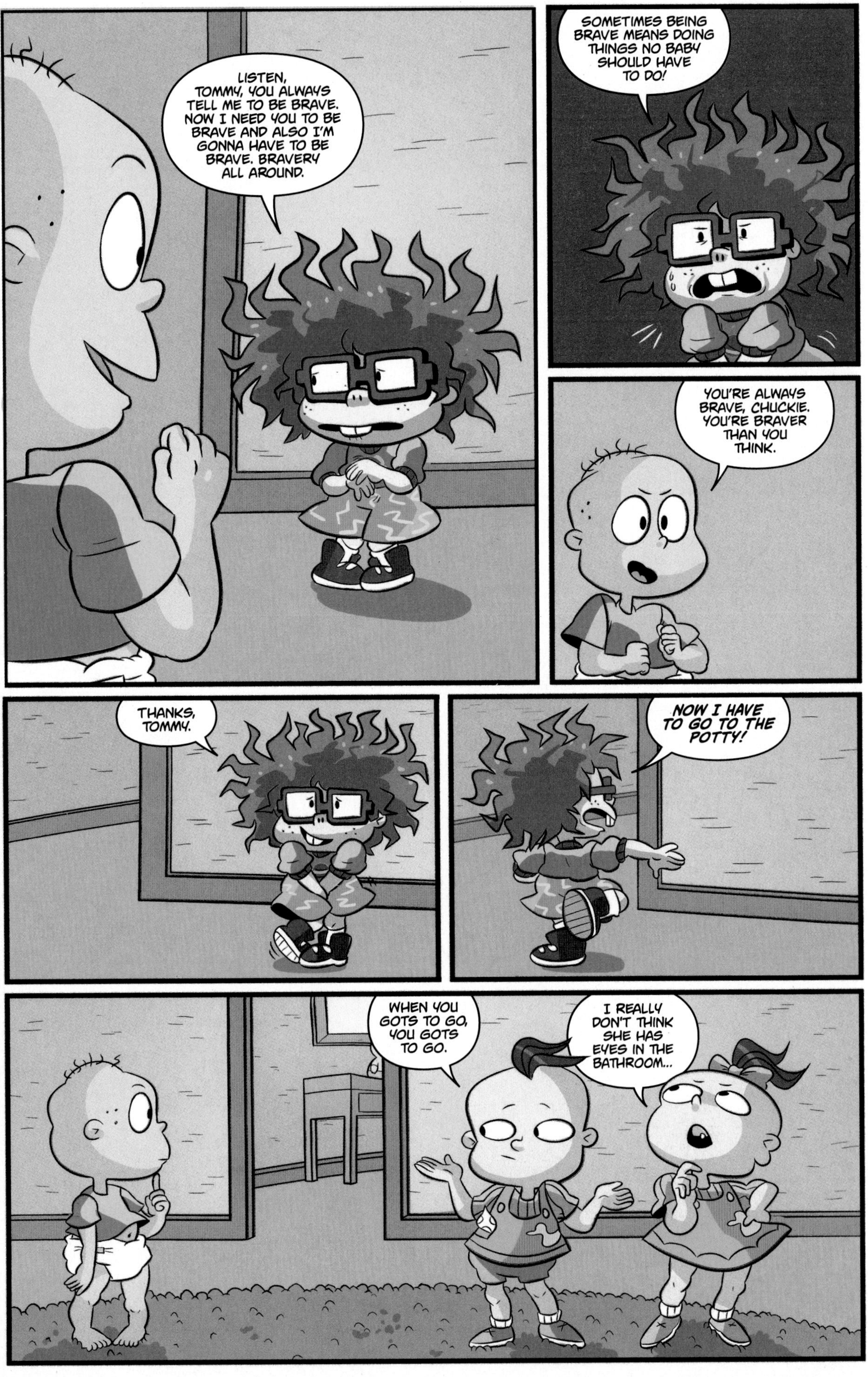
LISTEN, TOMMY, YOU ALWAYS TELL ME TO BE BRAVE. NOW I NEED YOU TO BE BRAVE AND ALSO I'M GONNA HAVE TO BE BRAVE. BRAVERY ALL AROUND.
SOMETIMES BEING BRAVE MEANS DOING THINGS NO BABY SHOULD HAVE TO DO!
YOU'RE ALWAYS BRAVE, CHUCKIE. YOU'RE BRAVER THAN YOU THINK.
THANKS, TOMMY.
NOW I HAVE TO GO TO THE POTTY!
WHEN YOU GOTS TO GO, YOU GOTS TO GO.
I REALLY DON'T THINK SHE HAS EYES IN THE BATHROOM...

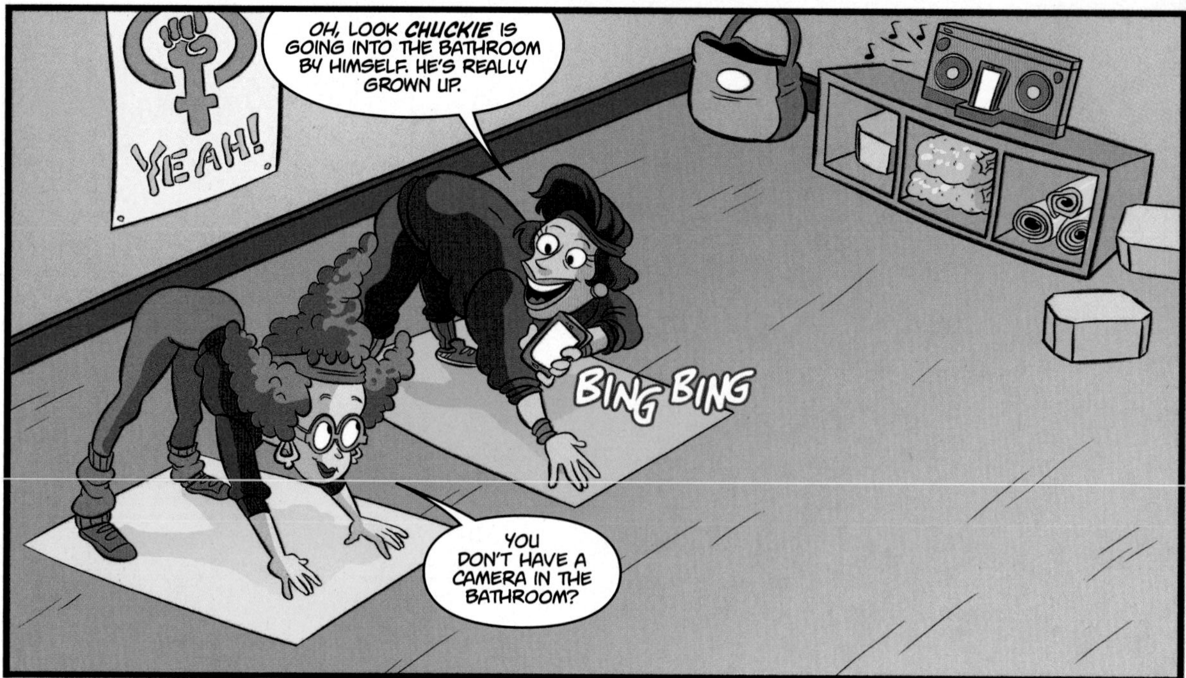
YEAH!
OH, LOOK CHUCKIE IS GOING INTO THE BATHROOM BY HIMSELF. HE'S REALLY GROWN UP.
BING BING
YOU DON'T HAVE A CAMERA IN THE BATHROOM?

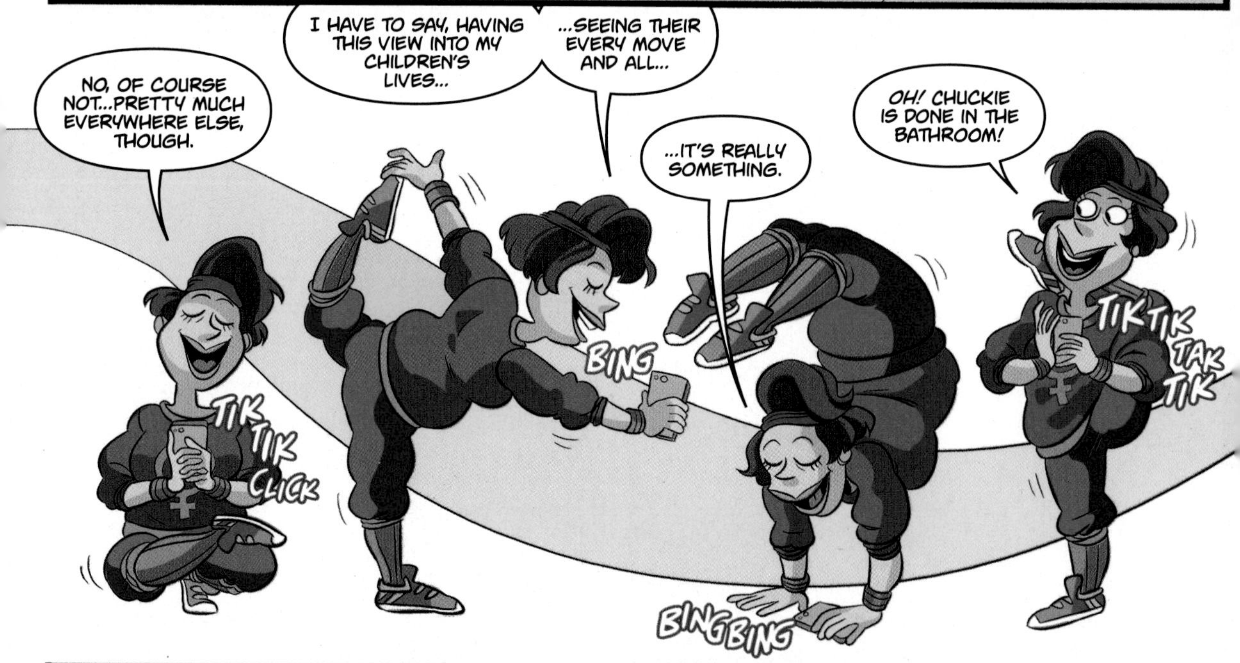
NO, OF COURSE NOT...PRETTY MUCH EVERYWHERE ELSE, THOUGH.
I HAVE TO SAY, HAVING THIS VIEW INTO MY CHILDREN'S LIVES...
...SEEING THEIR EVERY MOVE AND ALL...
...IT'S REALLY SOMETHING.
OH! CHUCKIE IS DONE IN THE BATHROOM!
TIK TIK CLICK
BING
BING BING
TIK TIK TAK TIK

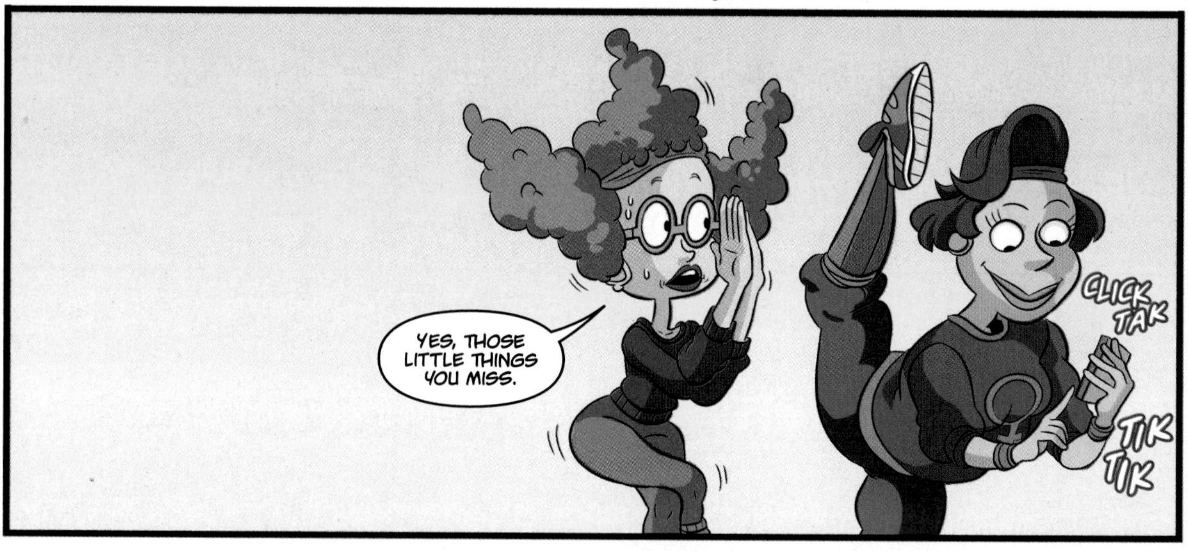
YES, THOSE LITTLE THINGS YOU MISS.
CLICK TAK
TIK TIK

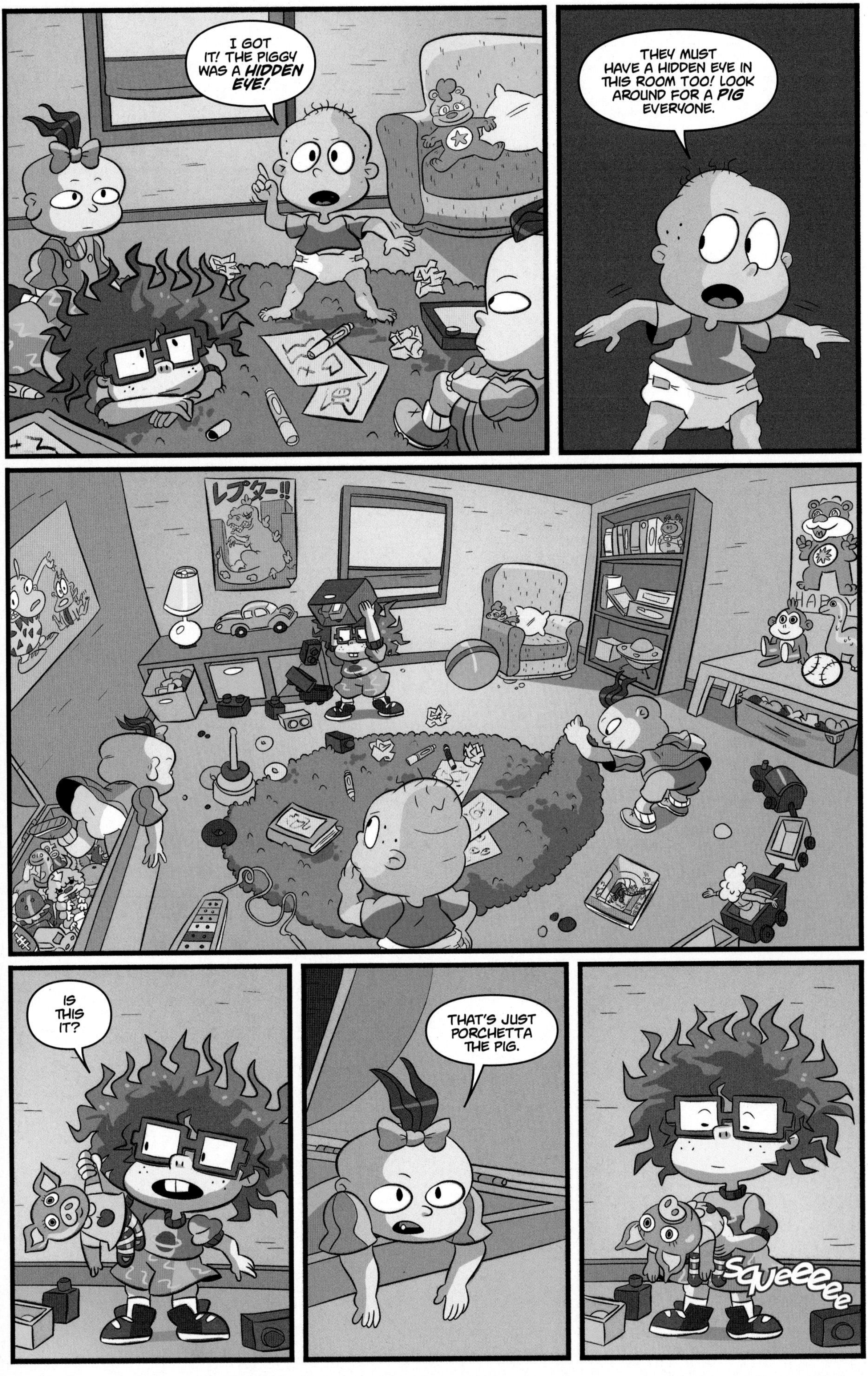
I GOT IT! THE PIGGY WAS A HIDDEN EYE!
THEY MUST HAVE A HIDDEN EYE IN THIS ROOM TOO! LOOK AROUND FOR A PIG EVERYONE.
レプター!!
IS THIS IT?
THAT'S JUST PORCHETTA THE PIG.
SQUEEEEEE

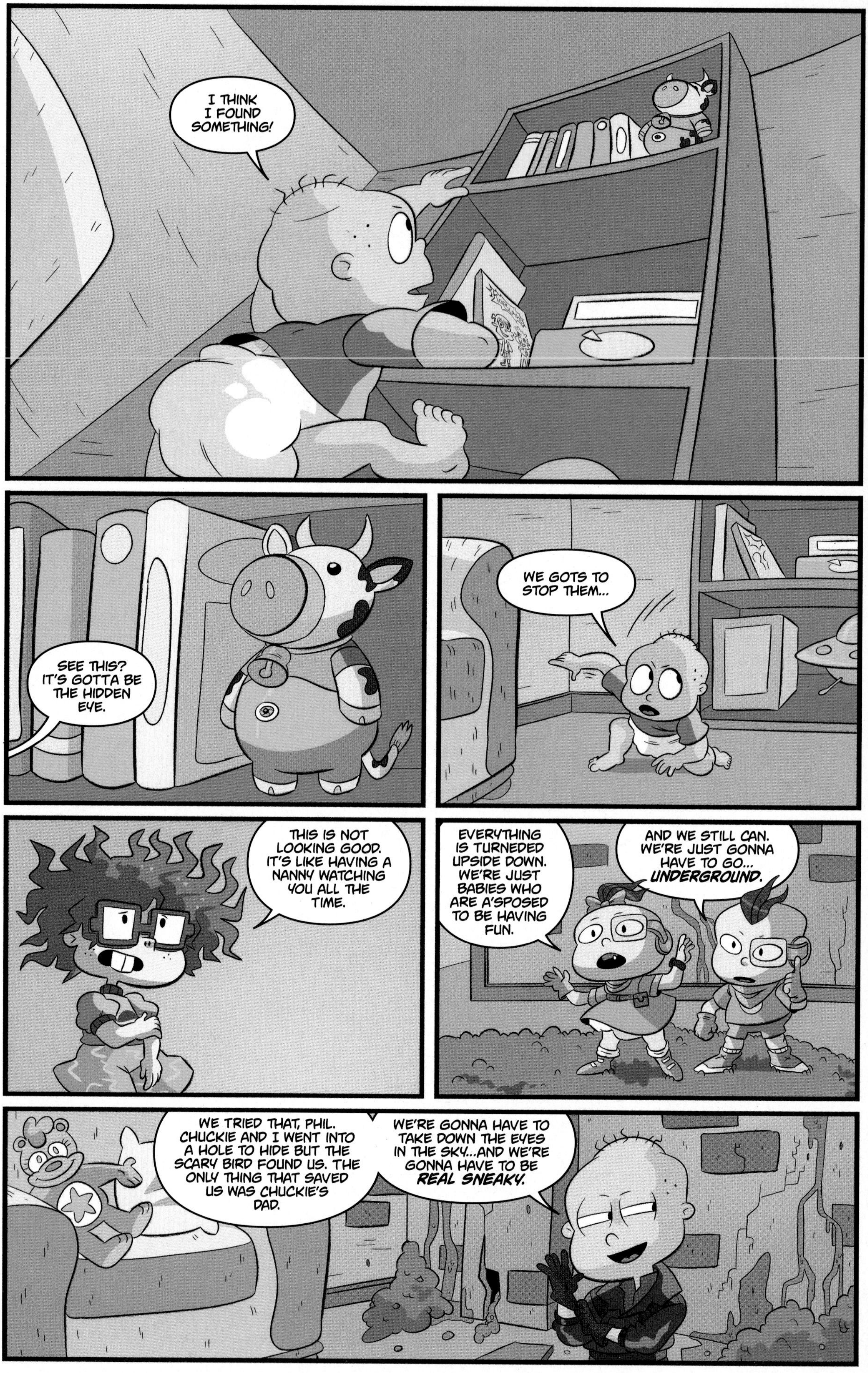
I THINK I FOUND SOMETHING!
SEE THIS? IT'S GOTTA BE THE HIDDEN EYE.
WE GOTS TO STOP THEM...
THIS IS NOT LOOKING GOOD. IT'S LIKE HAVING A NANNY WATCHING YOU ALL THE TIME.
EVERYTHING IS TURNEDED UPSIDE DOWN. WE'RE JUST BABIES WHO ARE A'SPOSED TO BE HAVING FUN.
AND WE STILL CAN. WE'RE JUST GONNA HAVE TO GO... ***UNDERGROUND.***
WE TRIED THAT, PHIL. CHUCKIE AND I WENT INTO A HOLE TO HIDE BUT THE SCARY BIRD FOUND US. THE ONLY THING THAT SAVED US WAS CHUCKIE'S DAD.
WE'RE GONNA HAVE TO TAKE DOWN THE EYES IN THE SKY...AND WE'RE GONNA HAVE TO BE ***REAL SNEAKY.***

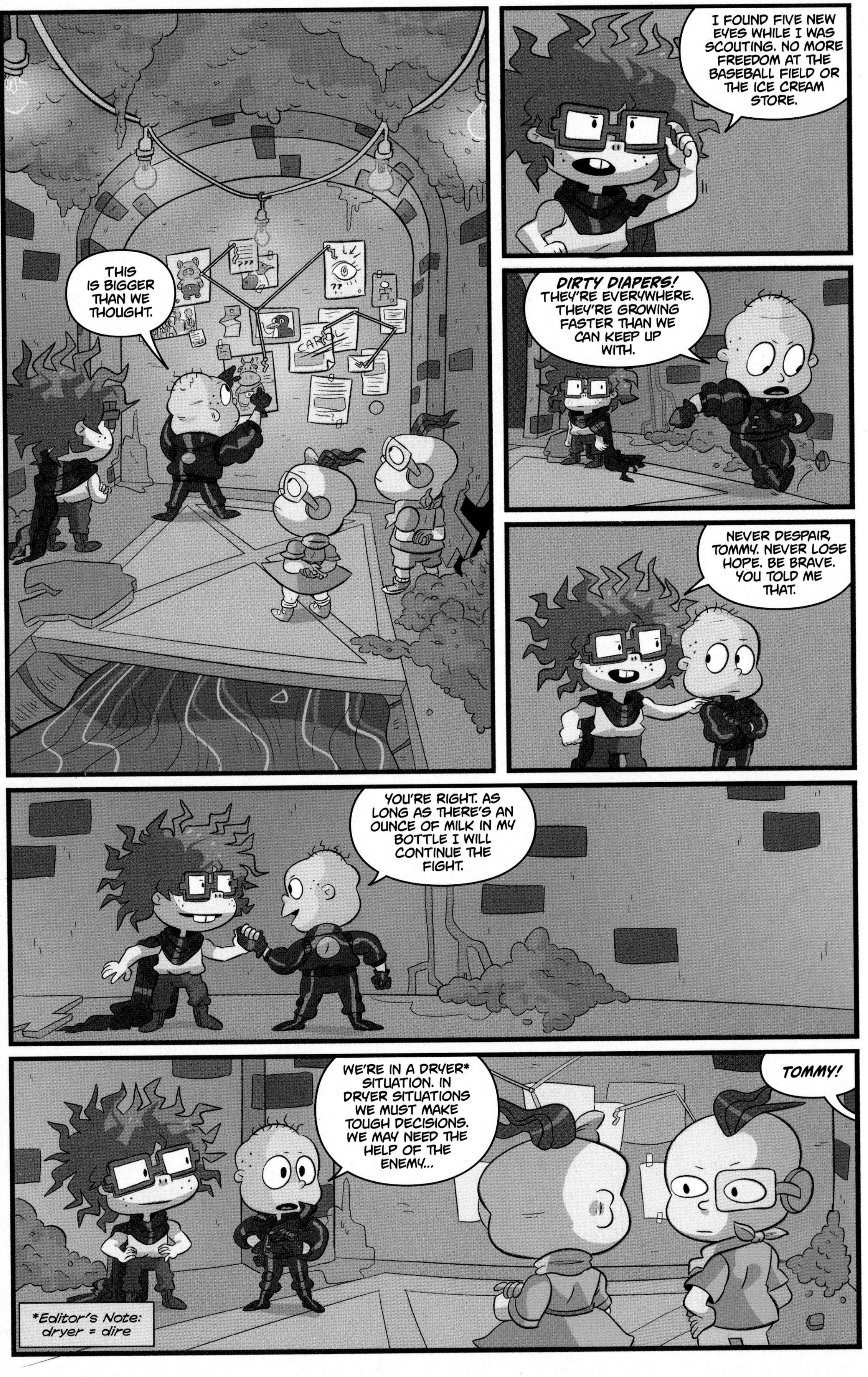
THIS IS BIGGER THAN WE THOUGHT.
CARROL
I FOUND FIVE NEW EYES WHILE I WAS SCOUTING. NO MORE FREEDOM AT THE BASEBALL FIELD OR THE ICE CREAM STORE.
DIRTY DIAPERS! THEY'RE EVERYWHERE. THEY'RE GROWING FASTER THAN WE CAN KEEP UP WITH.
NEVER DESPAIR, TOMMY. NEVER LOSE HOPE. BE BRAVE. YOU TOLD ME THAT.
YOU'RE RIGHT. AS LONG AS THERE'S AN OUNCE OF MILK IN MY BOTTLE I WILL CONTINUE THE FIGHT.
WE'RE IN A DRYER* SITUATION. IN DRYER SITUATIONS WE MUST MAKE TOUGH DECISIONS. WE MAY NEED THE HELP OF THE ENEMY...
TOMMY!
**Editor's Note: dryer = dire*

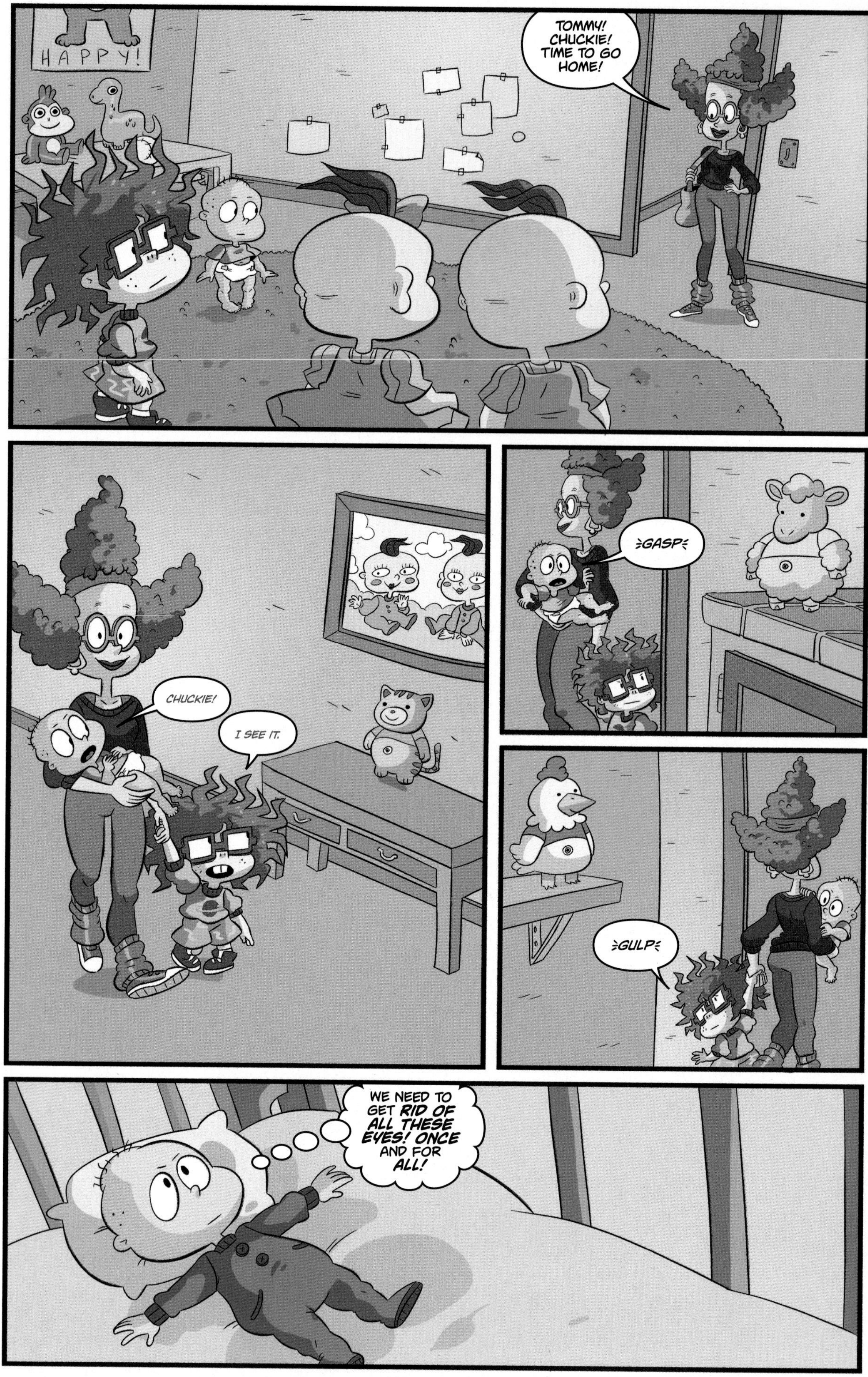
HAPPY!
TOMMY! CHUCKIE! TIME TO GO HOME!
CHUCKIE!
I SEE IT.
GASP
GULP
WE NEED TO GET RID OF ALL THESE EYES! ONCE AND FOR ALL!

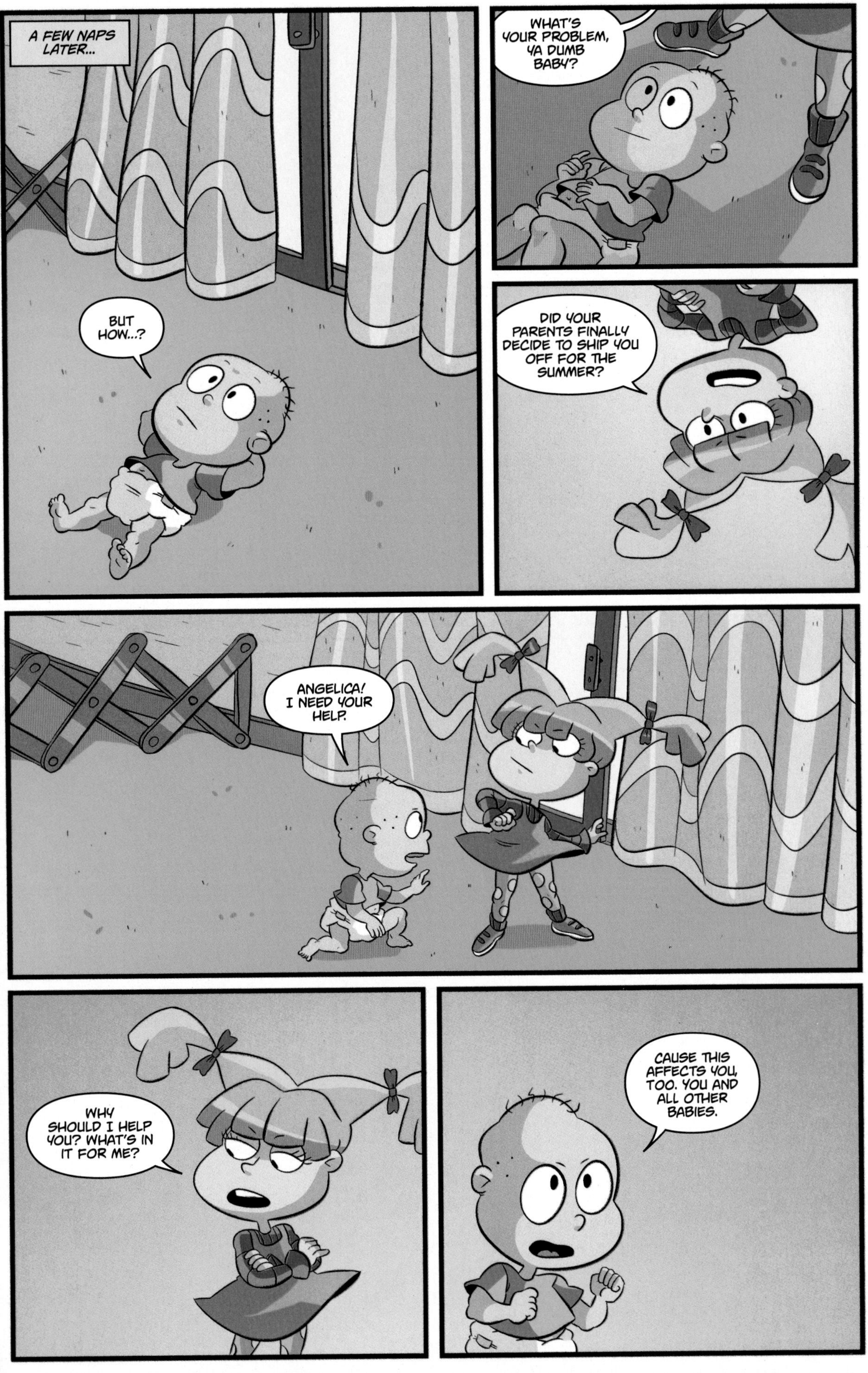
A FEW NAPS LATER...
BUT HOW...?
WHAT'S YOUR PROBLEM, YA DUMB BABY?
DID YOUR PARENTS FINALLY DECIDE TO SHIP YOU OFF FOR THE SUMMER?
ANGELICA! I NEED YOUR HELP.
WHY SHOULD I HELP YOU? WHAT'S IN IT FOR ME?
CAUSE THIS AFFECTS YOU, TOO. YOU AND ALL OTHER BABIES.

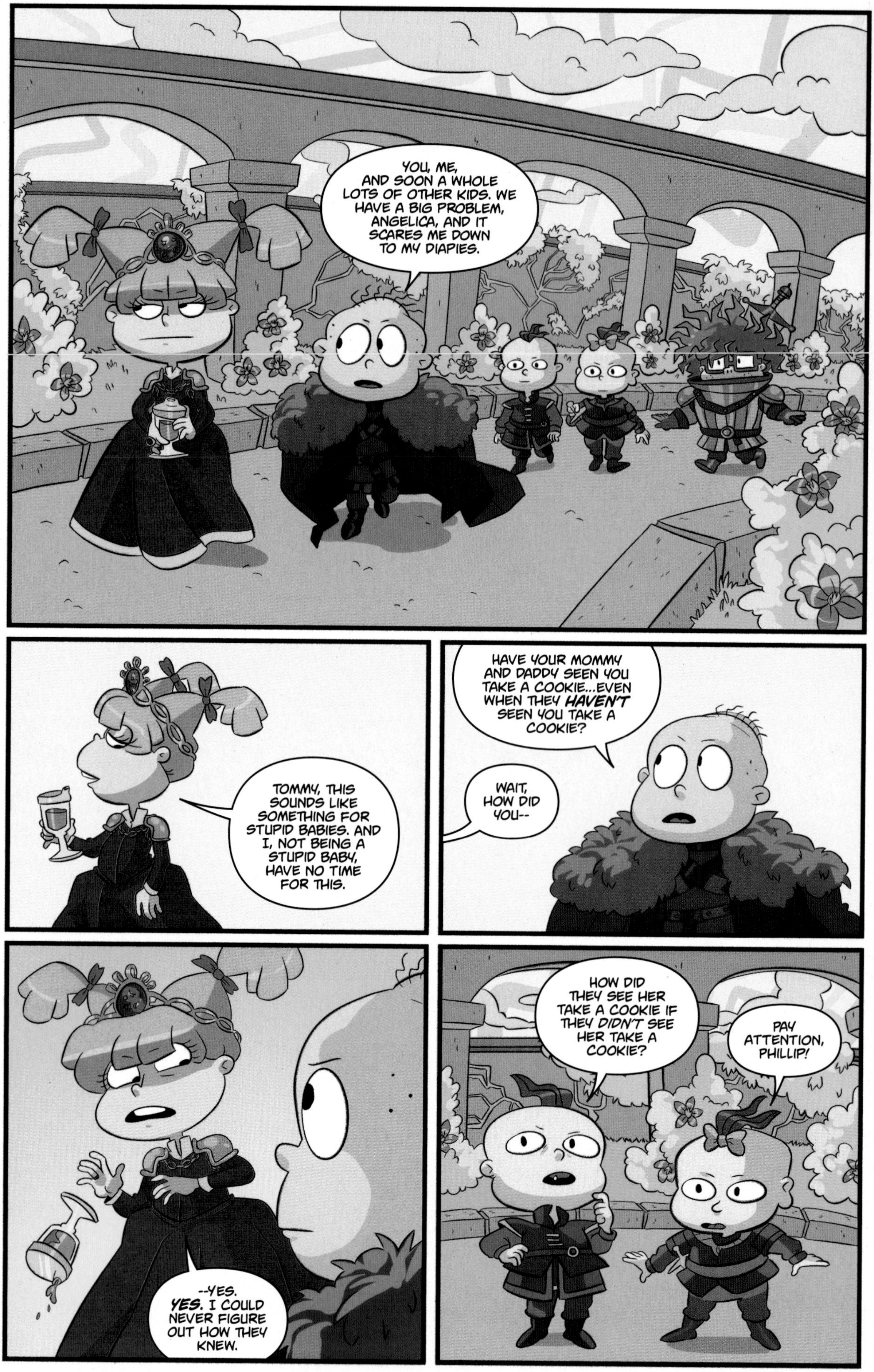
YOU, ME, AND SOON A WHOLE LOTS OF OTHER KIDS. WE HAVE A BIG PROBLEM, ANGELICA, AND IT SCARES ME DOWN TO MY DIAPIES.
TOMMY, THIS SOUNDS LIKE SOMETHING FOR STUPID BABIES. AND I, NOT BEING A STUPID BABY, HAVE NO TIME FOR THIS.
HAVE YOUR MOMMY AND DADDY SEEN YOU TAKE A COOKIE...EVEN WHEN THEY ***HAVEN'T*** SEEN YOU TAKE A COOKIE?
WAIT, HOW DID YOU--
--YES. ***YES.*** I COULD NEVER FIGURE OUT HOW THEY KNEW.
HOW DID THEY SEE HER TAKE A COOKIE IF THEY *DIDN'T* SEE HER TAKE A COOKIE?
PAY ATTENTION, PHILLIP!

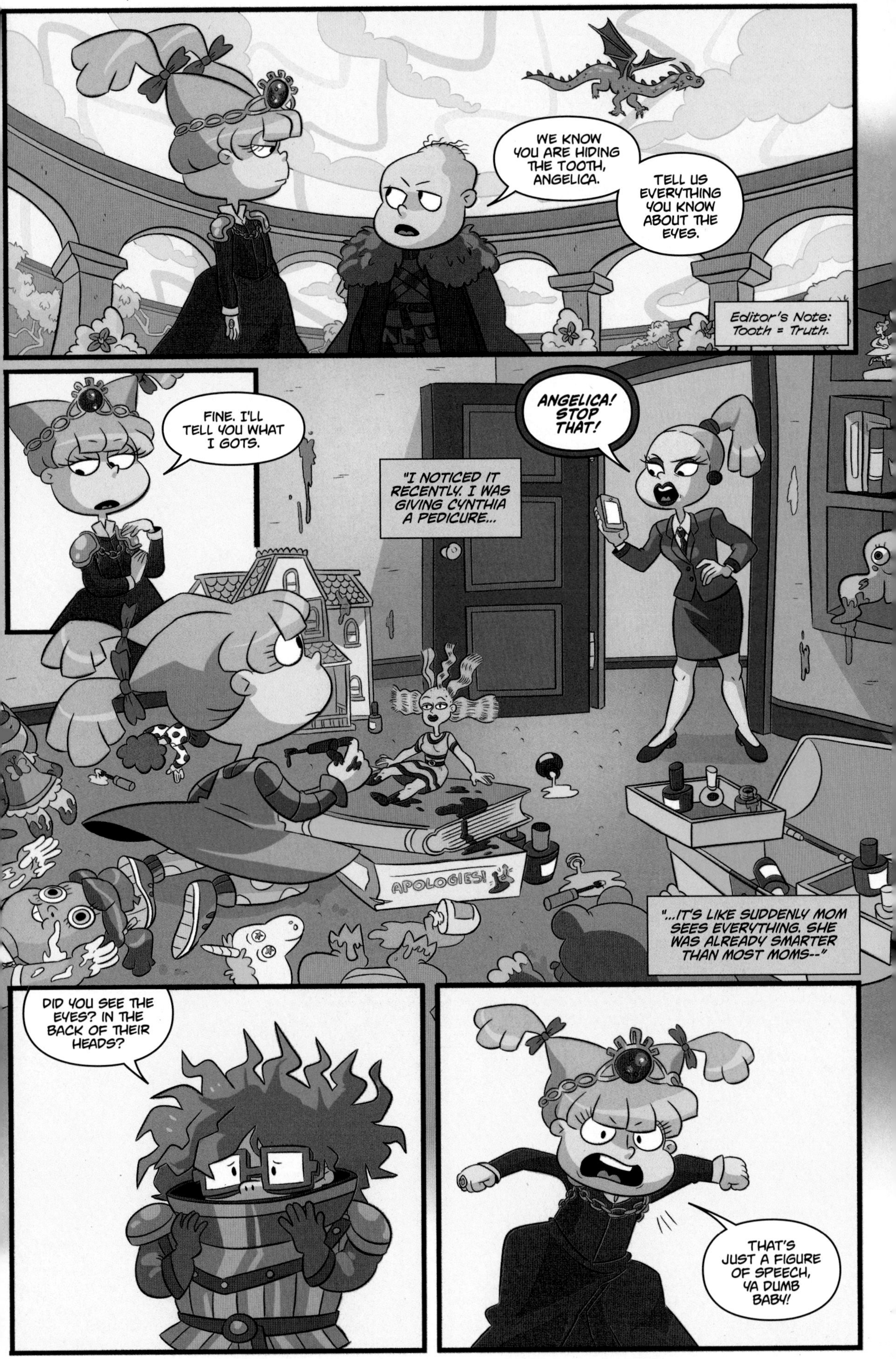

WE KNOW YOU ARE HIDING THE TOOTH, ANGELICA.
TELL US EVERYTHING YOU KNOW ABOUT THE EYES.
Editor's Note: Tooth = Truth.
FINE. I'LL TELL YOU WHAT I GOTS.
"I NOTICED IT RECENTLY. I WAS GIVING CYNTHIA A PEDICURE...
ANGELICA! STOP THAT!
APOLOGIES!
"...IT'S LIKE SUDDENLY MOM SEES EVERYTHING. SHE WAS ALREADY SMARTER THAN MOST MOMS--"
DID YOU SEE THE EYES? IN THE BACK OF THEIR HEADS?
THAT'S JUST A FIGURE OF SPEECH, YA DUMB BABY!

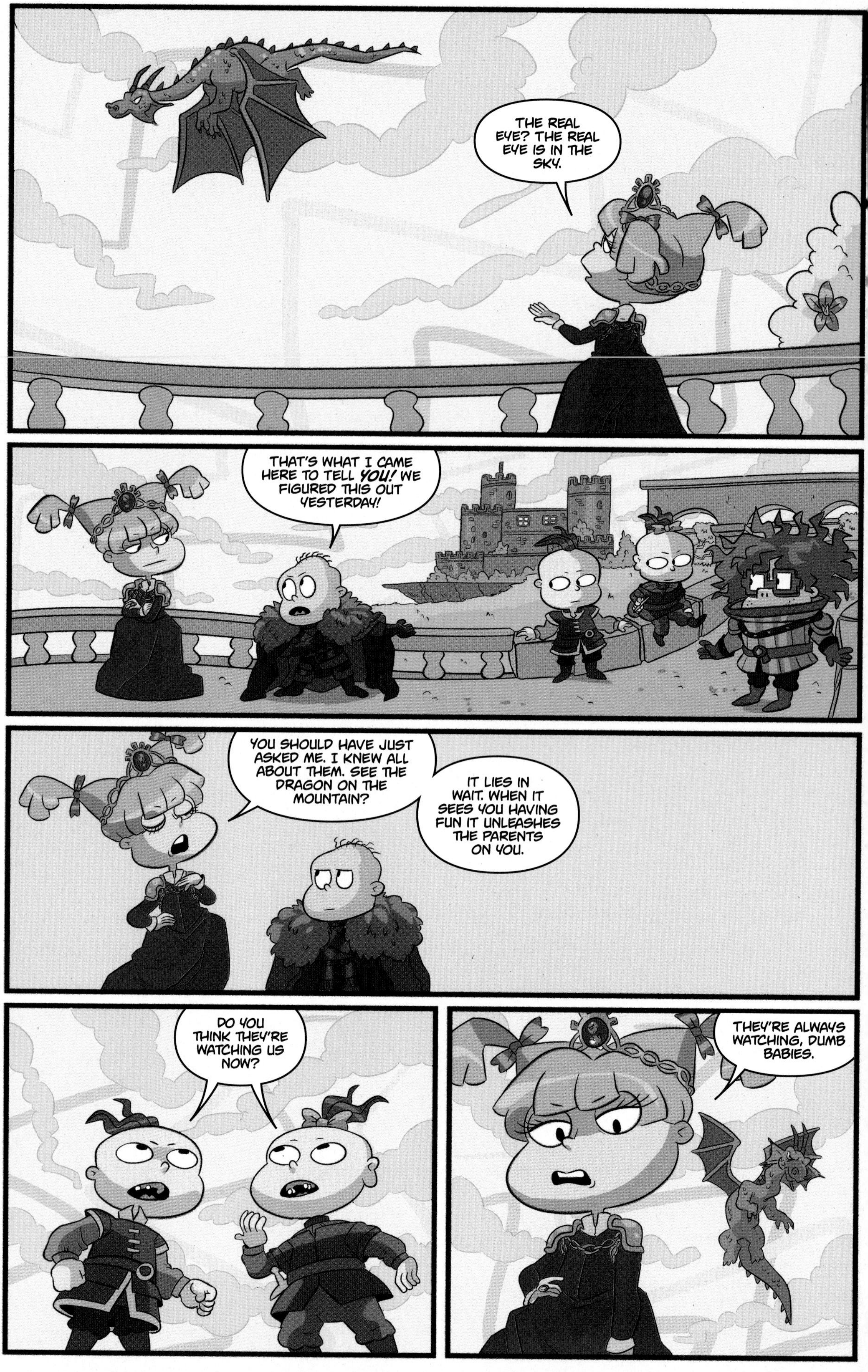
THE REAL EYE? THE REAL EYE IS IN THE SKY.
THAT'S WHAT I CAME HERE TO TELL *YOU!* WE FIGURED THIS OUT YESTERDAY!
YOU SHOULD HAVE JUST ASKED ME. I KNEW ALL ABOUT THEM. SEE THE DRAGON ON THE MOUNTAIN?
IT LIES IN WAIT. WHEN IT SEES YOU HAVING FUN IT UNLEASHES THE PARENTS ON YOU.
DO YOU THINK THEY'RE WATCHING US NOW?
THEY'RE ALWAYS WATCHING, DUMB BABIES.

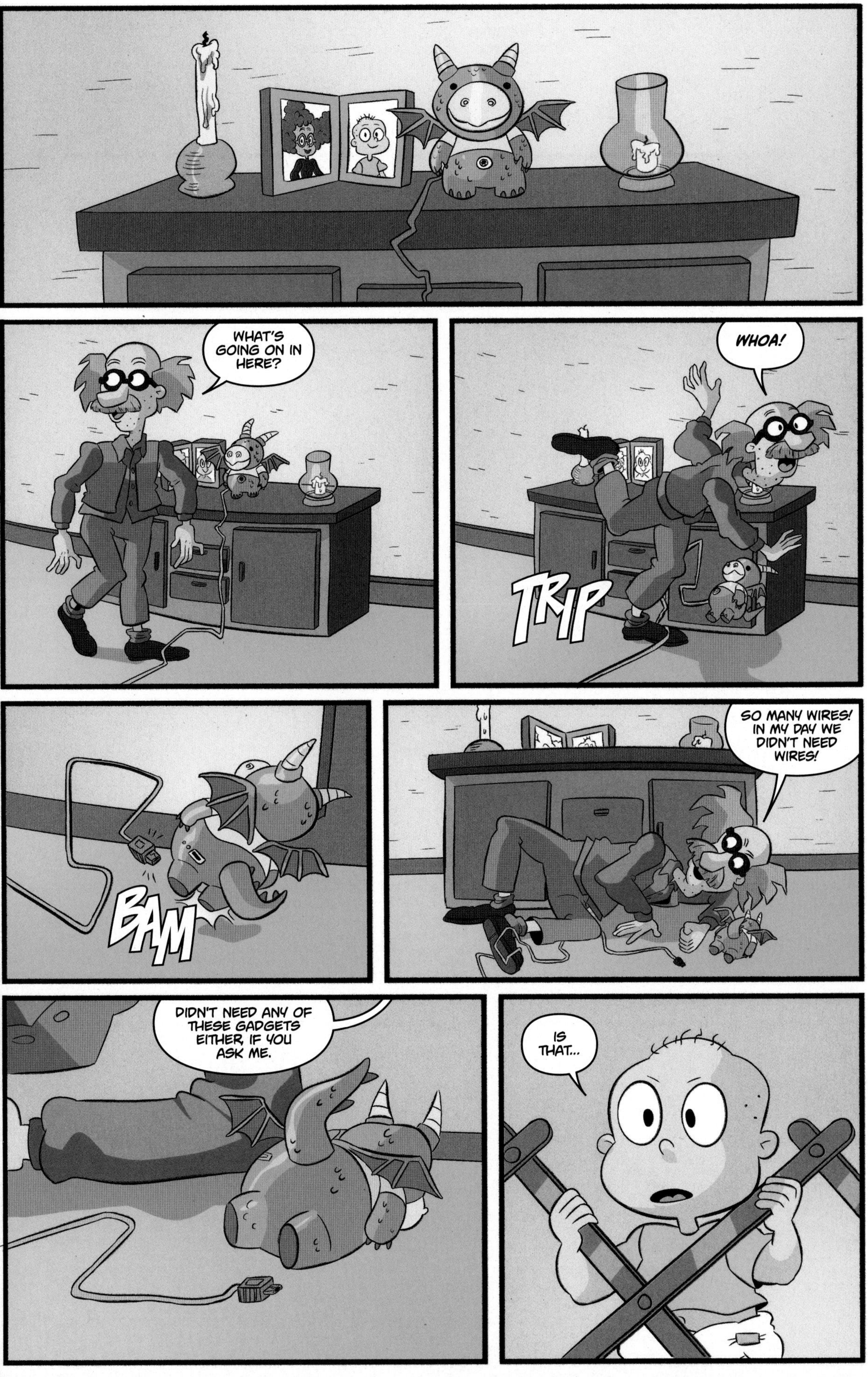
WHAT'S GOING ON IN HERE?
WHOA!
TRIP
BAM
SO MANY WIRES! IN MY DAY WE DIDN'T NEED WIRES!
DIDN'T NEED ANY OF THESE GADGETS EITHER, IF YOU ASK ME.
IS THAT...

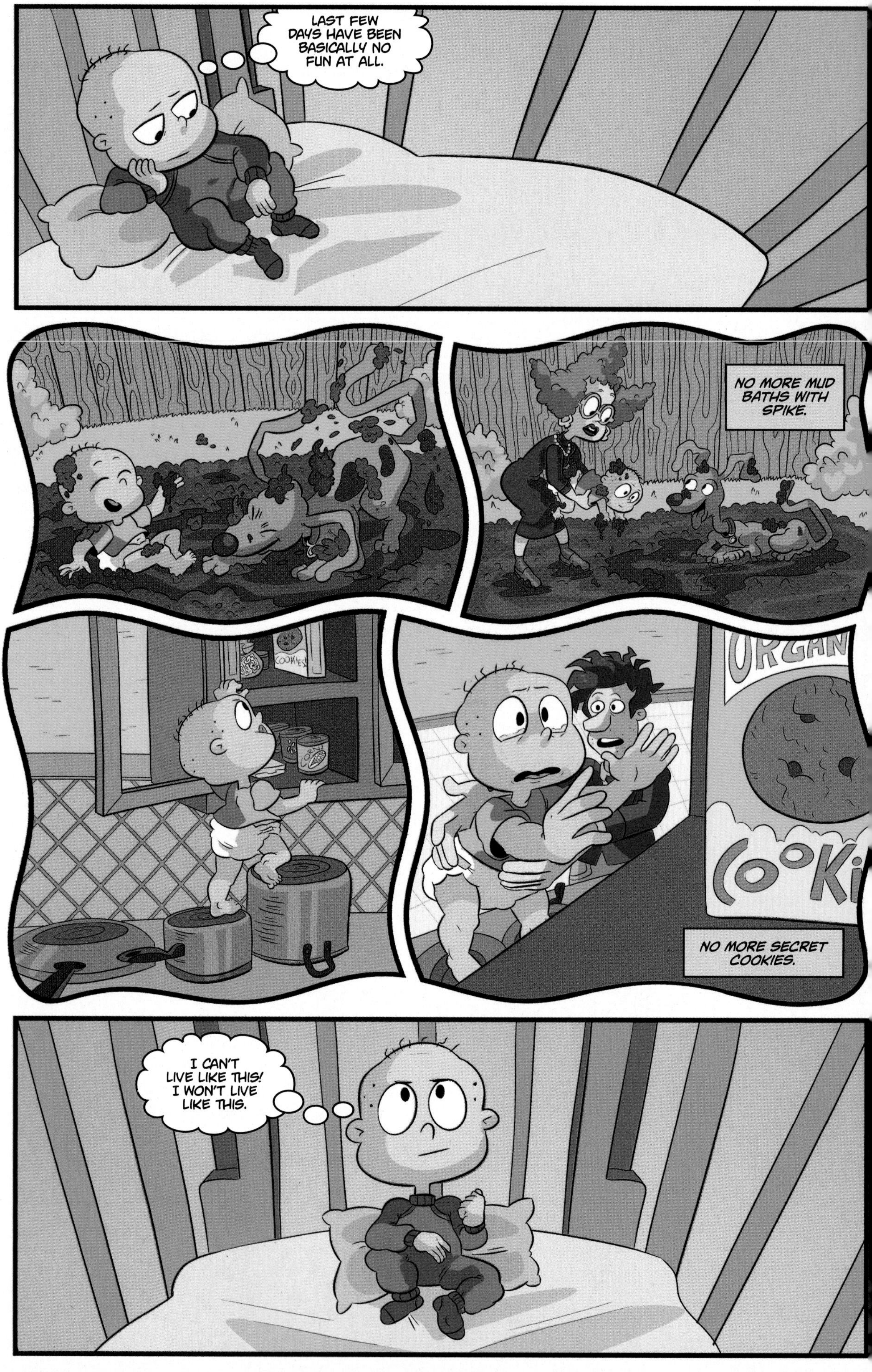
LAST FEW DAYS HAVE BEEN BASICALLY NO FUN AT ALL.
NO MORE MUD BATHS WITH SPIKE.
COOKIES
NO MORE SECRET COOKIES.
I CAN'T LIVE LIKE THIS! I WON'T LIVE LIKE THIS.

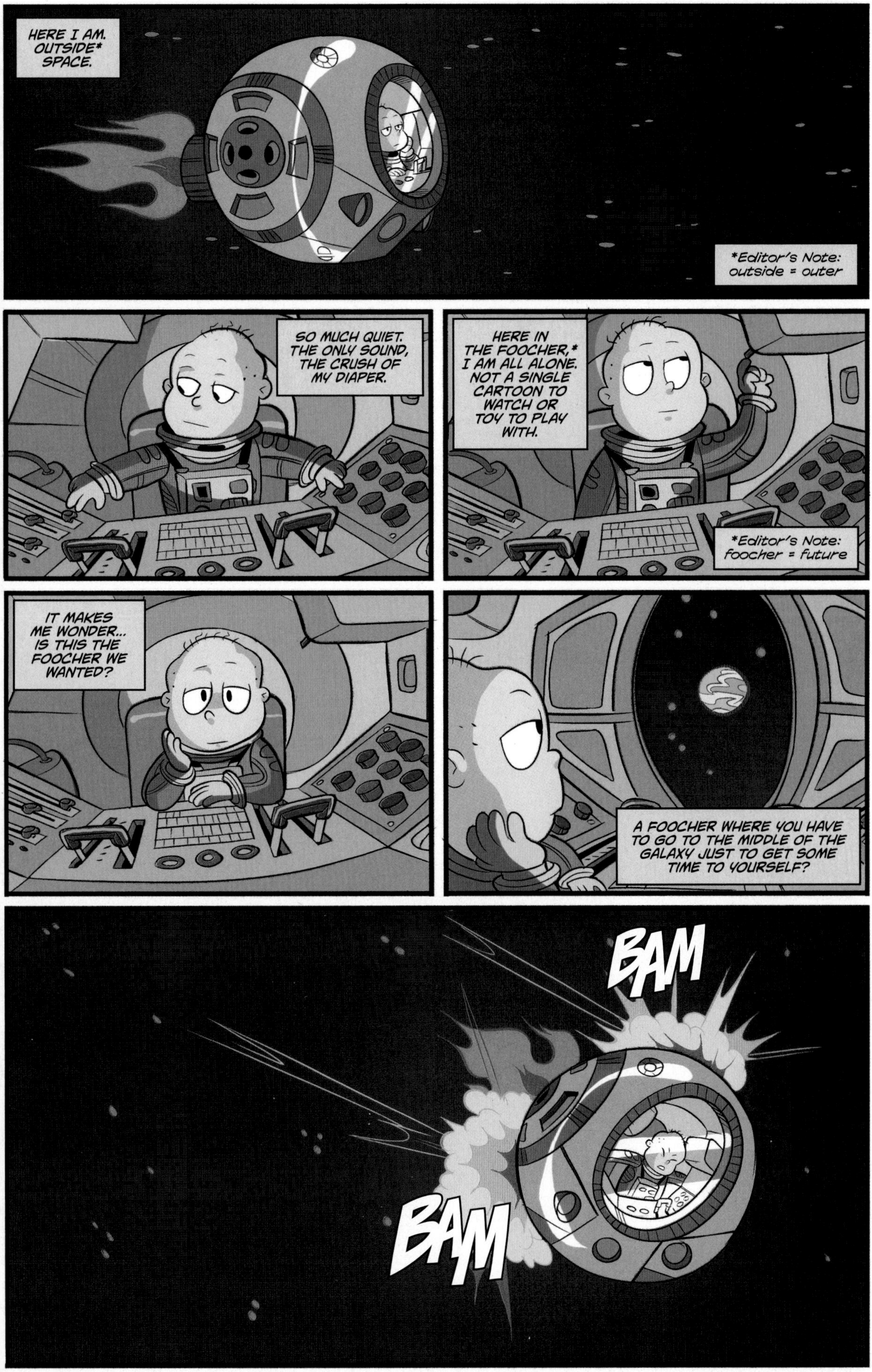
HERE I AM. OUTSIDE* SPACE.
*Editor's Note: outside = outer
SO MUCH QUIET. THE ONLY SOUND, THE CRUSH OF MY DIAPER.
HERE IN THE FOOCHER,* I AM ALL ALONE. NOT A SINGLE CARTOON TO WATCH OR TOY TO PLAY WITH.
*Editor's Note: foocher = future
IT MAKES ME WONDER... IS THIS THE FOOCHER WE WANTED?
A FOOCHER WHERE YOU HAVE TO GO TO THE MIDDLE OF THE GALAXY JUST TO GET SOME TIME TO YOURSELF?
BAM
BAM

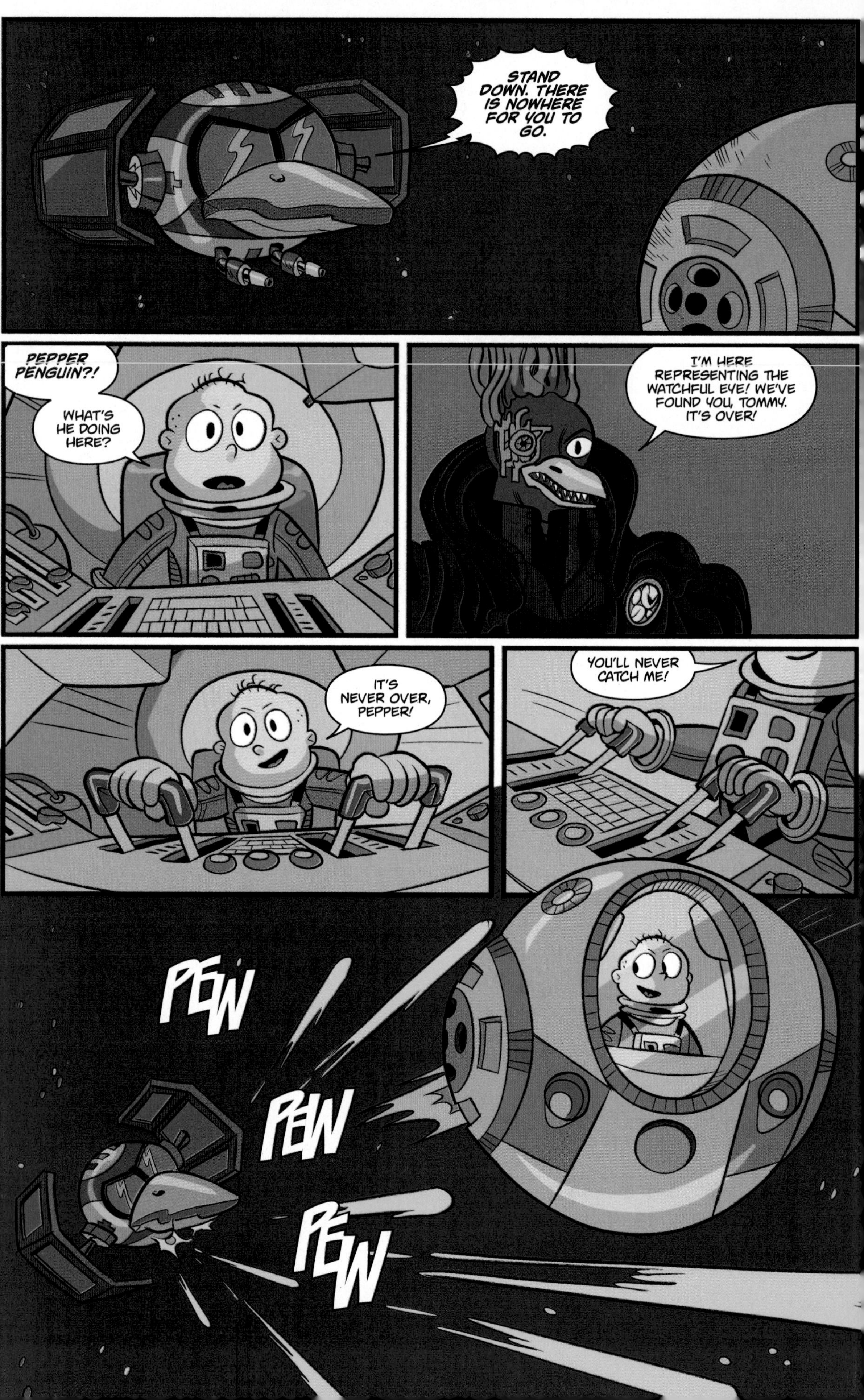
STAND DOWN. THERE IS NOWHERE FOR YOU TO GO.
PEPPER PENGUIN?!
WHAT'S HE DOING HERE?
I'M HERE REPRESENTING THE WATCHFUL EYE! WE'VE FOUND YOU, TOMMY. IT'S OVER!
IT'S NEVER OVER, PEPPER!
YOU'LL NEVER CATCH ME!
PEW
PEW
PEW

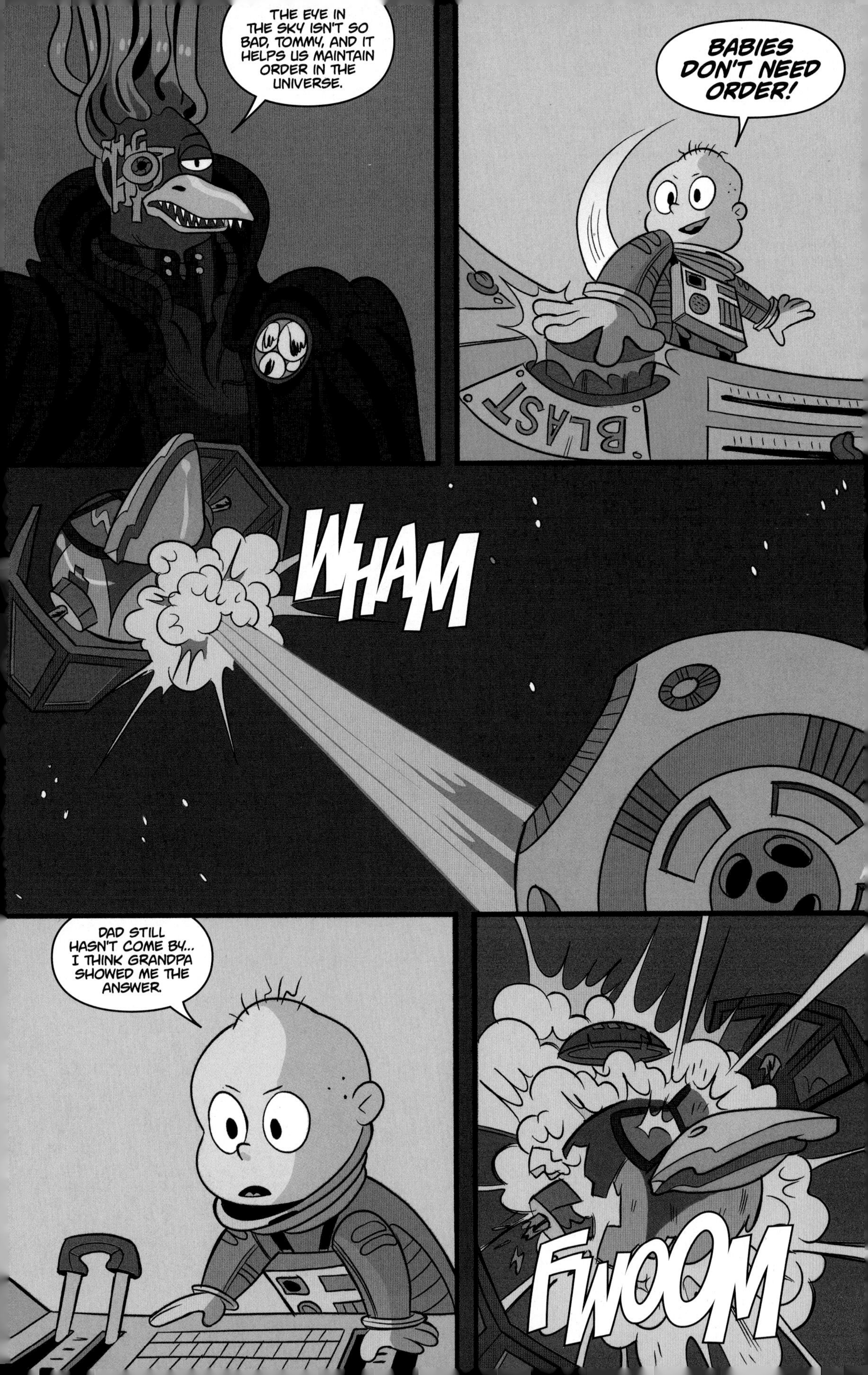
THE EYE IN THE SKY ISN'T SO BAD, TOMMY, AND IT HELPS US MAINTAIN ORDER IN THE UNIVERSE.
BABIES DON'T NEED ORDER!
BLAST
WHAM
DAD STILL HASN'T COME BY... I THINK GRANDPA SHOWED ME THE ANSWER.
FWOOM

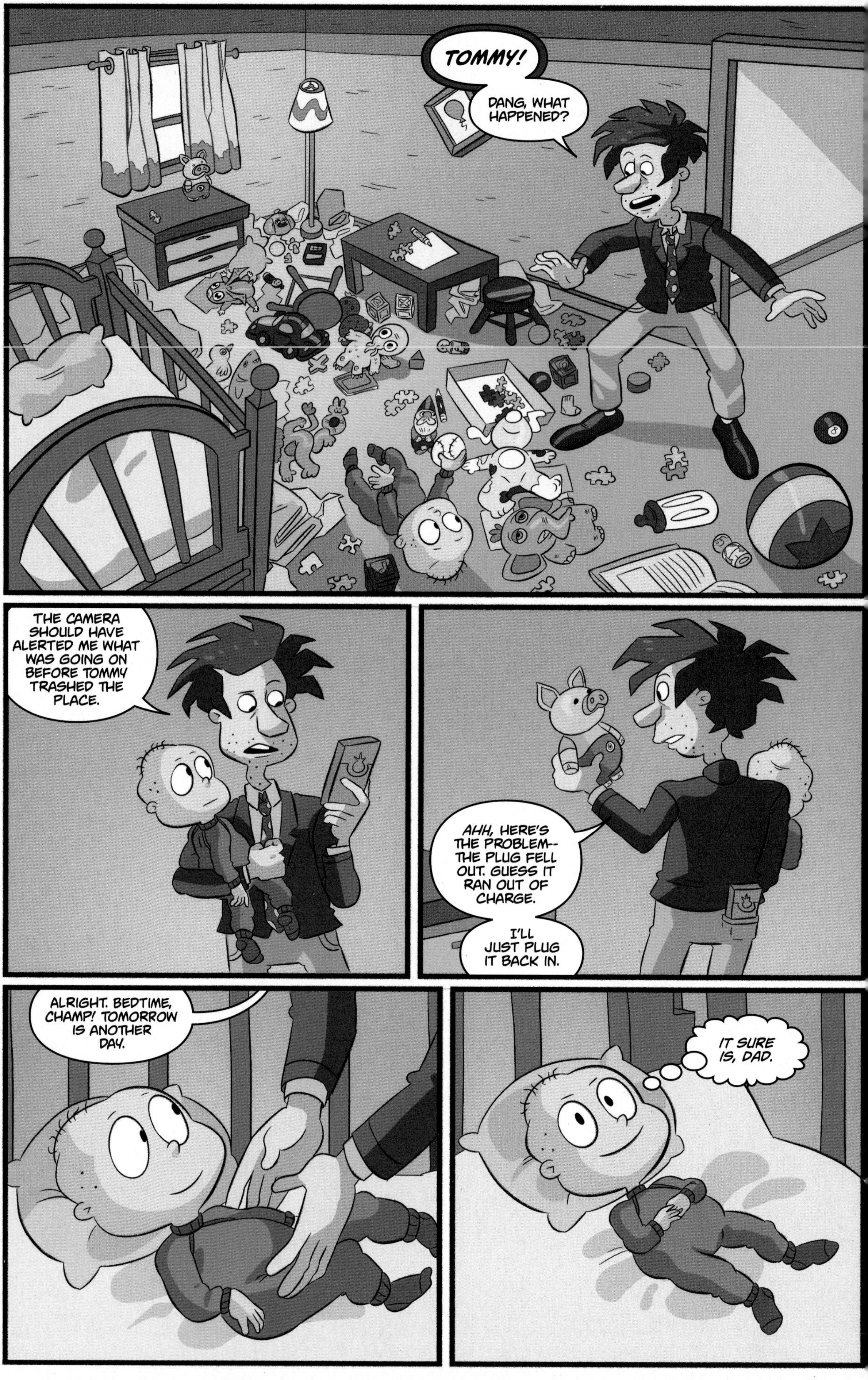
TOMMY!
DANG, WHAT HAPPENED?
THE CAMERA SHOULD HAVE ALERTED ME WHAT WAS GOING ON BEFORE TOMMY TRASHED THE PLACE.
AHH, HERE'S THE PROBLEM-- THE PLUG FELL OUT. GUESS IT RAN OUT OF CHARGE.
I'LL JUST PLUG IT BACK IN.
ALRIGHT. BEDTIME, CHAMP! TOMORROW IS ANOTHER DAY.
IT SURE IS, DAD.

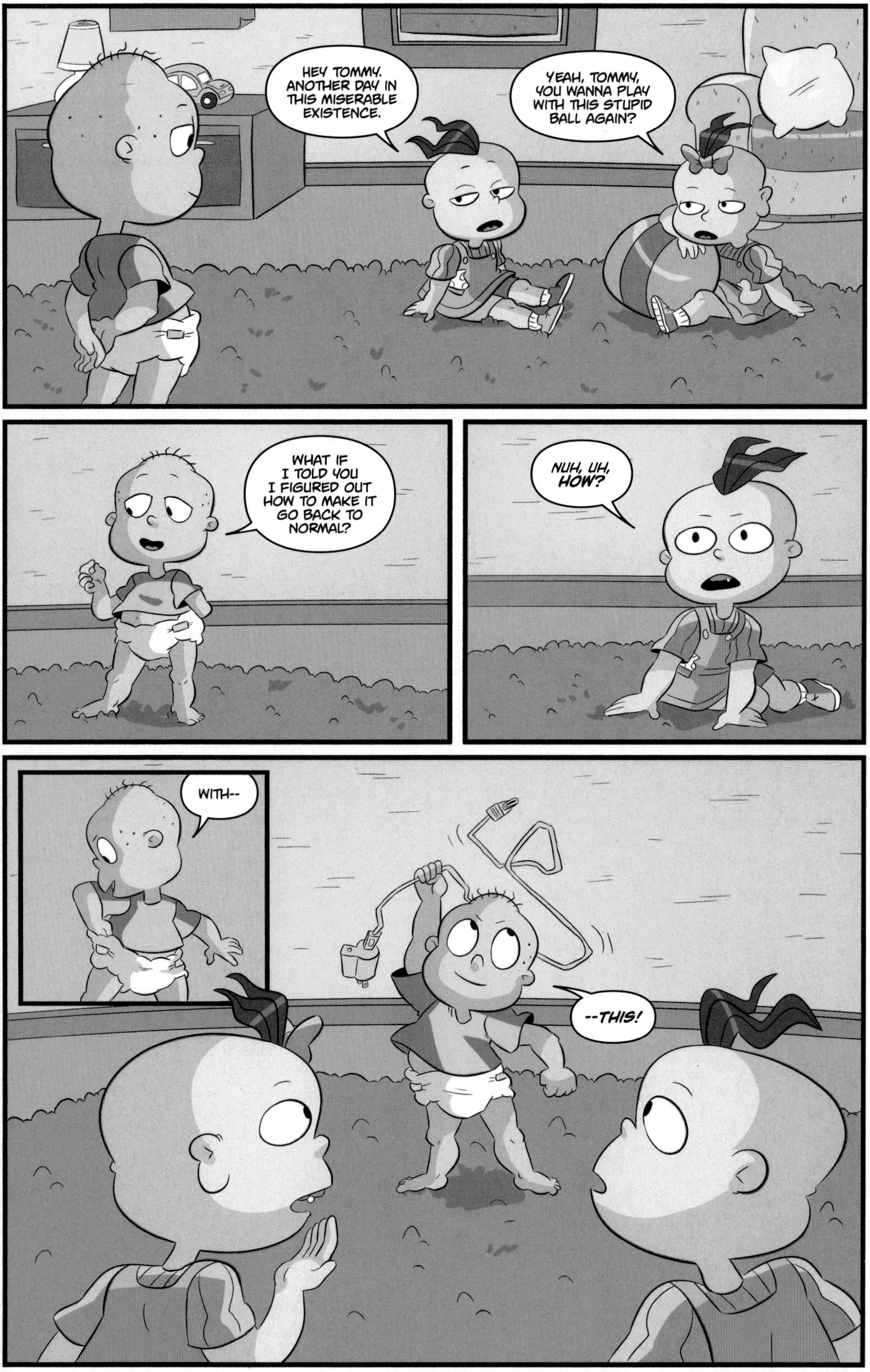
HEY TOMMY. ANOTHER DAY IN THIS MISERABLE EXISTENCE.
YEAH, TOMMY, YOU WANNA PLAY WITH THIS STUPID BALL AGAIN?
WHAT IF I TOLD YOU I FIGURED OUT HOW TO MAKE IT GO BACK TO NORMAL?
NUH, UH, HOW?
WITH--
--THIS!

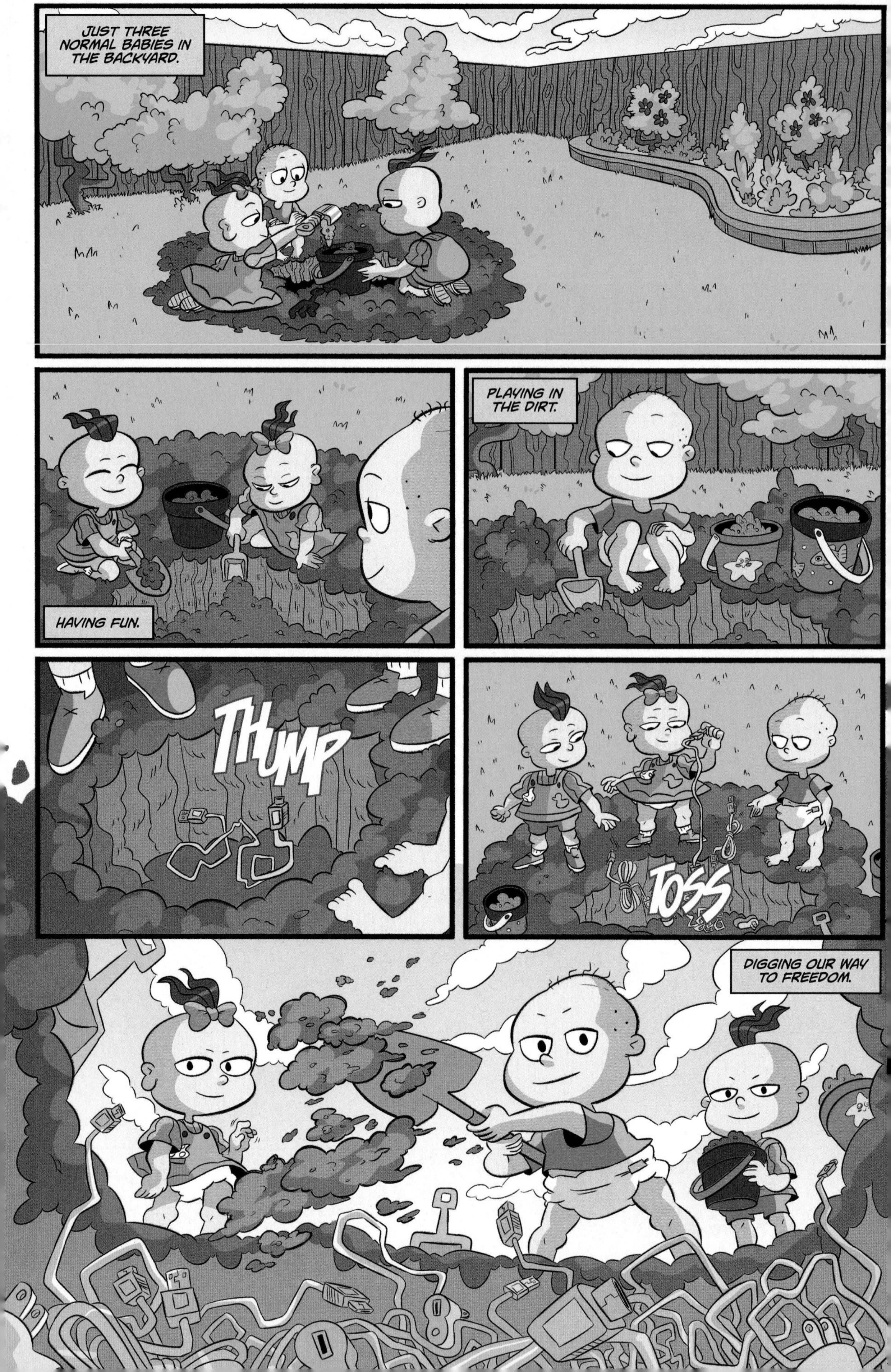
JUST THREE NORMAL BABIES IN THE BACKYARD.
HAVING FUN.
PLAYING IN THE DIRT.
THUMP
TOSS
DIGGING OUR WAY TO FREEDOM.

RIGHT NOW, THIS IS A
WAR OF NOLLIDGES!

CHAPTER
THREE

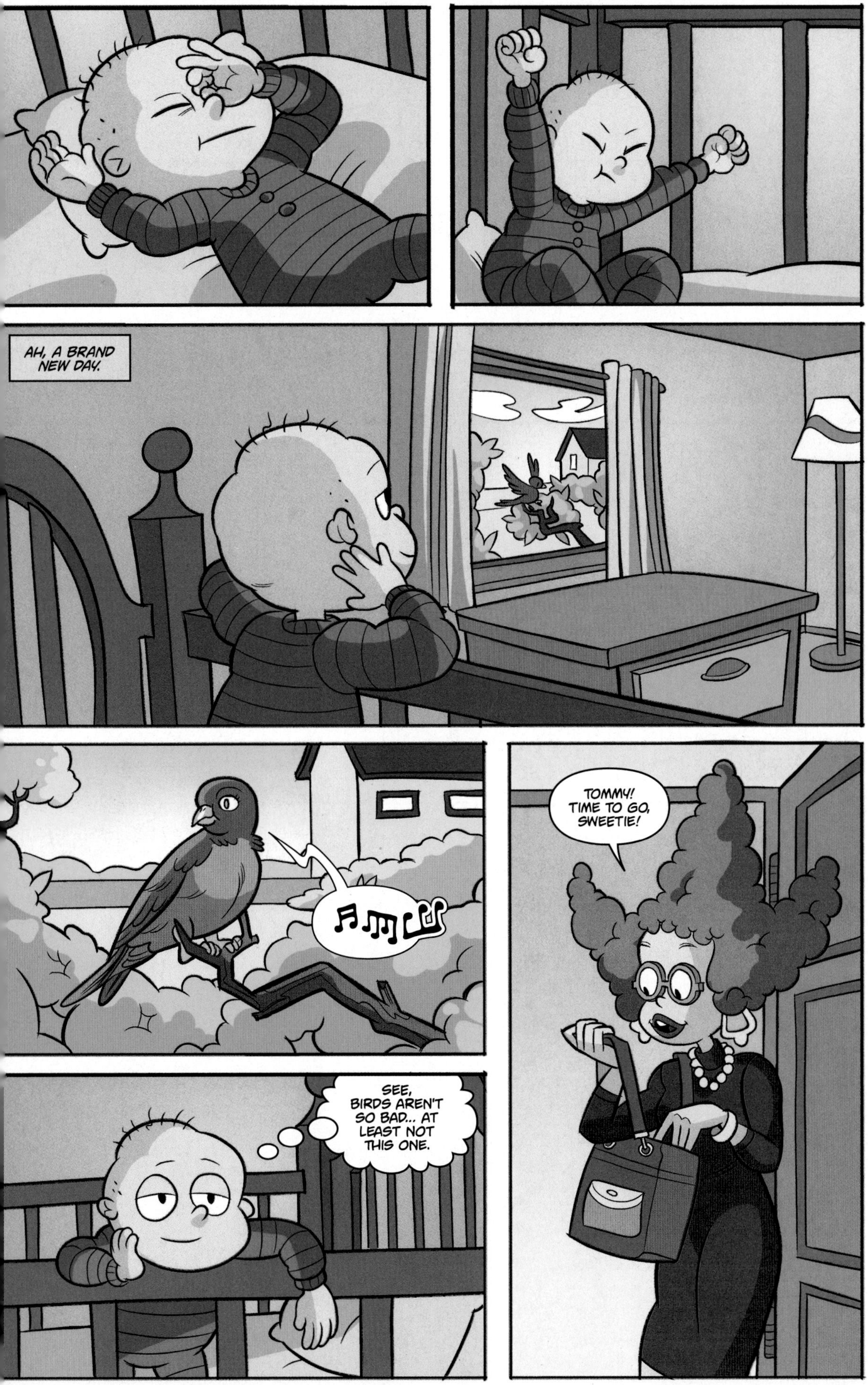
AH, A BRAND NEW DAY.
TOMMY! TIME TO GO, SWEETIE!
SEE, BIRDS AREN'T SO BAD... AT LEAST NOT THIS ONE.

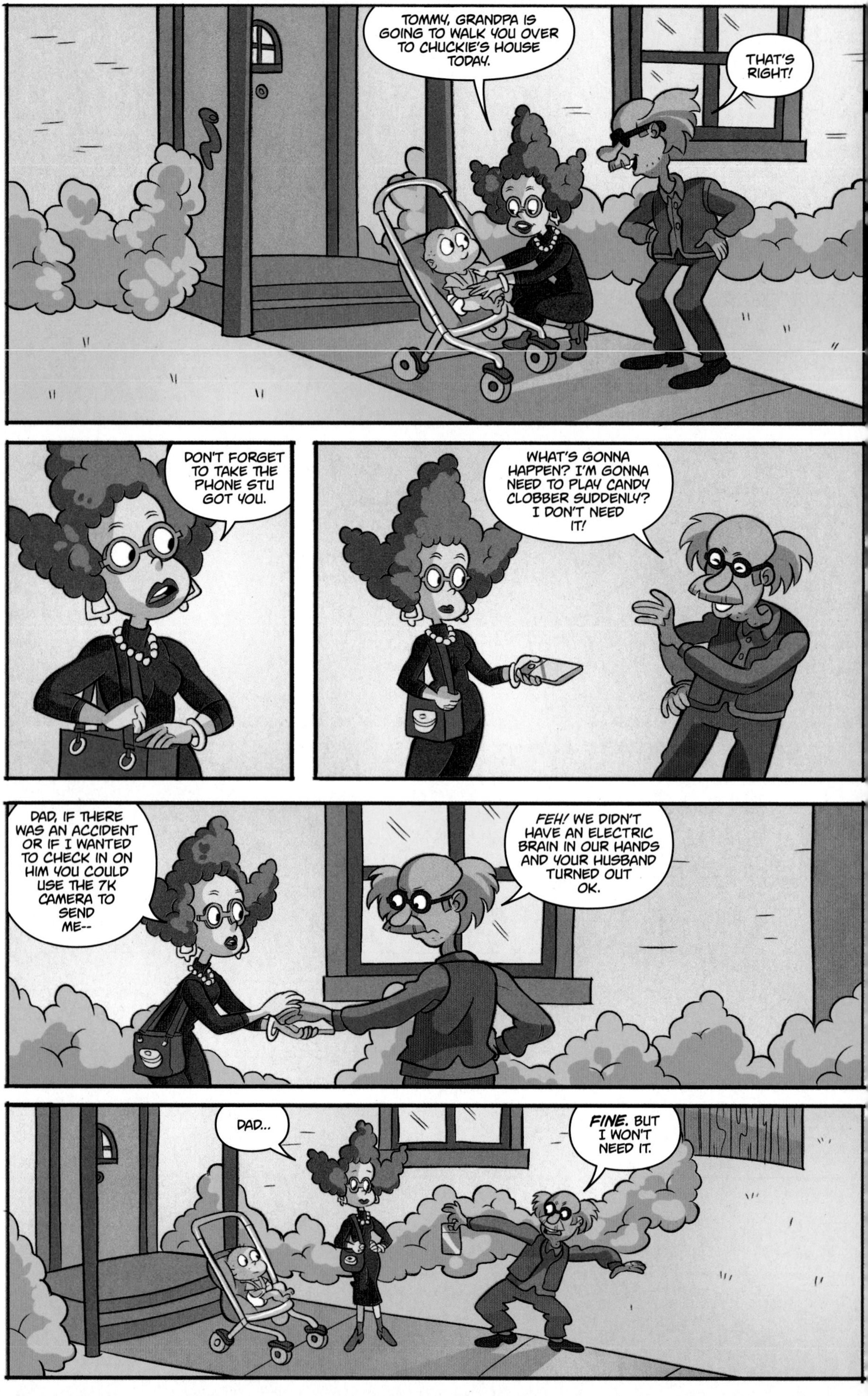
TOMMY, GRANDPA IS GOING TO WALK YOU OVER TO CHUCKIE'S HOUSE TODAY.
THAT'S RIGHT!
DON'T FORGET TO TAKE THE PHONE STU GOT YOU.
WHAT'S GONNA HAPPEN? I'M GONNA NEED TO PLAY CANDY CLOBBER SUDDENLY? I DON'T NEED IT!
DAD, IF THERE WAS AN ACCIDENT OR IF I WANTED TO CHECK IN ON HIM YOU COULD USE THE 7K CAMERA TO SEND ME--
FEH! WE DIDN'T HAVE AN ELECTRIC BRAIN IN OUR HANDS AND YOUR HUSBAND TURNED OUT OK.
DAD...
FINE. BUT I WON'T NEED IT.

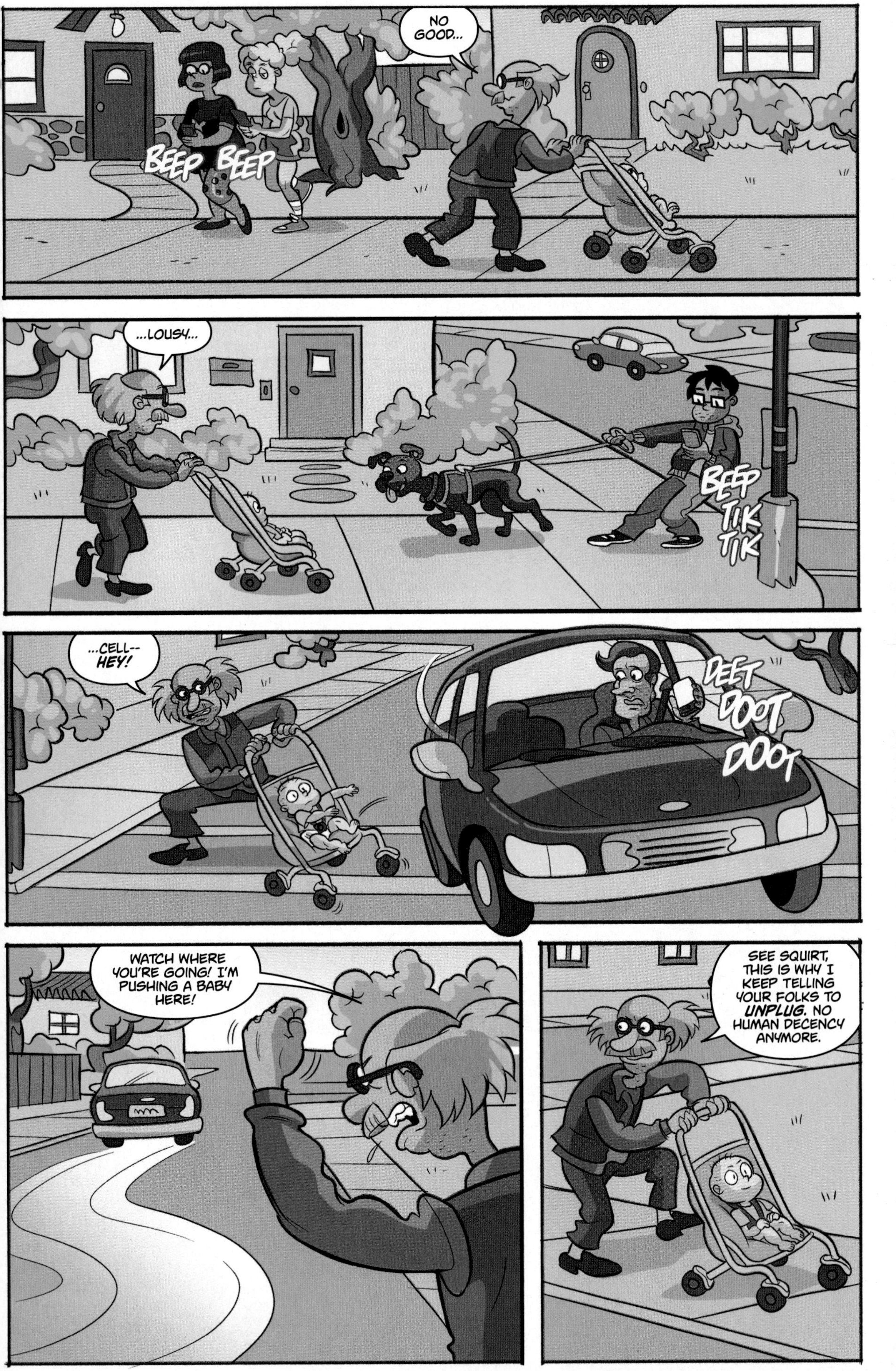
NO GOOD...
BEEP BEEP
...LOUSY...
BEEP TIK TIK
...CELL-- HEY!
DEET DOOT DOOT
WATCH WHERE YOU'RE GOING! I'M PUSHING A BABY HERE!
SEE SQUIRT, THIS IS WHY I KEEP TELLING YOUR FOLKS TO UNPLUG. NO HUMAN DECENCY ANYMORE.

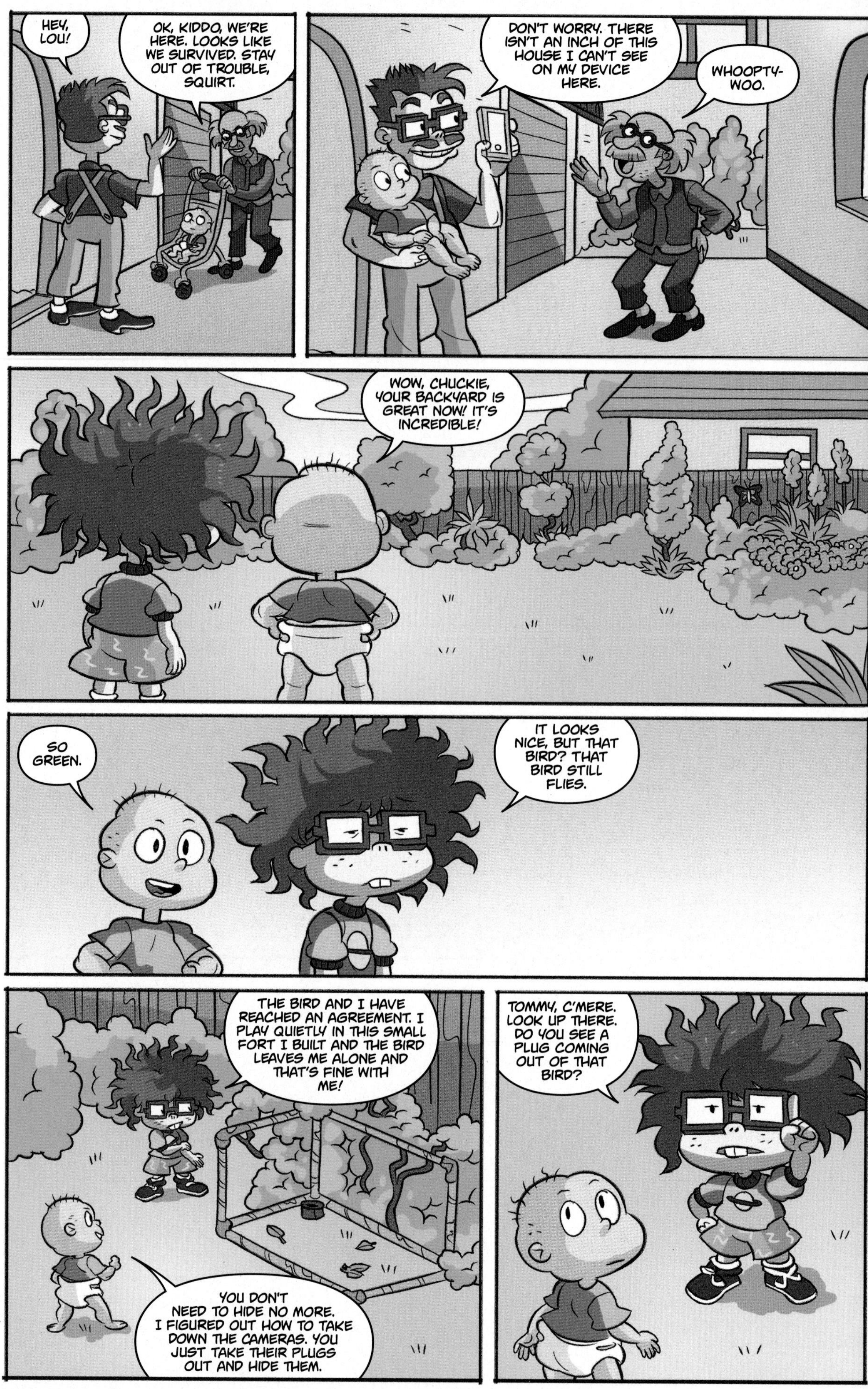
HEY, LOU!
OK, KIDDO, WE'RE HERE. LOOKS LIKE WE SURVIVED. STAY OUT OF TROUBLE, SQUIRT.
DON'T WORRY. THERE ISN'T AN INCH OF THIS HOUSE I CAN'T SEE ON MY DEVICE HERE.
WHOOPTY-WOO.
WOW, CHUCKIE, YOUR BACKYARD IS GREAT NOW! IT'S INCREDIBLE!
SO GREEN.
IT LOOKS NICE, BUT THAT BIRD? THAT BIRD STILL FLIES.
THE BIRD AND I HAVE REACHED AN AGREEMENT. I PLAY QUIETLY IN THIS SMALL FORT I BUILT AND THE BIRD LEAVES ME ALONE AND THAT'S FINE WITH ME!
YOU DON'T NEED TO HIDE NO MORE. I FIGURED OUT HOW TO TAKE DOWN THE CAMERAS. YOU JUST TAKE THEIR PLUGS OUT AND HIDE THEM.
TOMMY, C'MERE. LOOK UP THERE. DO YOU SEE A PLUG COMING OUT OF THAT BIRD?

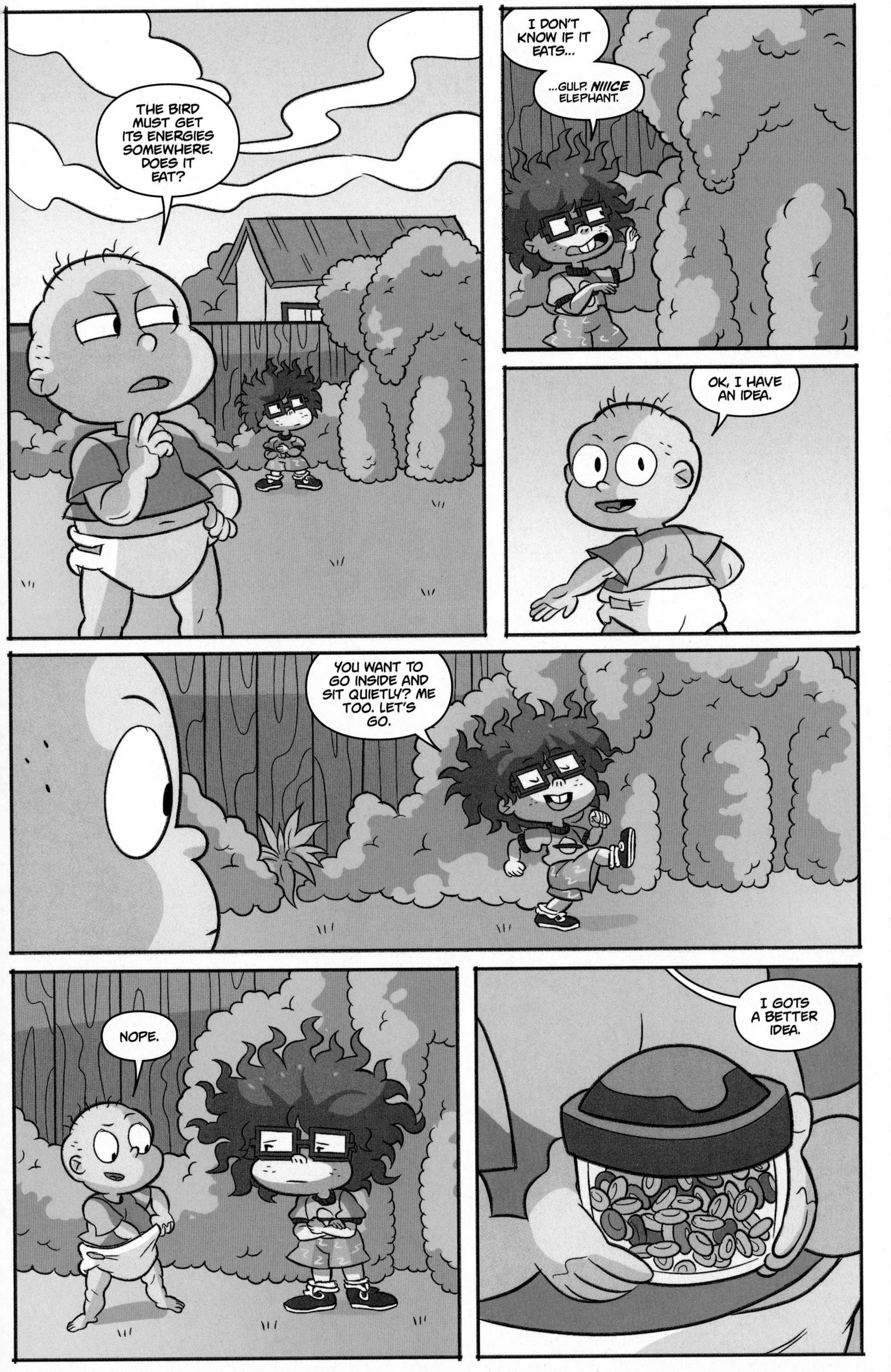
THE BIRD MUST GET ITS ENERGIES SOMEWHERE. DOES IT EAT?
I DON'T KNOW IF IT EATS...
...GULP. NIIICE ELEPHANT.
OK, I HAVE AN IDEA.
YOU WANT TO GO INSIDE AND SIT QUIETLY? ME TOO. LET'S GO.
NOPE.
I GOTS A BETTER IDEA.

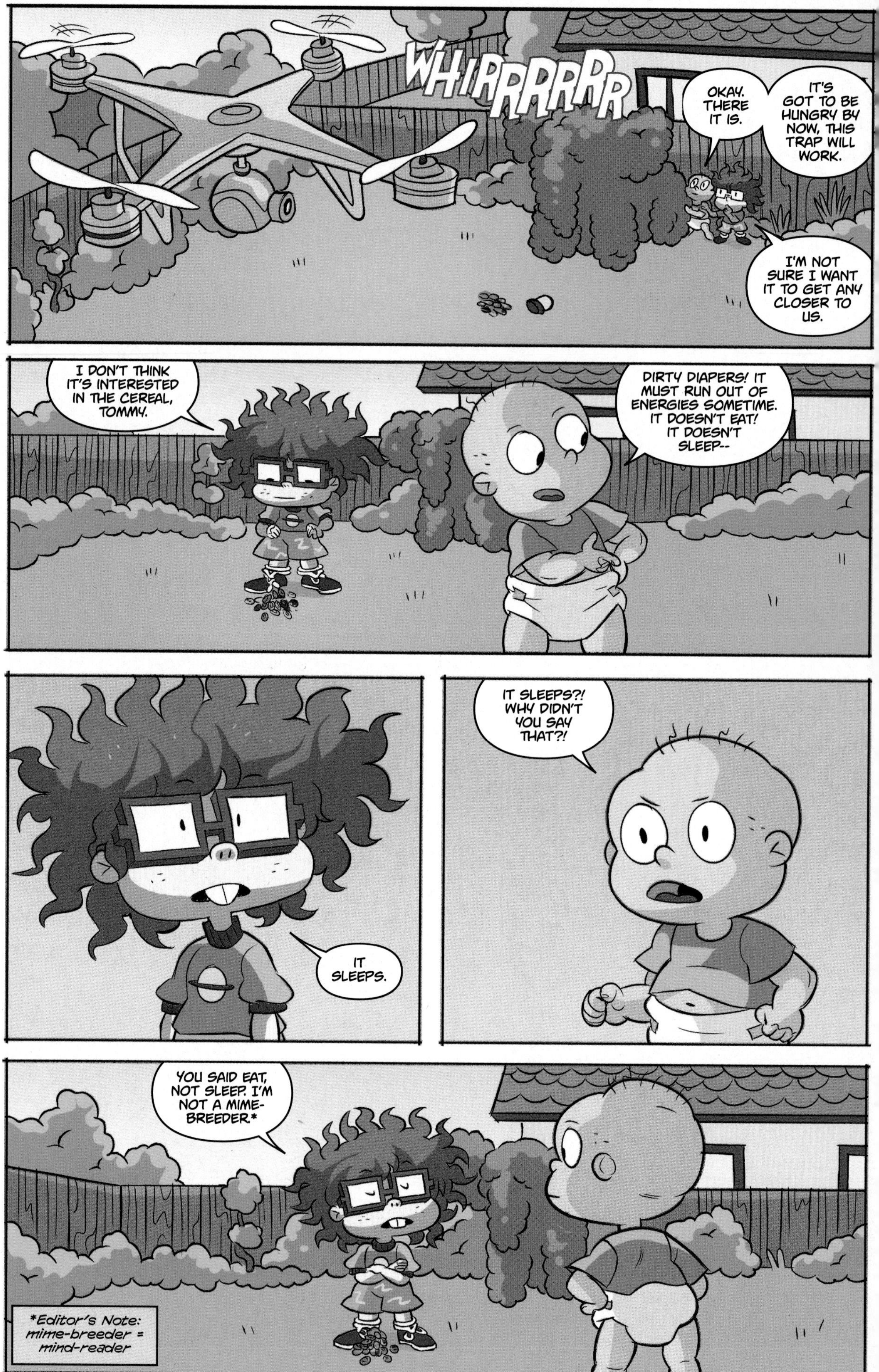
WHIRRRRRRR
OKAY. THERE IT IS.
IT'S GOT TO BE HUNGRY BY NOW, THIS TRAP WILL WORK.
I'M NOT SURE I WANT IT TO GET ANY CLOSER TO US.
I DON'T THINK IT'S INTERESTED IN THE CEREAL, TOMMY.
DIRTY DIAPERS! IT MUST RUN OUT OF ENERGIES SOMETIME. IT DOESN'T EAT! IT DOESN'T SLEEP--
IT SLEEPS.
IT SLEEPS?! WHY DIDN'T YOU SAY THAT?!
YOU SAID EAT, NOT SLEEP. I'M NOT A MIME-BREEDER.*
*Editor's Note: mime-breeder = mind-reader

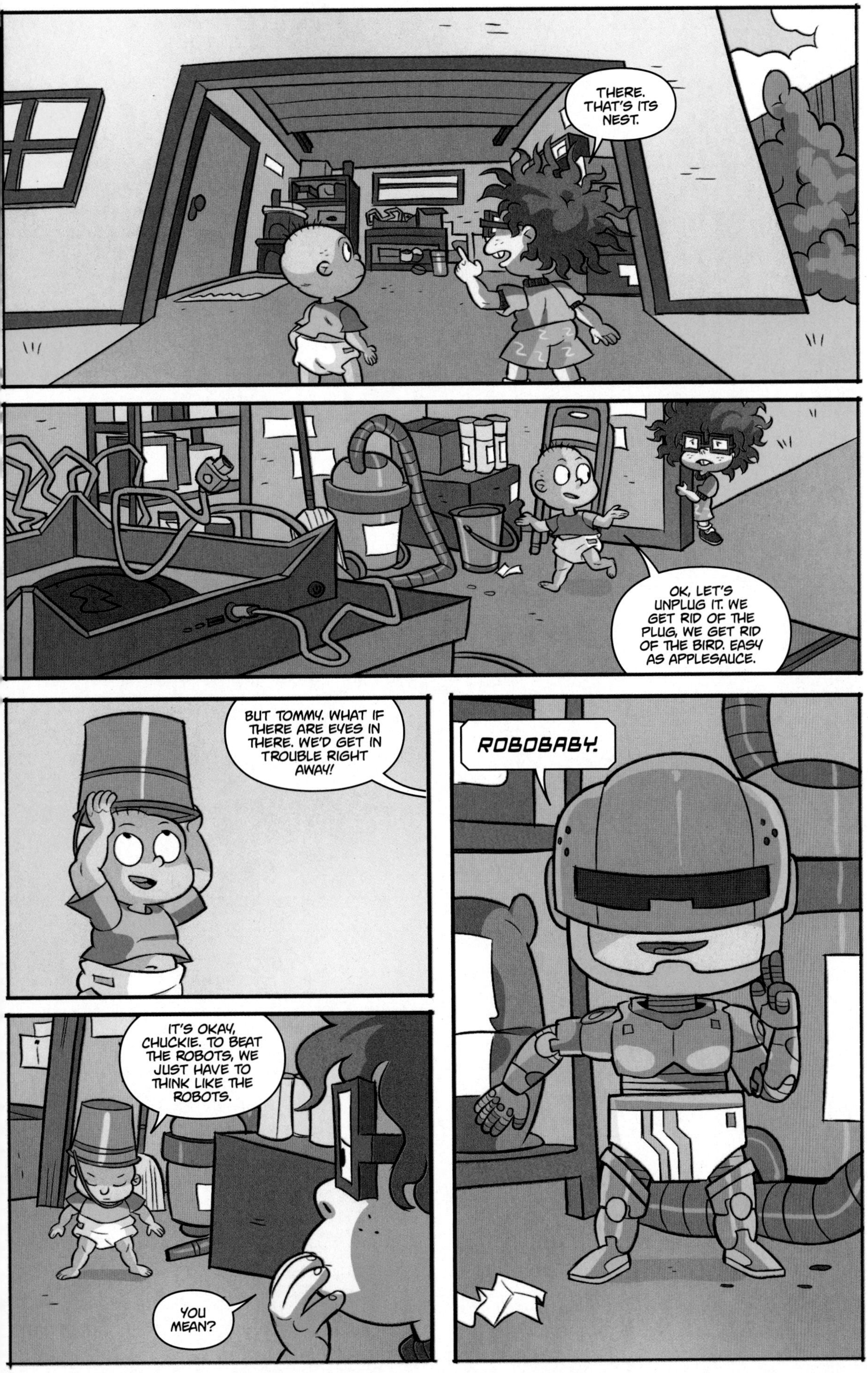
THERE. THAT'S ITS NEST.
OK, LET'S UNPLUG IT. WE GET RID OF THE PLUG, WE GET RID OF THE BIRD. EASY AS APPLESAUCE.
BUT TOMMY. WHAT IF THERE ARE EYES IN THERE. WE'D GET IN TROUBLE RIGHT AWAY!
IT'S OKAY, CHUCKIE. TO BEAT THE ROBOTS, WE JUST HAVE TO THINK LIKE THE ROBOTS.
YOU MEAN?
ROBOBABY.

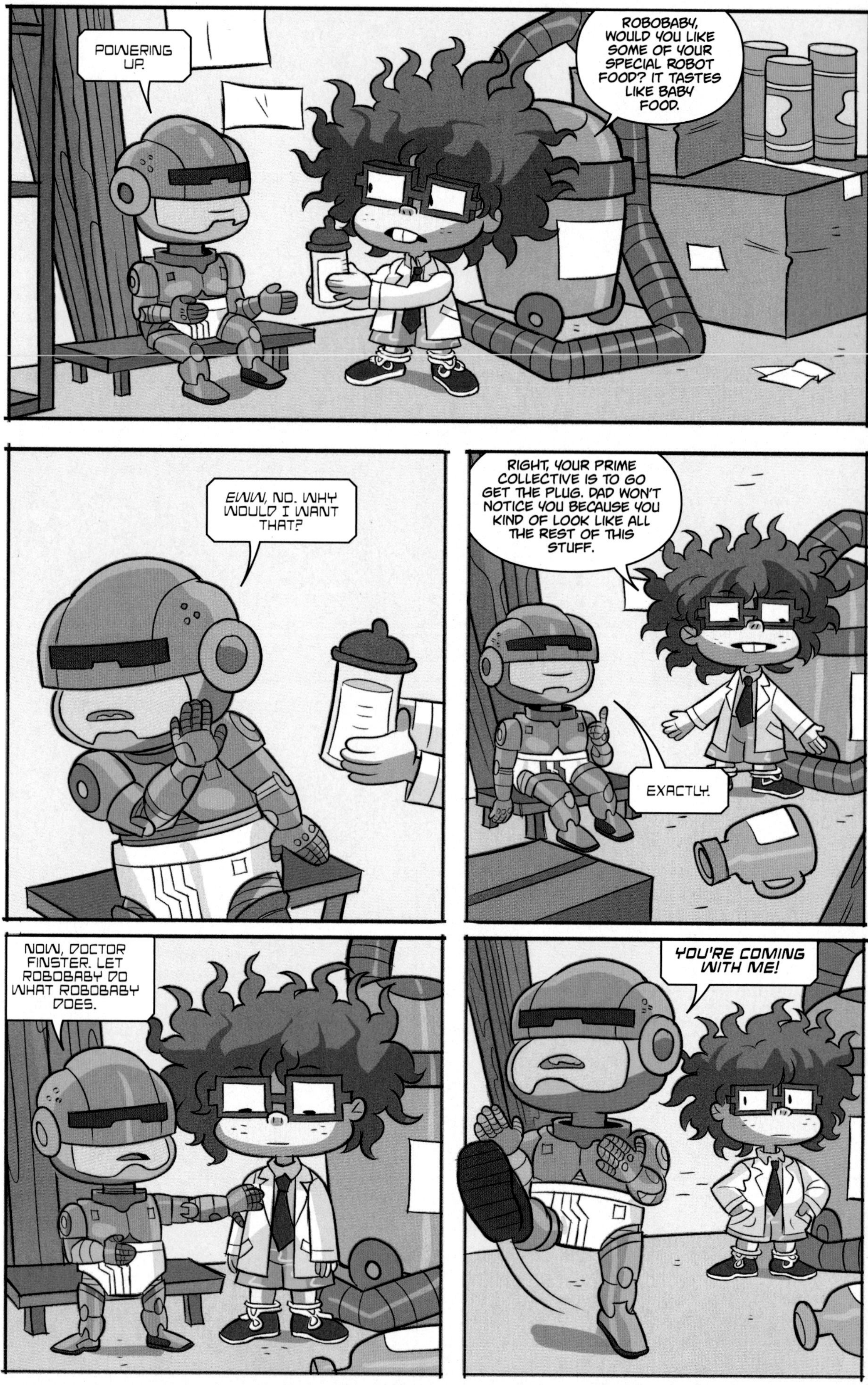
POWERING UP.
ROBOBABY, WOULD YOU LIKE SOME OF YOUR SPECIAL ROBOT FOOD? IT TASTES LIKE BABY FOOD.
EWW, NO. WHY WOULD I WANT THAT?
RIGHT, YOUR PRIME COLLECTIVE IS TO GO GET THE PLUG. DAD WON'T NOTICE YOU BECAUSE YOU KIND OF LOOK LIKE ALL THE REST OF THIS STUFF.
EXACTLY.
NOW, DOCTOR FINSTER. LET ROBOBABY DO WHAT ROBOBABY DOES.
YOU'RE COMING WITH ME!

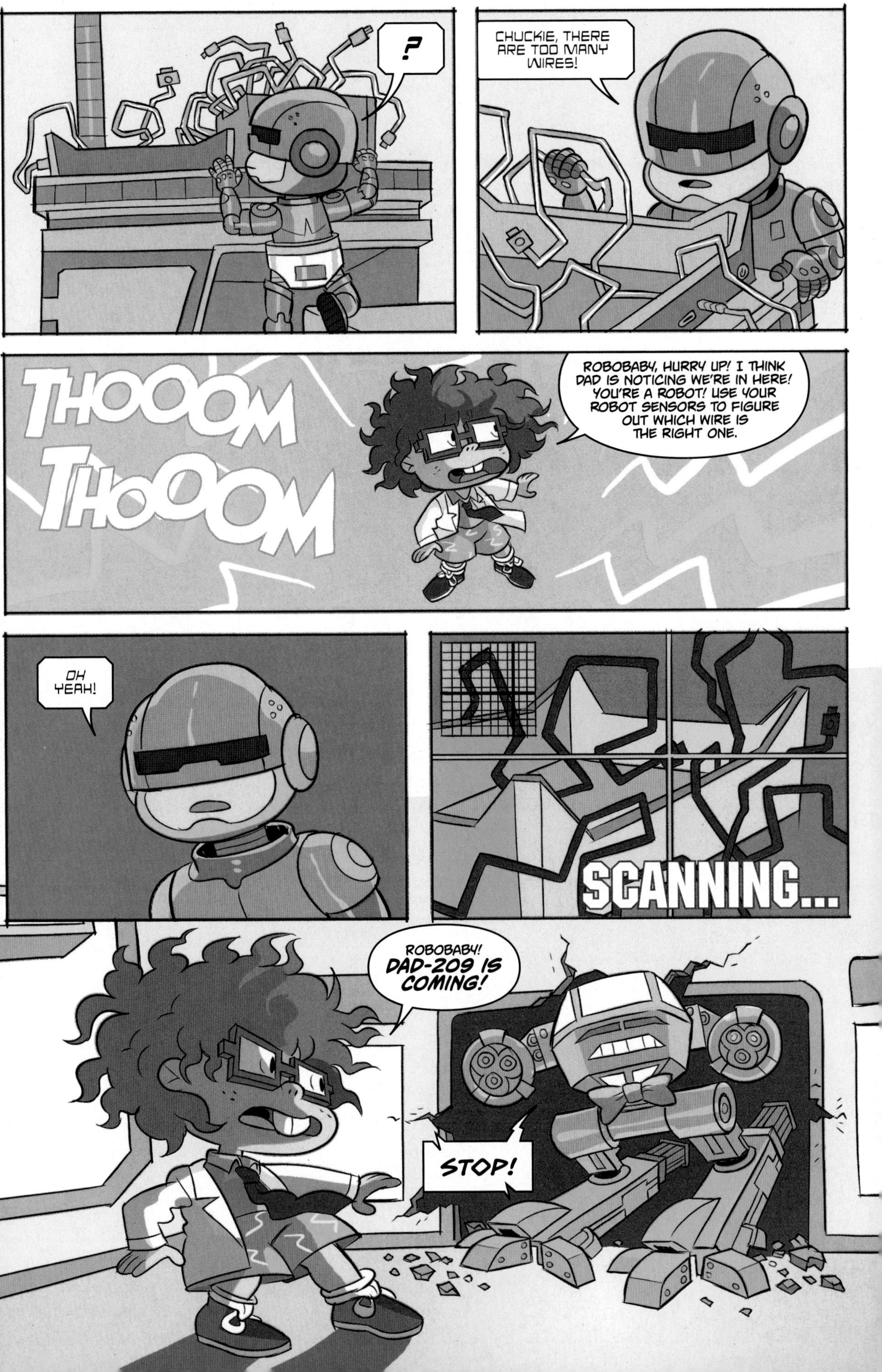
?
CHUCKIE, THERE ARE TOO MANY WIRES!
THOOOM THOOOM
ROBOBABY, HURRY UP! I THINK DAD IS NOTICING WE'RE IN HERE! YOU'RE A ROBOT! USE YOUR ROBOT SENSORS TO FIGURE OUT WHICH WIRE IS THE RIGHT ONE.
OH YEAH!
SCANNING...
ROBOBABY! DAD-209 IS COMING!
STOP!

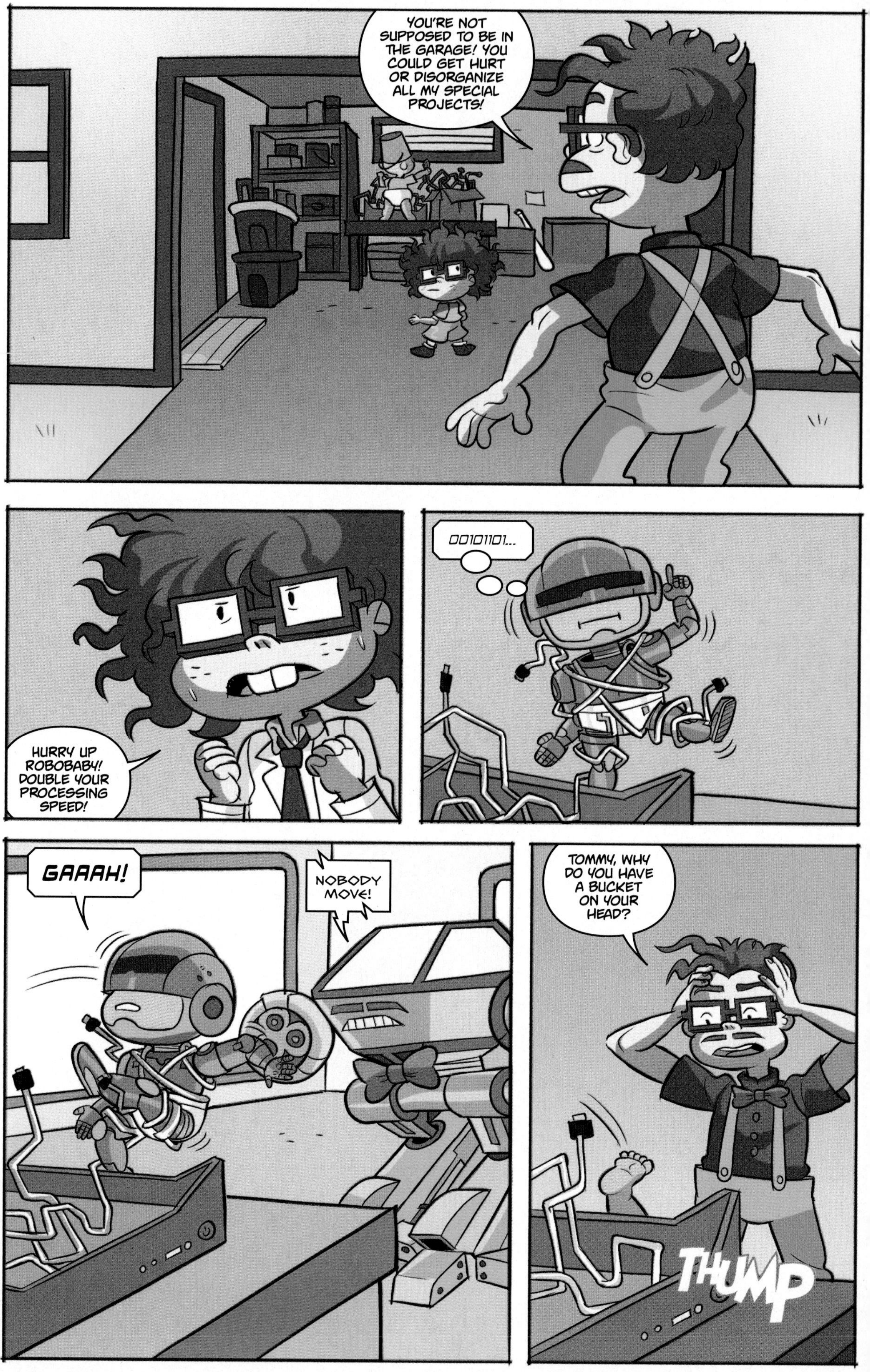
YOU'RE NOT SUPPOSED TO BE IN THE GARAGE! YOU COULD GET HURT OR DISORGANIZE ALL MY SPECIAL PROJECTS!
HURRY UP ROBOBABY! DOUBLE YOUR PROCESSING SPEED!
00101101...
GAAAH!
NOBODY MOVE!
TOMMY, WHY DO YOU HAVE A BUCKET ON YOUR HEAD?
THUMP

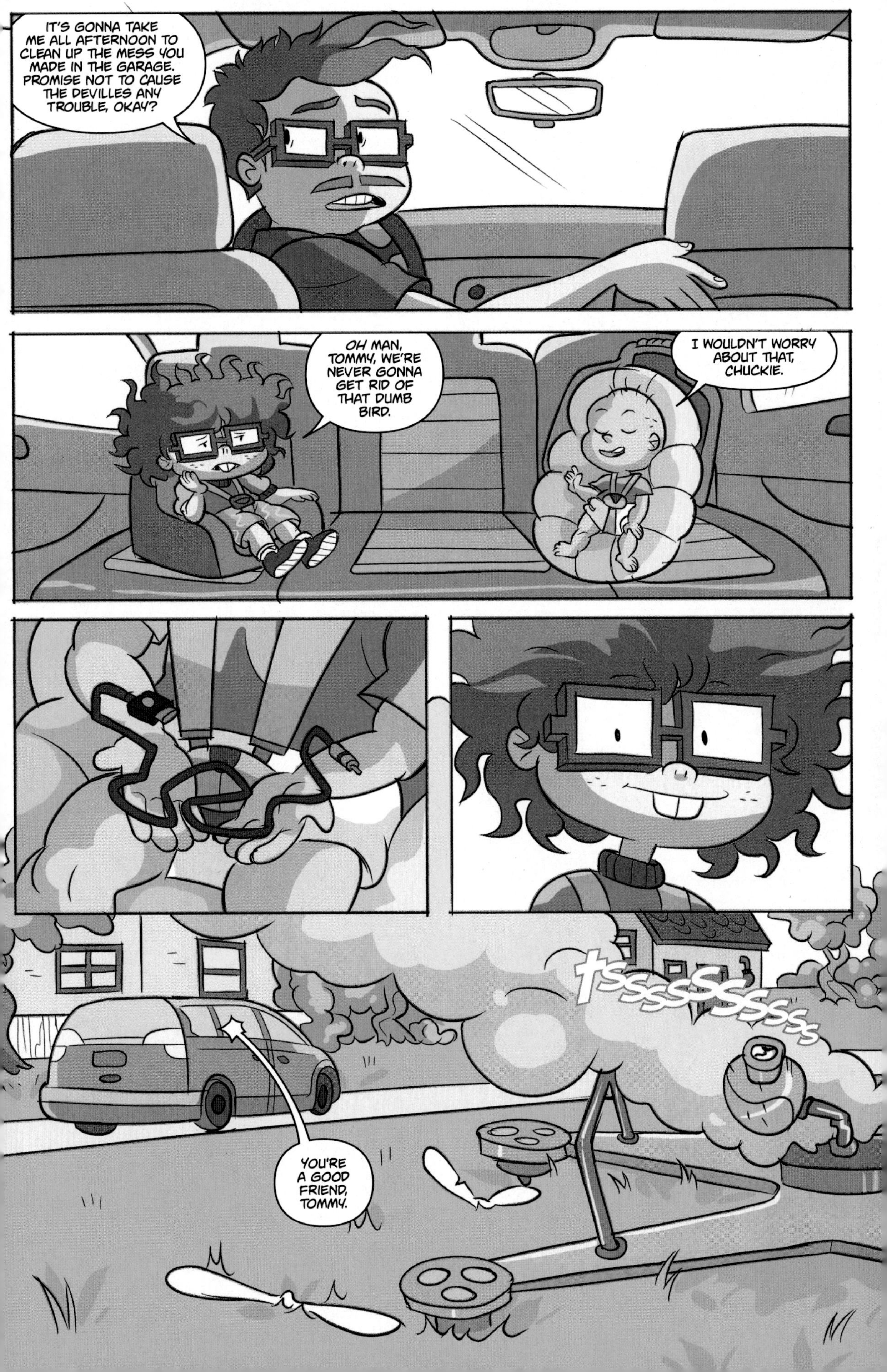
IT'S GONNA TAKE ME ALL AFTERNOON TO CLEAN UP THE MESS YOU MADE IN THE GARAGE. PROMISE NOT TO CAUSE THE DEVILLES ANY TROUBLE, OKAY?
OH MAN, TOMMY, WE'RE NEVER GONNA GET RID OF THAT DUMB BIRD.
I WOULDN'T WORRY ABOUT THAT, CHUCKIE.
tssssSSSSSsss
YOU'RE A GOOD FRIEND, TOMMY.

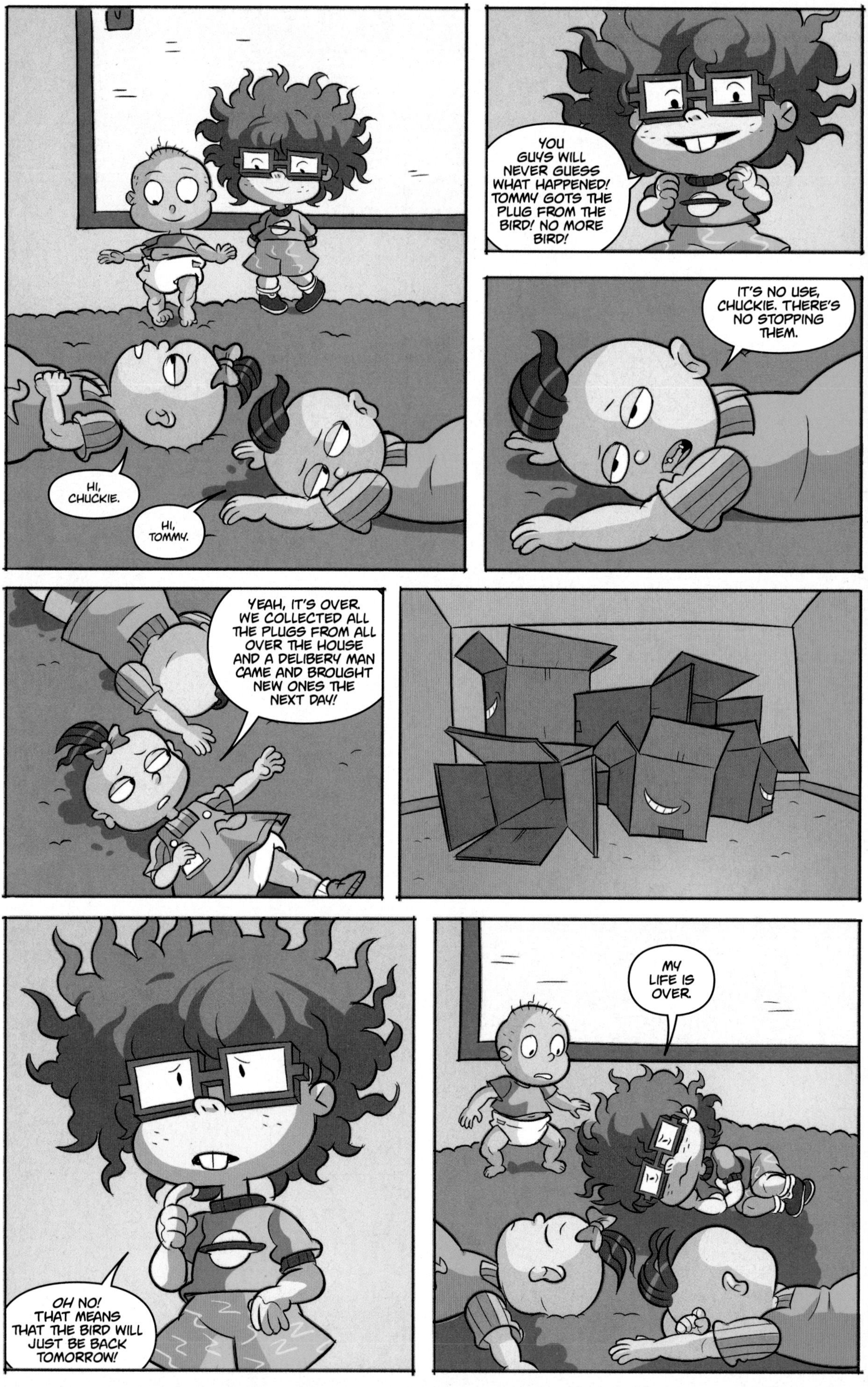
HI, CHUCKIE.
HI, TOMMY.
YOU GUYS WILL NEVER GUESS WHAT HAPPENED! TOMMY GOTS THE PLUG FROM THE BIRD! NO MORE BIRD!
IT'S NO USE, CHUCKIE. THERE'S NO STOPPING THEM.
YEAH, IT'S OVER. WE COLLECTED ALL THE PLUGS FROM ALL OVER THE HOUSE AND A DELIBERY MAN CAME AND BROUGHT NEW ONES THE NEXT DAY!
OH NO! THAT MEANS THAT THE BIRD WILL JUST BE BACK TOMORROW!
MY LIFE IS OVER.

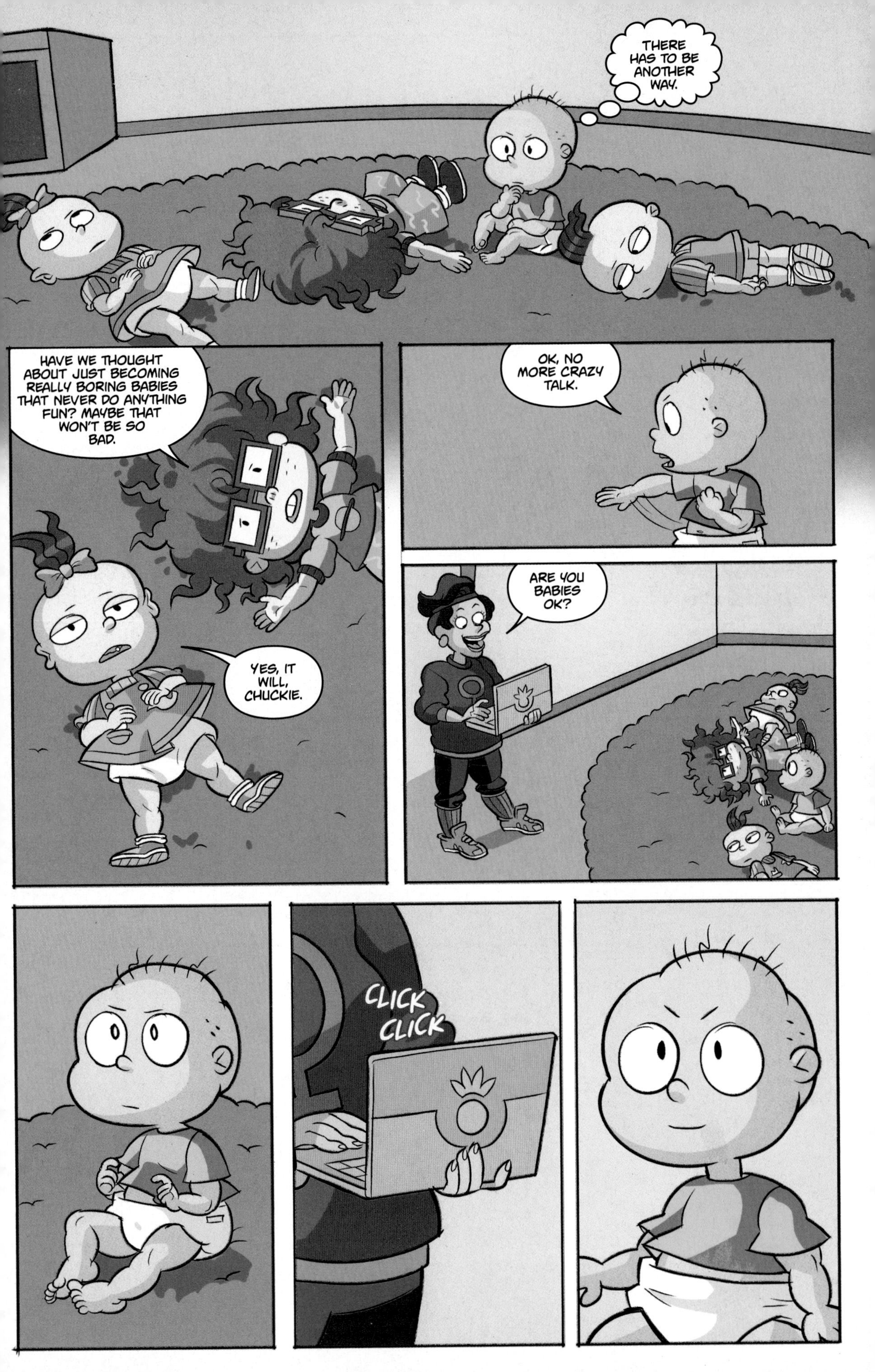
THERE HAS TO BE ANOTHER WAY.
HAVE WE THOUGHT ABOUT JUST BECOMING REALLY BORING BABIES THAT NEVER DO ANYTHING FUN? MAYBE THAT WON'T BE SO BAD.
YES, IT WILL, CHUCKIE.
OK, NO MORE CRAZY TALK.
ARE YOU BABIES OK?
CLICK
CLICK

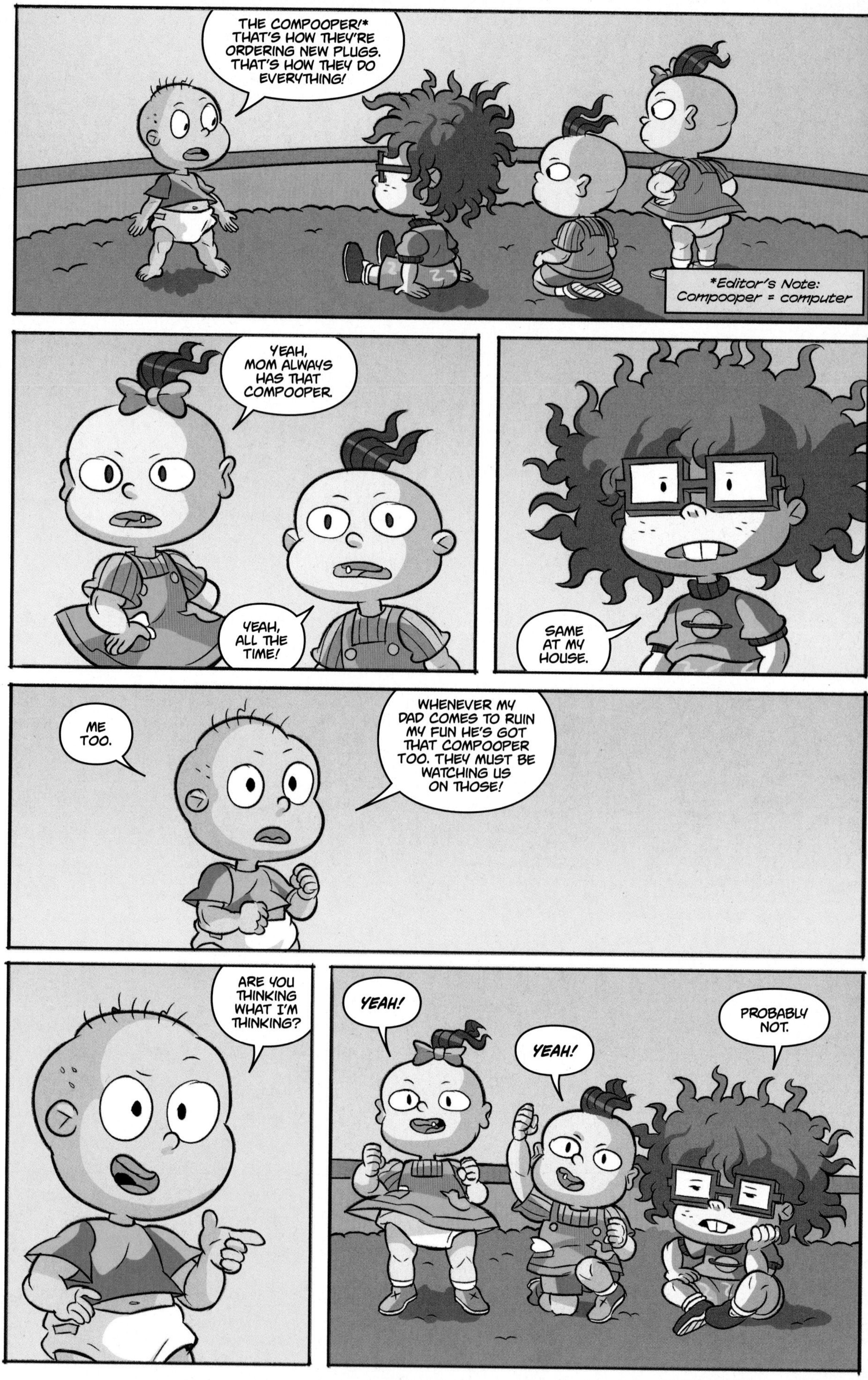
THE COMPOOPER!* THAT'S HOW THEY'RE ORDERING NEW PLUGS. THAT'S HOW THEY DO EVERYTHING!
*Editor's Note: Compooper = computer
YEAH, MOM ALWAYS HAS THAT COMPOOPER.
YEAH, ALL THE TIME!
SAME AT MY HOUSE.
ME TOO.
WHENEVER MY DAD COMES TO RUIN MY FUN HE'S GOT THAT COMPOOPER TOO. THEY MUST BE WATCHING US ON THOSE!
ARE YOU THINKING WHAT I'M THINKING?
YEAH!
YEAH!
PROBABLY NOT.

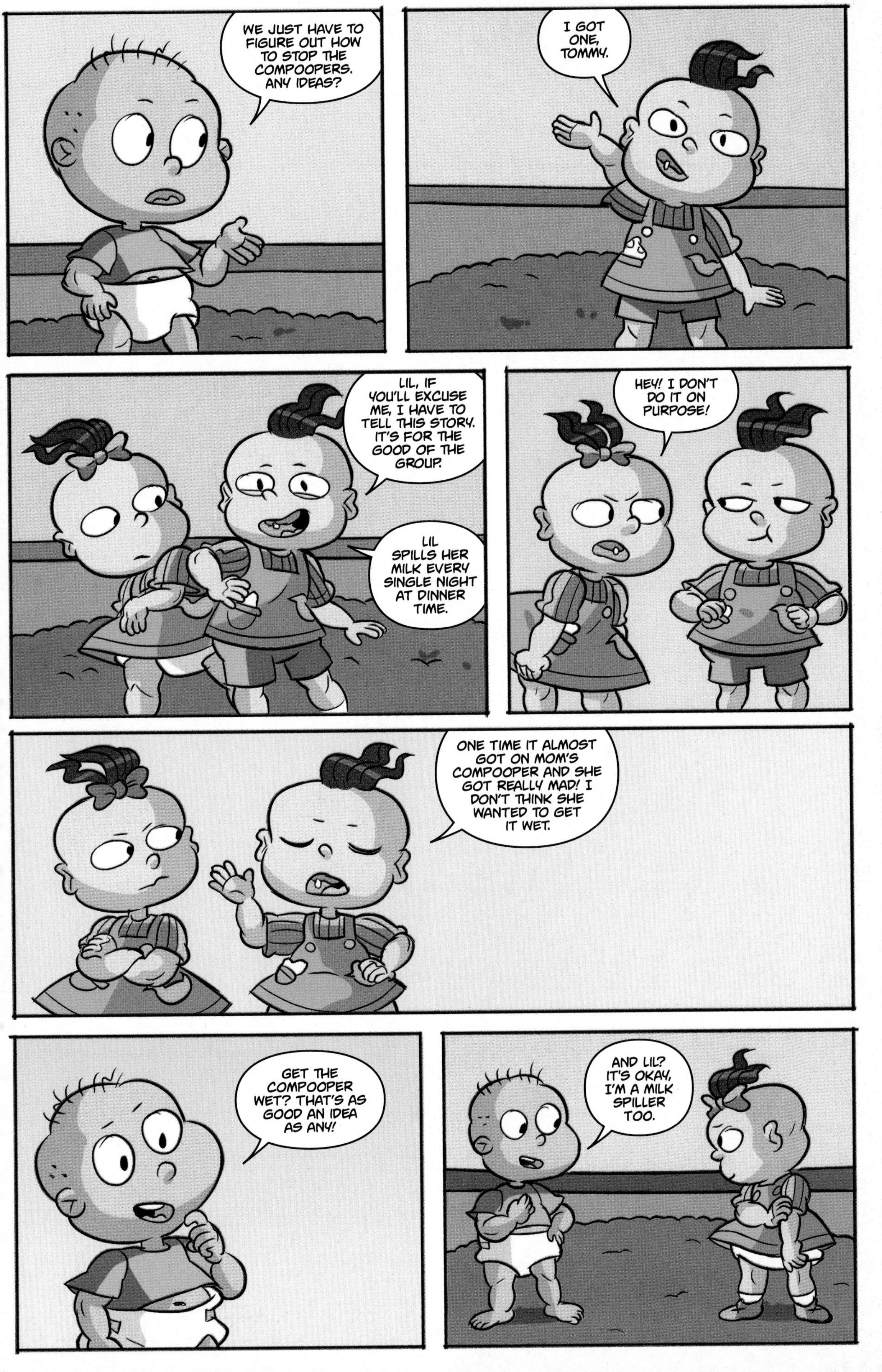
WE JUST HAVE TO FIGURE OUT HOW TO STOP THE COMPOOPERS. ANY IDEAS?
I GOT ONE, TOMMY.
LIL, IF YOU'LL EXCUSE ME, I HAVE TO TELL THIS STORY. IT'S FOR THE GOOD OF THE GROUP.
LIL SPILLS HER MILK EVERY SINGLE NIGHT AT DINNER TIME.
HEY! I DON'T DO IT ON PURPOSE!
ONE TIME IT ALMOST GOT ON MOM'S COMPOOPER AND SHE GOT REALLY MAD! I DON'T THINK SHE WANTED TO GET IT WET.
GET THE COMPOOPER WET? THAT'S AS GOOD AN IDEA AS ANY!
AND LIL? IT'S OKAY, I'M A MILK SPILLER TOO.

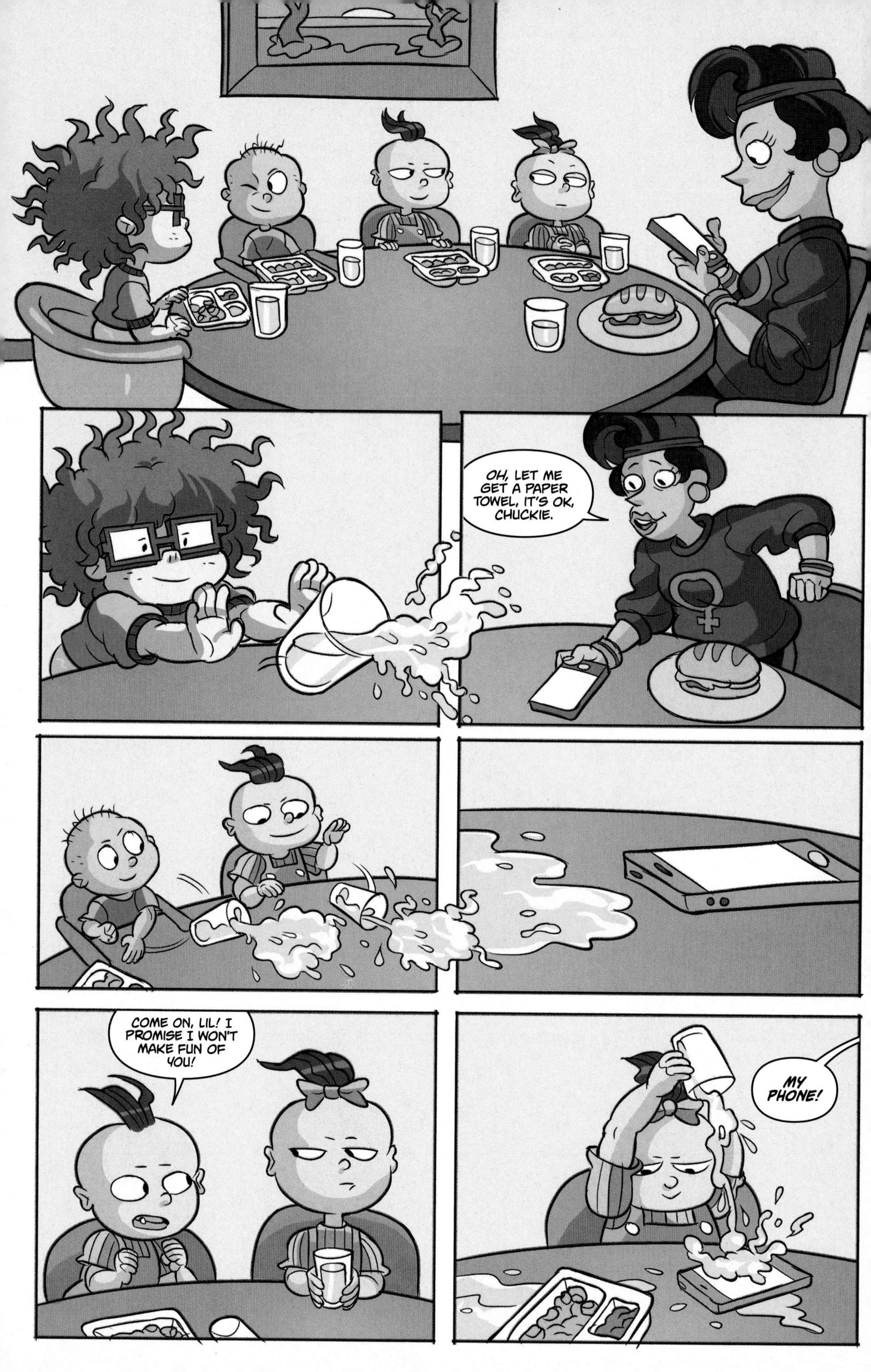
OH, LET ME GET A PAPER TOWEL, IT'S OK, CHUCKIE.
COME ON, LIL! I PROMISE I WON'T MAKE FUN OF YOU!
MY PHONE!

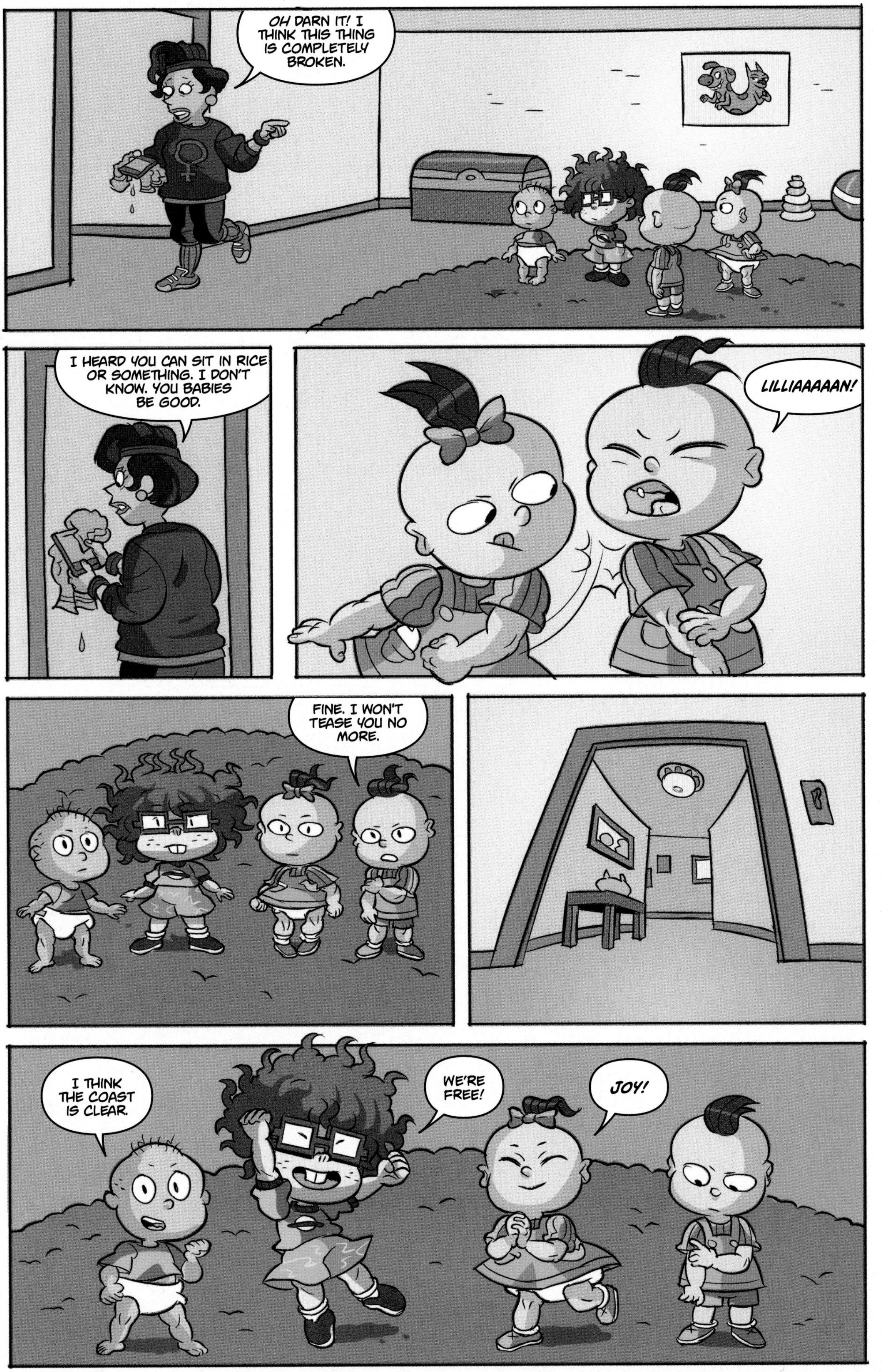
OH DARN IT! I THINK THIS THING IS COMPLETELY BROKEN.
I HEARD YOU CAN SIT IN RICE OR SOMETHING. I DON'T KNOW. YOU BABIES BE GOOD.
LILLIAAAAAN!
FINE. I WON'T TEASE YOU NO MORE.
I THINK THE COAST IS CLEAR.
WE'RE FREE!
JOY!

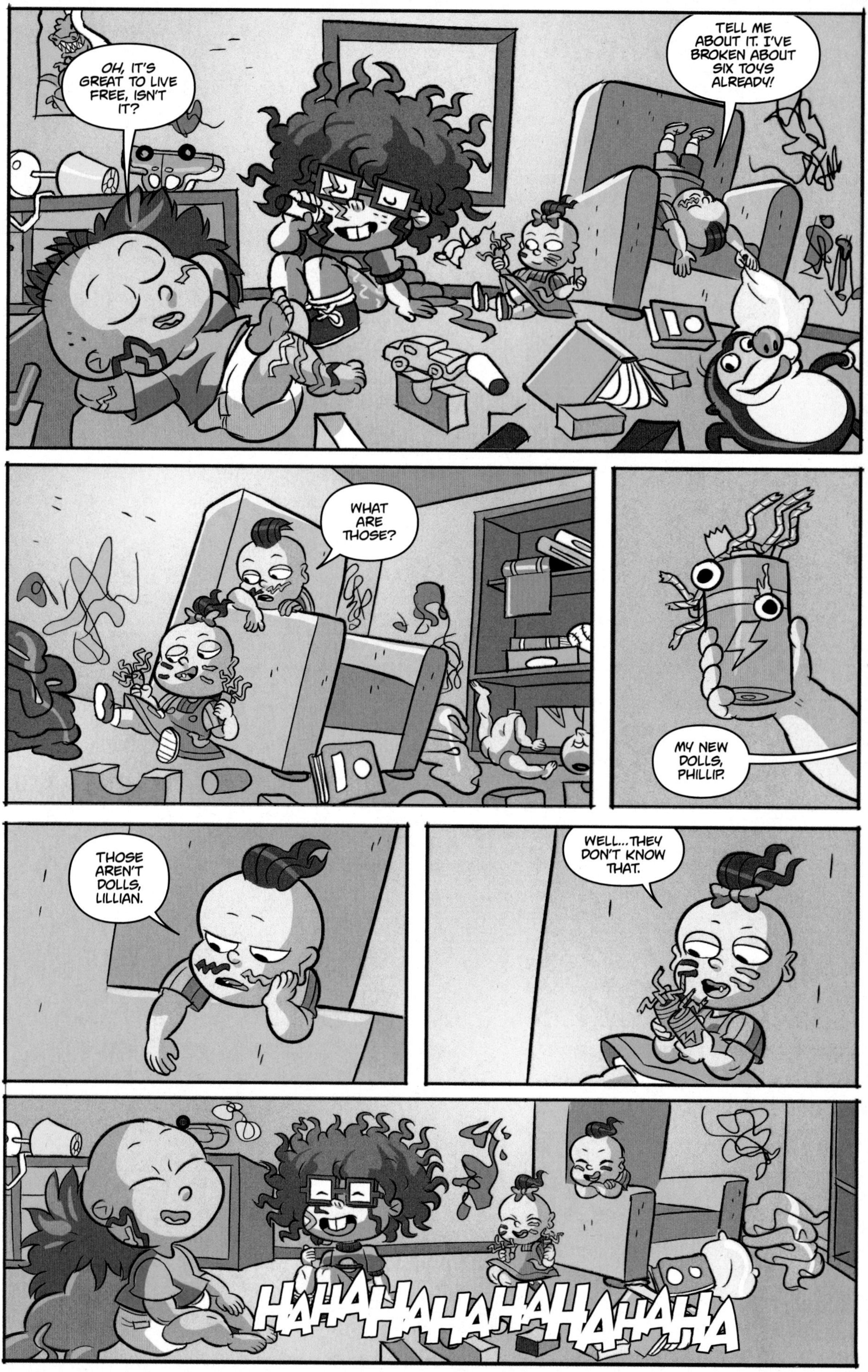
OH, IT'S GREAT TO LIVE FREE, ISN'T IT?
TELL ME ABOUT IT. I'VE BROKEN ABOUT SIX TOYS ALREADY!
WHAT ARE THOSE?
MY NEW DOLLS, PHILLIP.
THOSE AREN'T DOLLS, LILLIAN.
WELL...THEY DON'T KNOW THAT.
HAHAHAHAHAHAHAHAHAHA

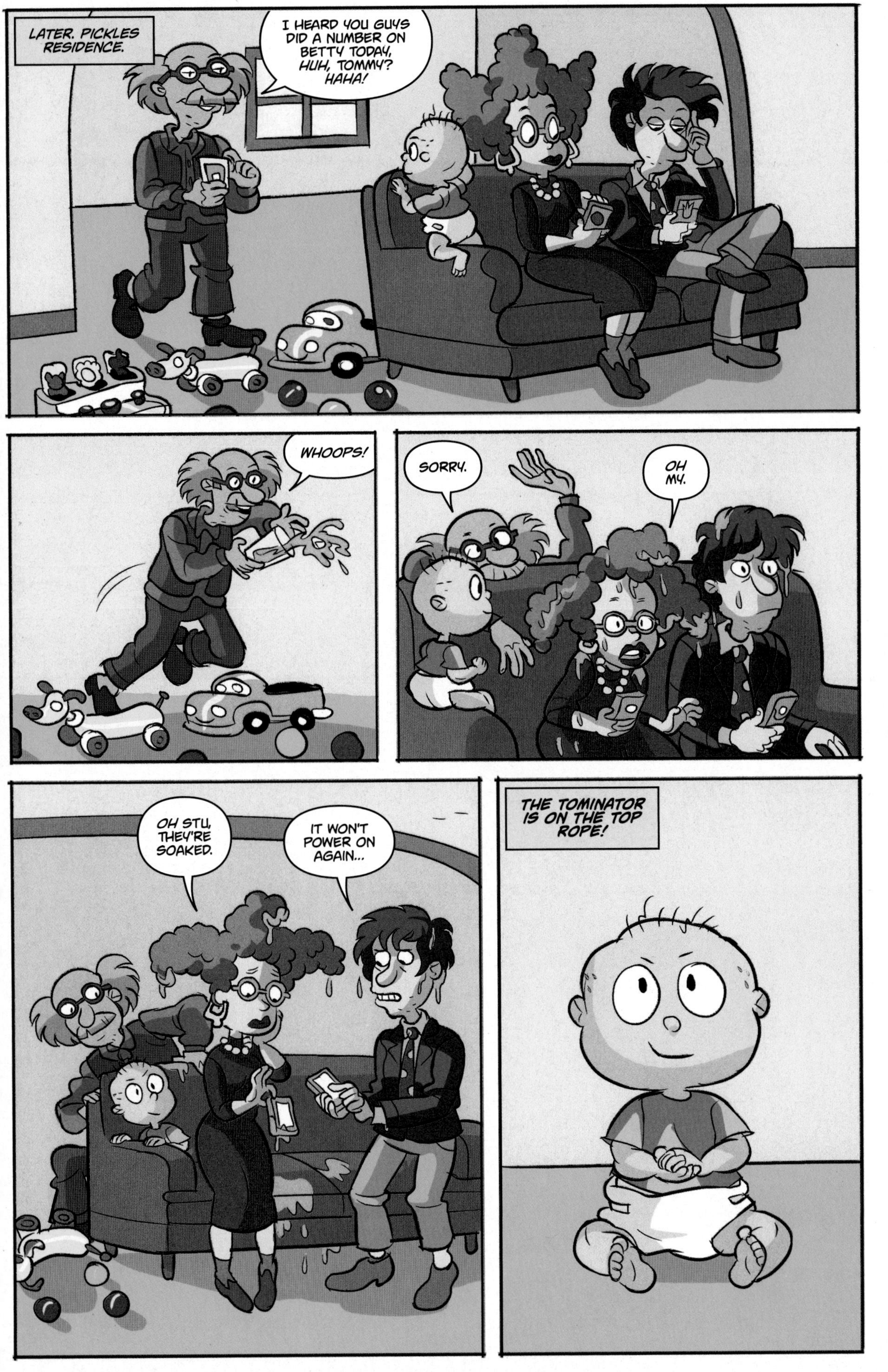
LATER. PICKLES RESIDENCE.
I HEARD YOU GUYS DID A NUMBER ON BETTY TODAY, HUH, TOMMY? HAHA!
WHOOPS!
SORRY.
OH MY.
OH STU, THEY'RE SOAKED.
IT WON'T POWER ON AGAIN...
THE TOMINATOR IS ON THE TOP ROPE!

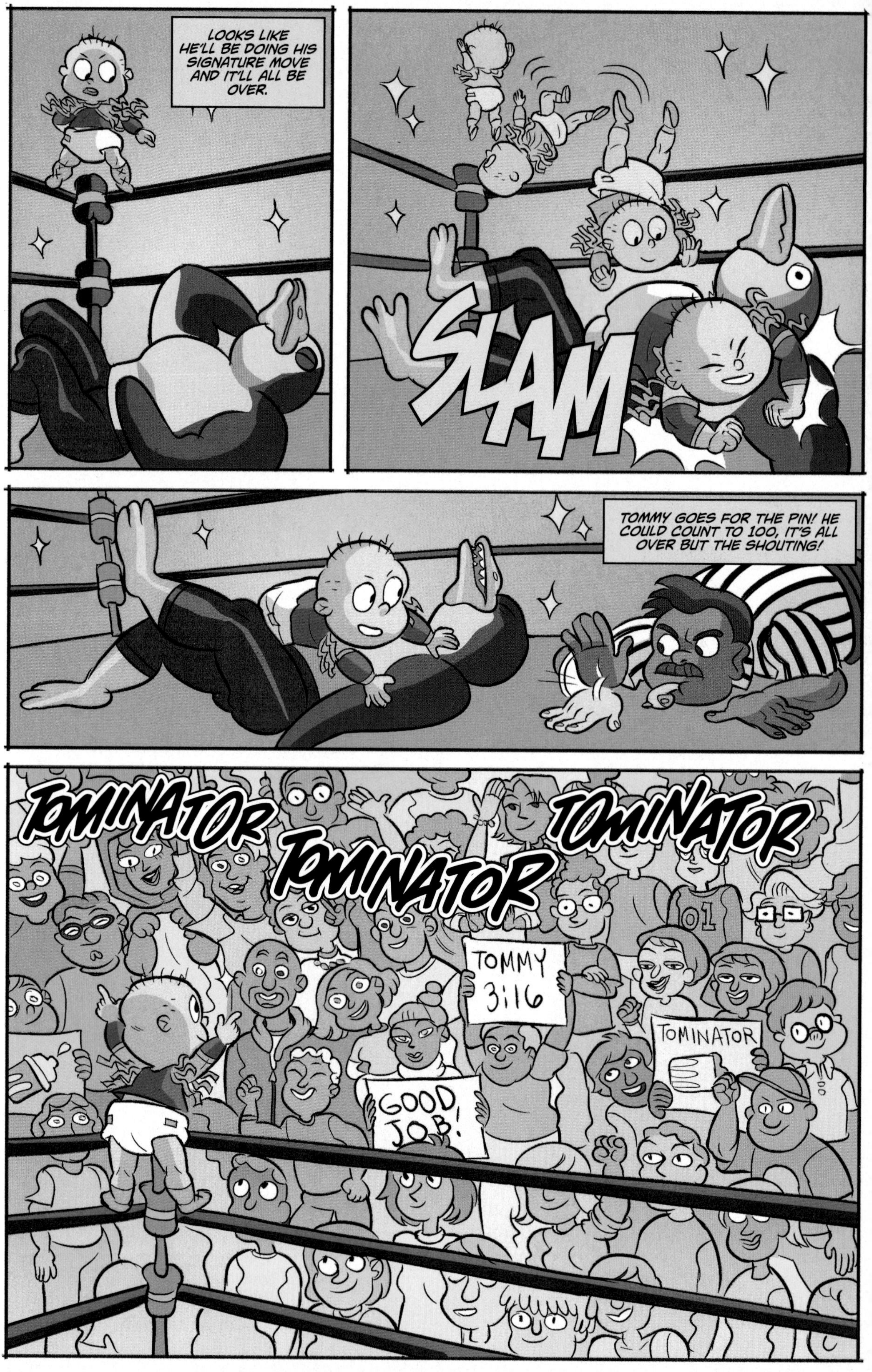
LOOKS LIKE HE'LL BE DOING HIS SIGNATURE MOVE AND IT'LL ALL BE OVER.
SLAM
TOMMY GOES FOR THE PIN! HE COULD COUNT TO 100, IT'S ALL OVER BUT THE SHOUTING!
TOMINATOR
TOMINATOR
TOMINATOR
01
TOMMY 3:16
TOMINATOR
GOOD JOB!

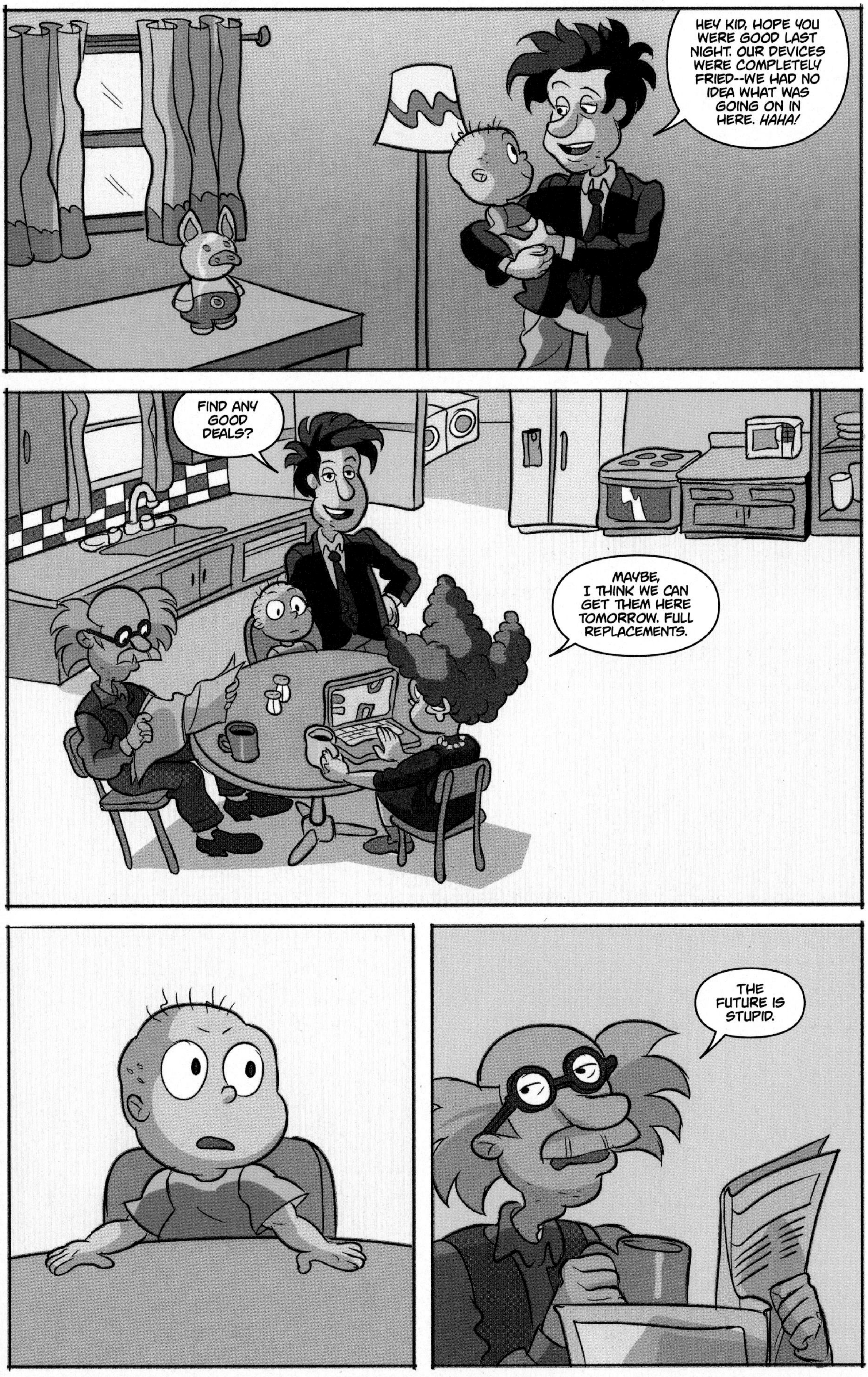
HEY KID, HOPE YOU WERE GOOD LAST NIGHT. OUR DEVICES WERE COMPLETELY FRIED--WE HAD NO IDEA WHAT WAS GOING ON IN HERE. HAHA!
FIND ANY GOOD DEALS?
MAYBE, I THINK WE CAN GET THEM HERE TOMORROW. FULL REPLACEMENTS.
THE FUTURE IS STUPID.

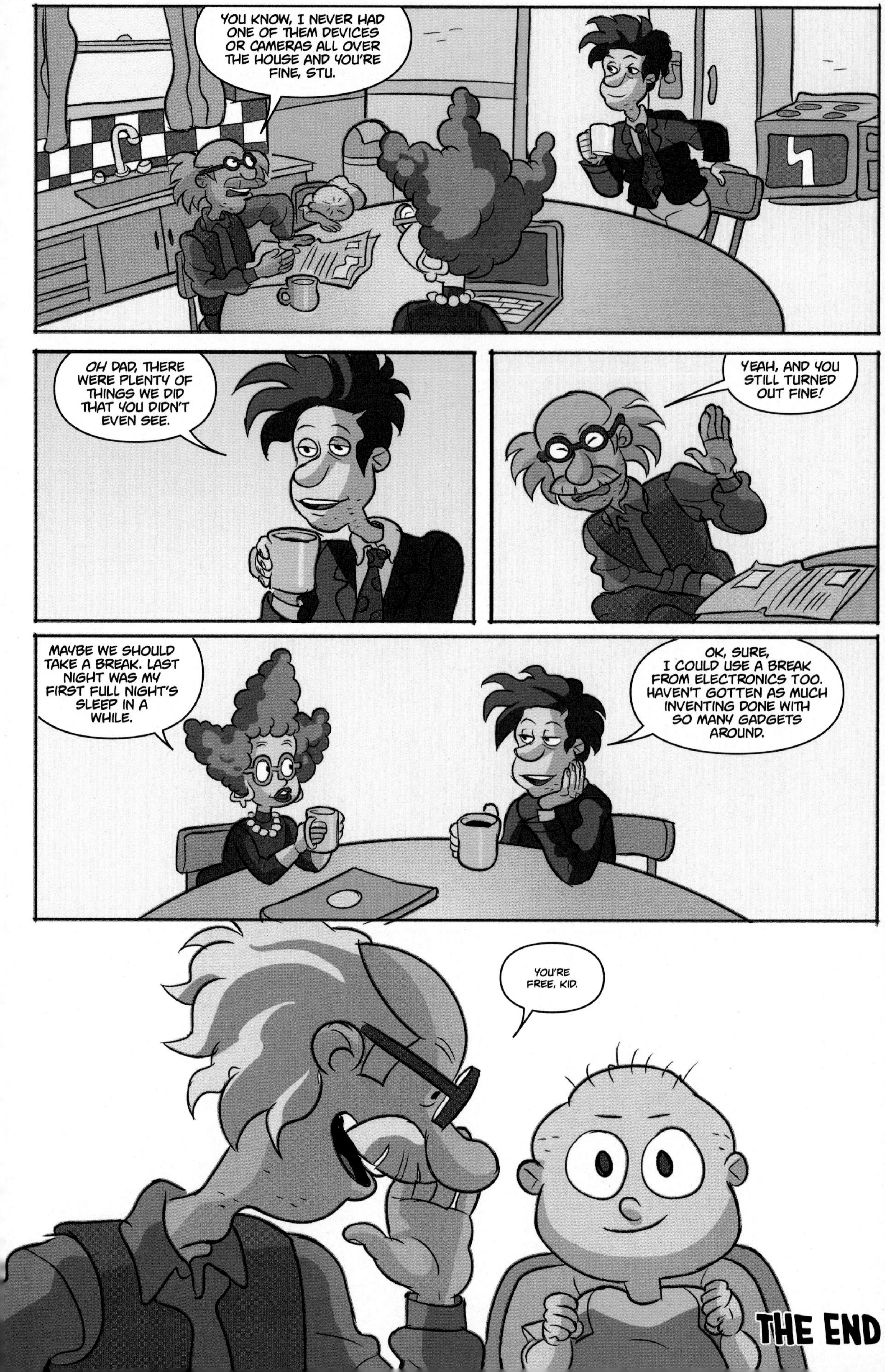
YOU KNOW, I NEVER HAD ONE OF THEM DEVICES OR CAMERAS ALL OVER THE HOUSE AND YOU'RE FINE, STU.
OH DAD, THERE WERE PLENTY OF THINGS WE DID THAT YOU DIDN'T EVEN SEE.
YEAH, AND YOU STILL TURNED OUT FINE!
MAYBE WE SHOULD TAKE A BREAK. LAST NIGHT WAS MY FIRST FULL NIGHT'S SLEEP IN A WHILE.
OK, SURE, I COULD USE A BREAK FROM ELECTRONICS TOO. HAVEN'T GOTTEN AS MUCH INVENTING DONE WITH SO MANY GADGETS AROUND.
YOU'RE FREE, KID.
THE END

THE COMPOOPER!
THAT'S HOW THEY'RE
ORDERING NEW PLUGS.

DESPERATELY SEEKING
CYNTHIA

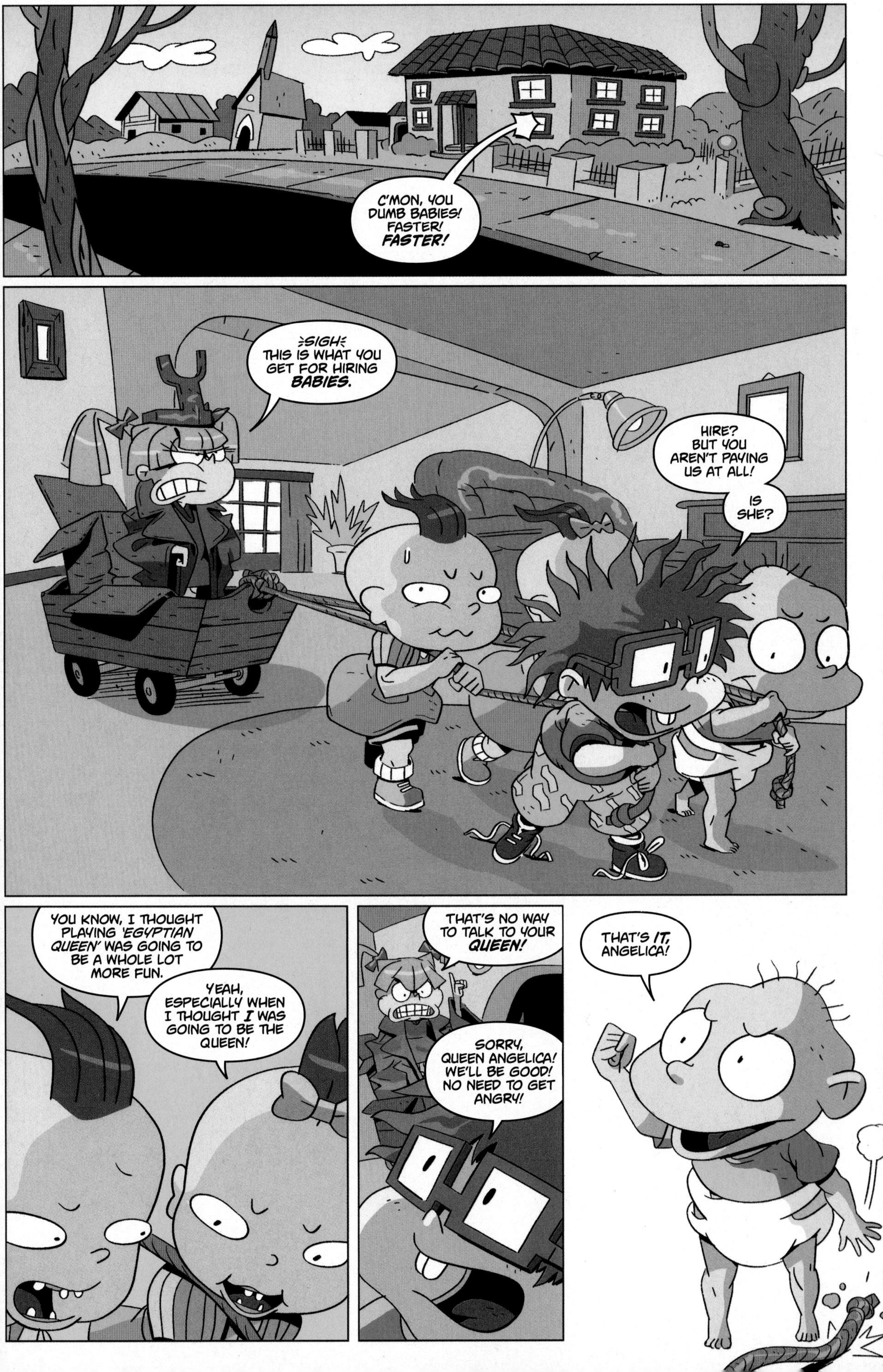
C'MON, YOU DUMB BABIES! FASTER! FASTER!
SIGH THIS IS WHAT YOU GET FOR HIRING BABIES.
HIRE? BUT YOU AREN'T PAYING US AT ALL!
IS SHE?
YOU KNOW, I THOUGHT PLAYING 'EGYPTIAN QUEEN' WAS GOING TO BE A WHOLE LOT MORE FUN.
YEAH, ESPECIALLY WHEN I THOUGHT I WAS GOING TO BE THE QUEEN!
THAT'S NO WAY TO TALK TO YOUR QUEEN!
SORRY, QUEEN ANGELICA! WE'LL BE GOOD! NO NEED TO GET ANGRY!
THAT'S IT, ANGELICA!

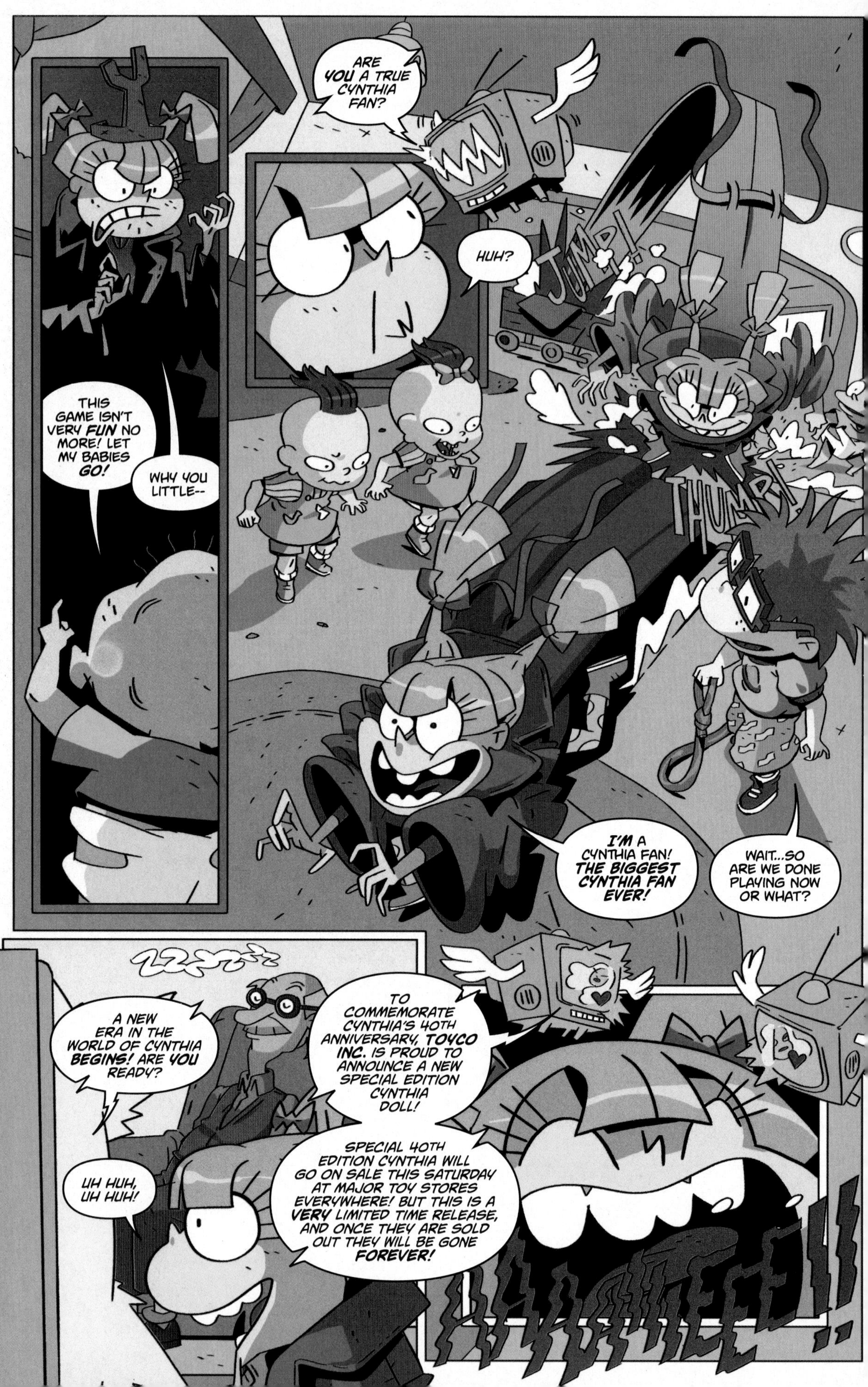
ARE YOU A TRUE CYNTHIA FAN?
HUH?
JUMP!
THIS GAME ISN'T VERY FUN NO MORE! LET MY BABIES GO!
WHY YOU LITTLE--
THUMP!
I'M A CYNTHIA FAN! THE BIGGEST CYNTHIA FAN EVER!
WAIT...SO ARE WE DONE PLAYING NOW OR WHAT?
ZZZZZZZ
A NEW ERA IN THE WORLD OF CYNTHIA BEGINS! ARE YOU READY?
TO COMMEMORATE CYNTHIA'S 40TH ANNIVERSARY, TOYCO INC. IS PROUD TO ANNOUNCE A NEW SPECIAL EDITION CYNTHIA DOLL!
UH HUH, UH HUH!
SPECIAL 40TH EDITION CYNTHIA WILL GO ON SALE THIS SATURDAY AT MAJOR TOY STORES EVERYWHERE! BUT THIS IS A VERY LIMITED TIME RELEASE, AND ONCE THEY ARE SOLD OUT THEY WILL BE GONE FOREVER!
HAAAAEEE!!

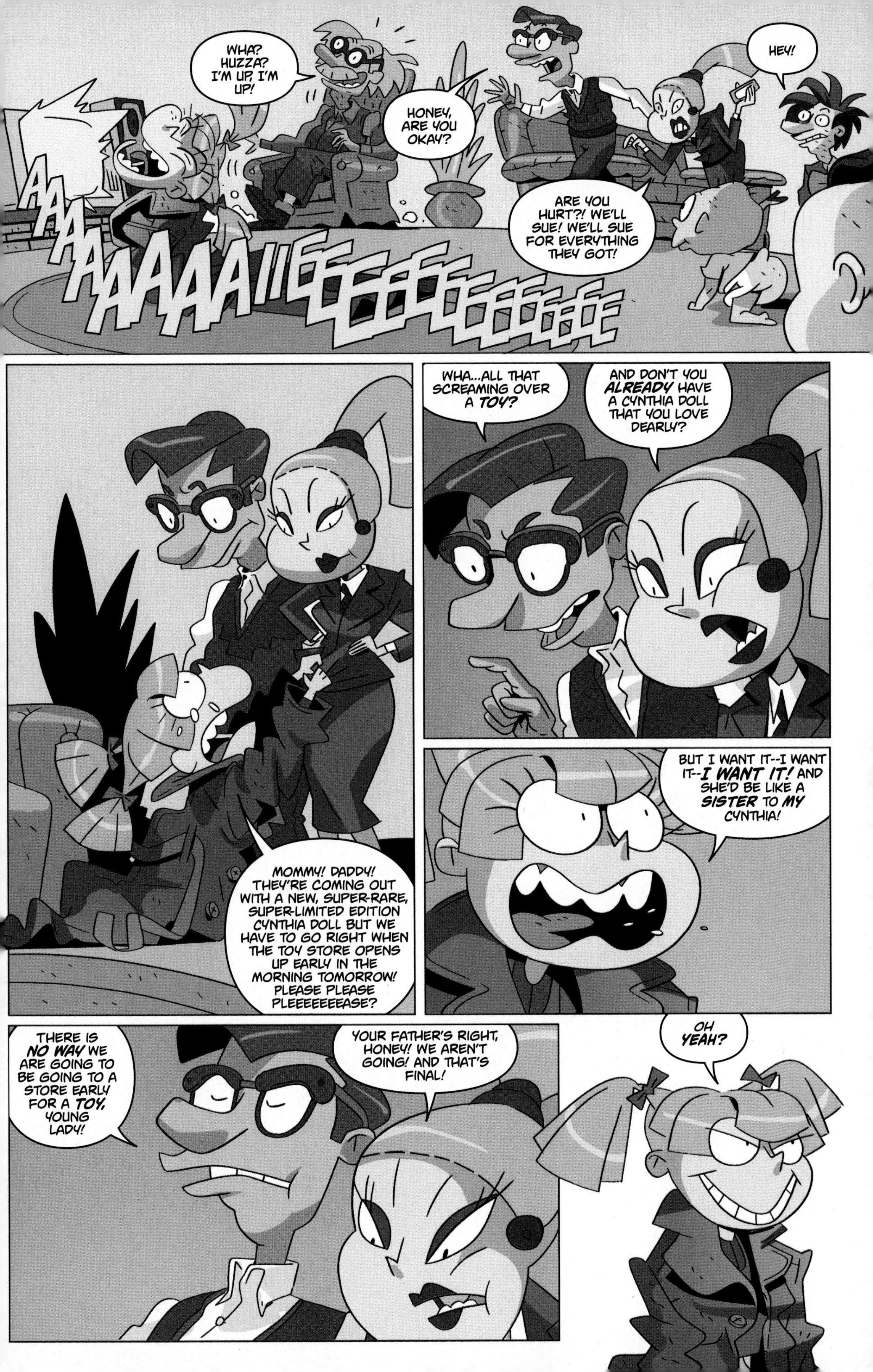
AAAAAAAAIIEEEEEEEEEEEEEEEE
WHA? HUZZA? I'M UP, I'M UP!
HONEY, ARE YOU OKAY?
ARE YOU HURT?! WE'LL SUE! WE'LL SUE FOR EVERYTHING THEY GOT!
HEY!
MOMMY! DADDY! THEY'RE COMING OUT WITH A NEW, SUPER-RARE, SUPER-LIMITED EDITION CYNTHIA DOLL BUT WE HAVE TO GO RIGHT WHEN THE TOY STORE OPENS UP EARLY IN THE MORNING TOMORROW! PLEASE PLEASE PLEEEEEEEEASE?
WHA...ALL THAT SCREAMING OVER A TOY?
AND DON'T YOU ALREADY HAVE A CYNTHIA DOLL THAT YOU LOVE DEARLY?
BUT I WANT IT--I WANT IT--I WANT IT! AND SHE'D BE LIKE A SISTER TO MY CYNTHIA!
THERE IS NO WAY WE ARE GOING TO BE GOING TO A STORE EARLY FOR A TOY, YOUNG LADY!
YOUR FATHER'S RIGHT, HONEY! WE AREN'T GOING! AND THAT'S FINAL!
OH YEAH?

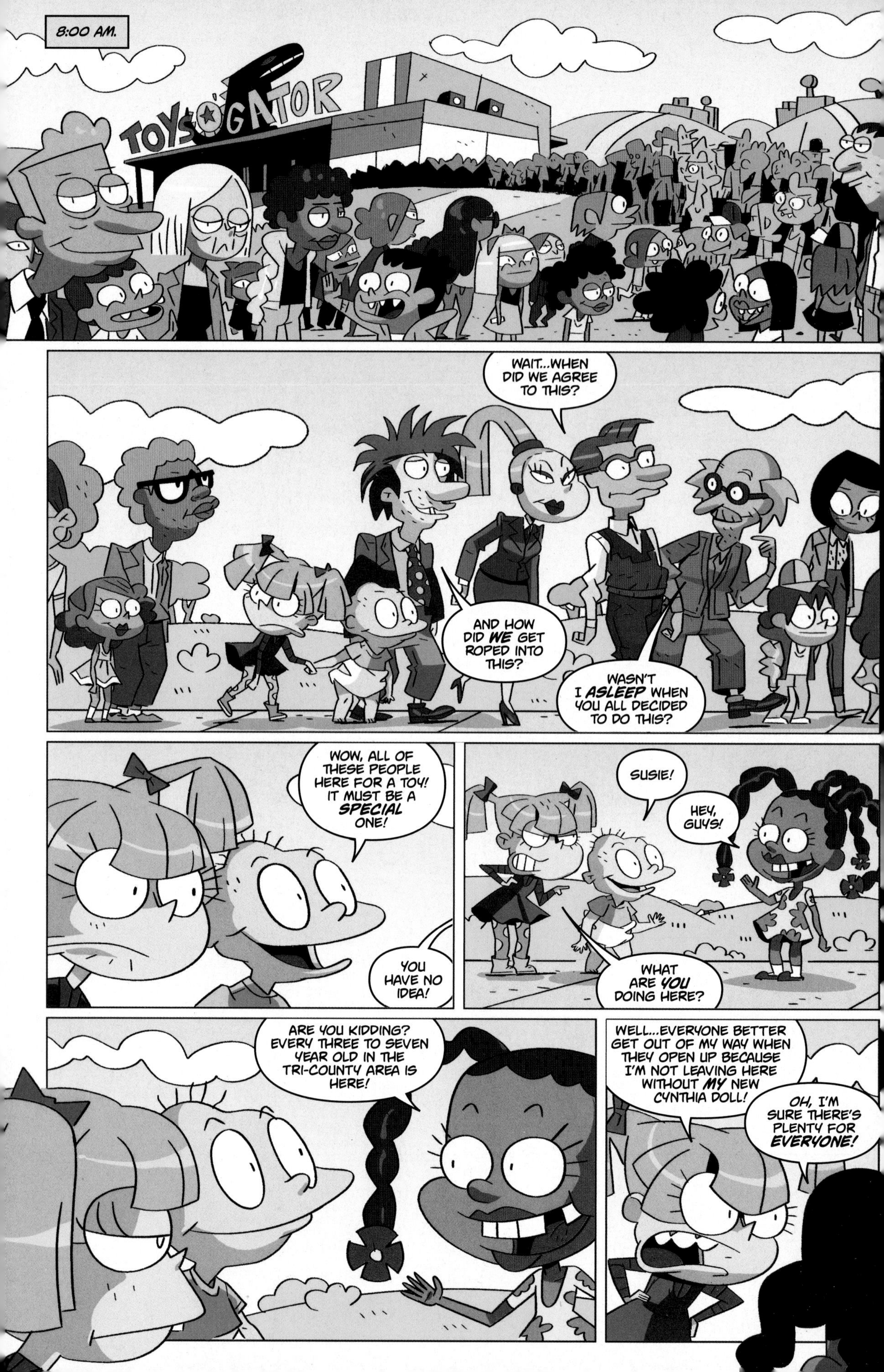
8:00 AM.
TOYS 'O' GATOR
WAIT...WHEN DID WE AGREE TO THIS?
AND HOW DID WE GET ROPED INTO THIS?
WASN'T I ASLEEP WHEN YOU ALL DECIDED TO DO THIS?
WOW, ALL OF THESE PEOPLE HERE FOR A TOY! IT MUST BE A SPECIAL ONE!
YOU HAVE NO IDEA!
SUSIE!
HEY, GUYS!
WHAT ARE YOU DOING HERE?
ARE YOU KIDDING? EVERY THREE TO SEVEN YEAR OLD IN THE TRI-COUNTY AREA IS HERE!
WELL...EVERYONE BETTER GET OUT OF MY WAY WHEN THEY OPEN UP BECAUSE I'M NOT LEAVING HERE WITHOUT MY NEW CYNTHIA DOLL!
OH, I'M SURE THERE'S PLENTY FOR EVERYONE!

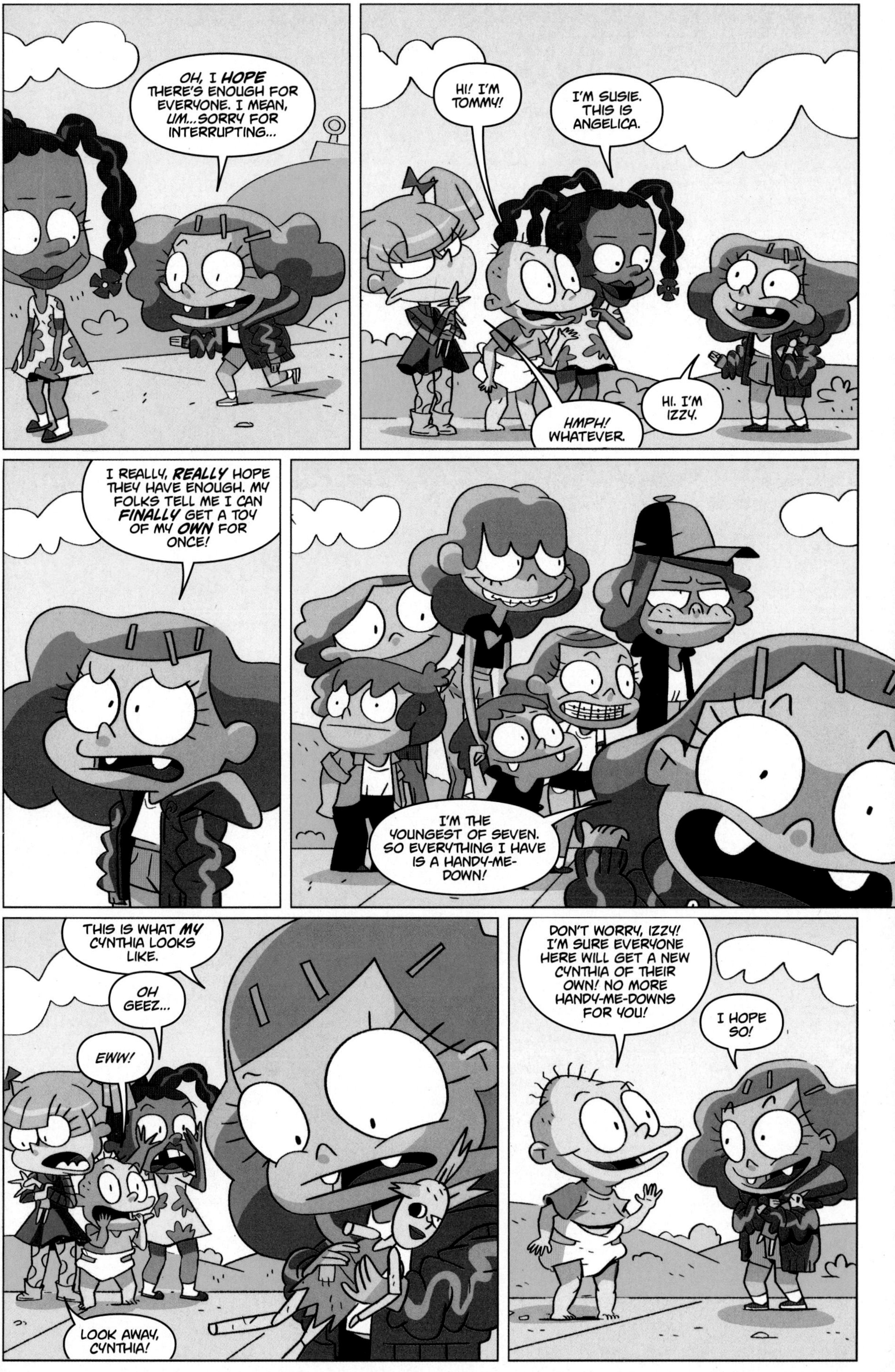
OH, I HOPE THERE'S ENOUGH FOR EVERYONE. I MEAN, UM...SORRY FOR INTERRUPTING...
HI! I'M TOMMY!
I'M SUSIE. THIS IS ANGELICA.
HMPH! WHATEVER.
HI. I'M IZZY.
I REALLY, REALLY HOPE THEY HAVE ENOUGH. MY FOLKS TELL ME I CAN FINALLY GET A TOY OF MY OWN FOR ONCE!
I'M THE YOUNGEST OF SEVEN. SO EVERYTHING I HAVE IS A HANDY-ME-DOWN!
THIS IS WHAT MY CYNTHIA LOOKS LIKE.
OH GEEZ...
EWW!
LOOK AWAY, CYNTHIA!
DON'T WORRY, IZZY! I'M SURE EVERYONE HERE WILL GET A NEW CYNTHIA OF THEIR OWN! NO MORE HANDY-ME-DOWNS FOR YOU!
I HOPE SO!

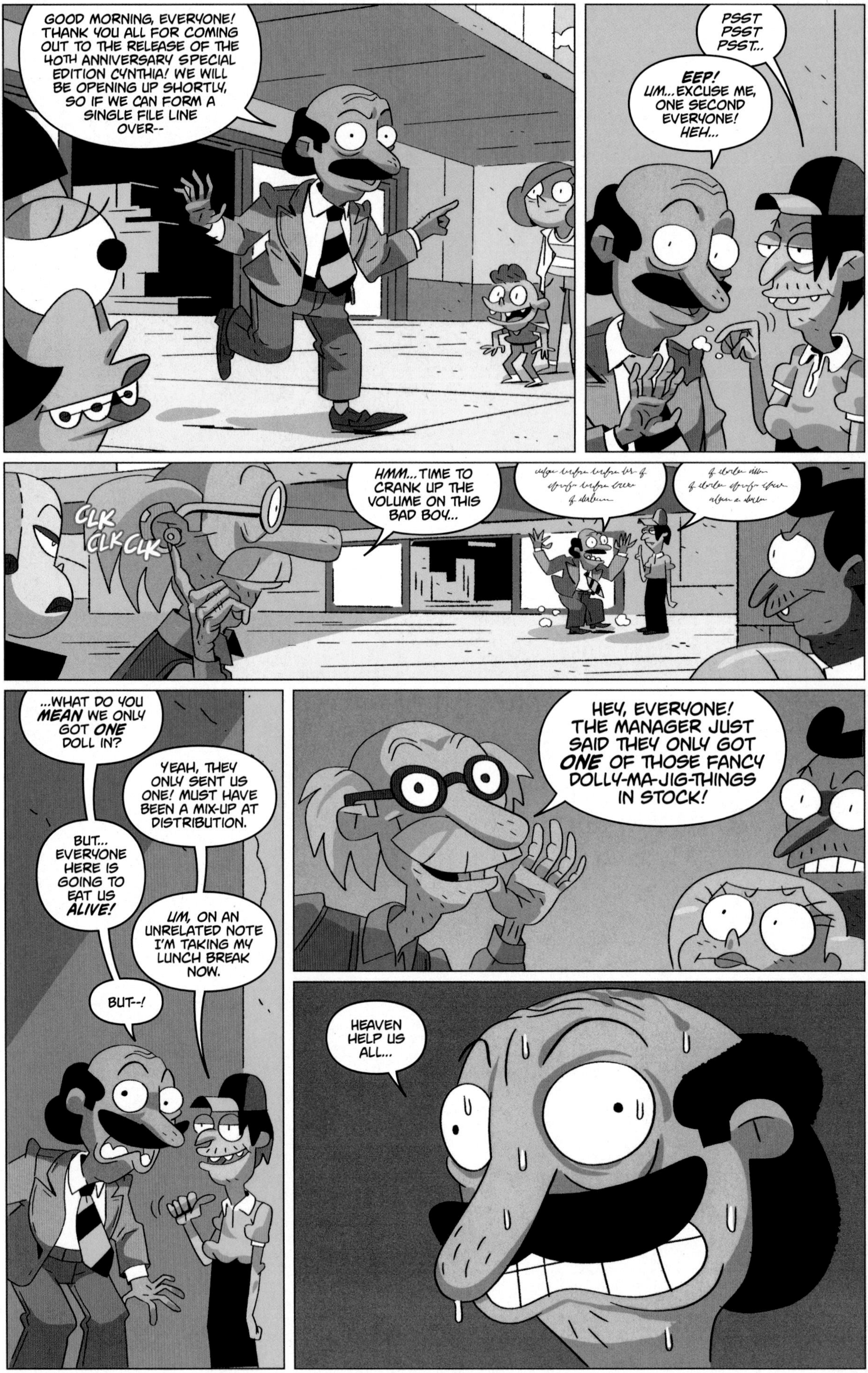
GOOD MORNING, EVERYONE! THANK YOU ALL FOR COMING OUT TO THE RELEASE OF THE 40TH ANNIVERSARY SPECIAL EDITION CYNTHIA! WE WILL BE OPENING UP SHORTLY, SO IF WE CAN FORM A SINGLE FILE LINE OVER--
PSST PSST PSST...
EEP! UM... EXCUSE ME, ONE SECOND EVERYONE! HEH...
CLK CLK CLK
HMM... TIME TO CRANK UP THE VOLUME ON THIS BAD BOY...
...WHAT DO YOU MEAN WE ONLY GOT ONE DOLL IN?
YEAH, THEY ONLY SENT US ONE! MUST HAVE BEEN A MIX-UP AT DISTRIBUTION.
BUT... EVERYONE HERE IS GOING TO EAT US ALIVE!
UM, ON AN UNRELATED NOTE I'M TAKING MY LUNCH BREAK NOW.
BUT--!
HEY, EVERYONE! THE MANAGER JUST SAID THEY ONLY GOT ONE OF THOSE FANCY DOLLY-MA-JIG-THINGS IN STOCK!
HEAVEN HELP US ALL...

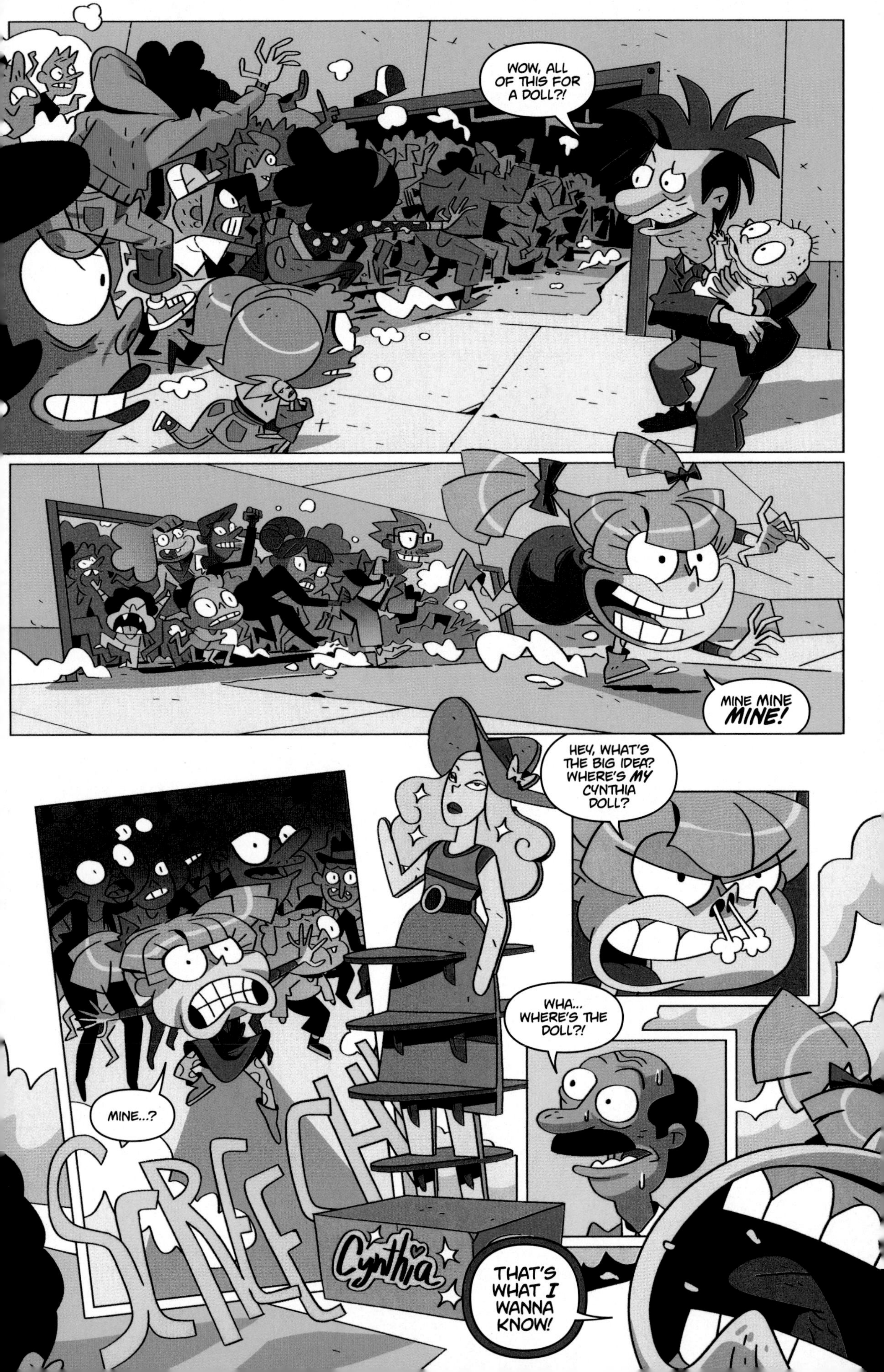
WOW, ALL OF THIS FOR A DOLL?!
MINE MINE MINE!
HEY, WHAT'S THE BIG IDEA? WHERE'S MY CYNTHIA DOLL?
WHA... WHERE'S THE DOLL?!
MINE...?
SCREECH
Cynthia
THAT'S WHAT I WANNA KNOW!

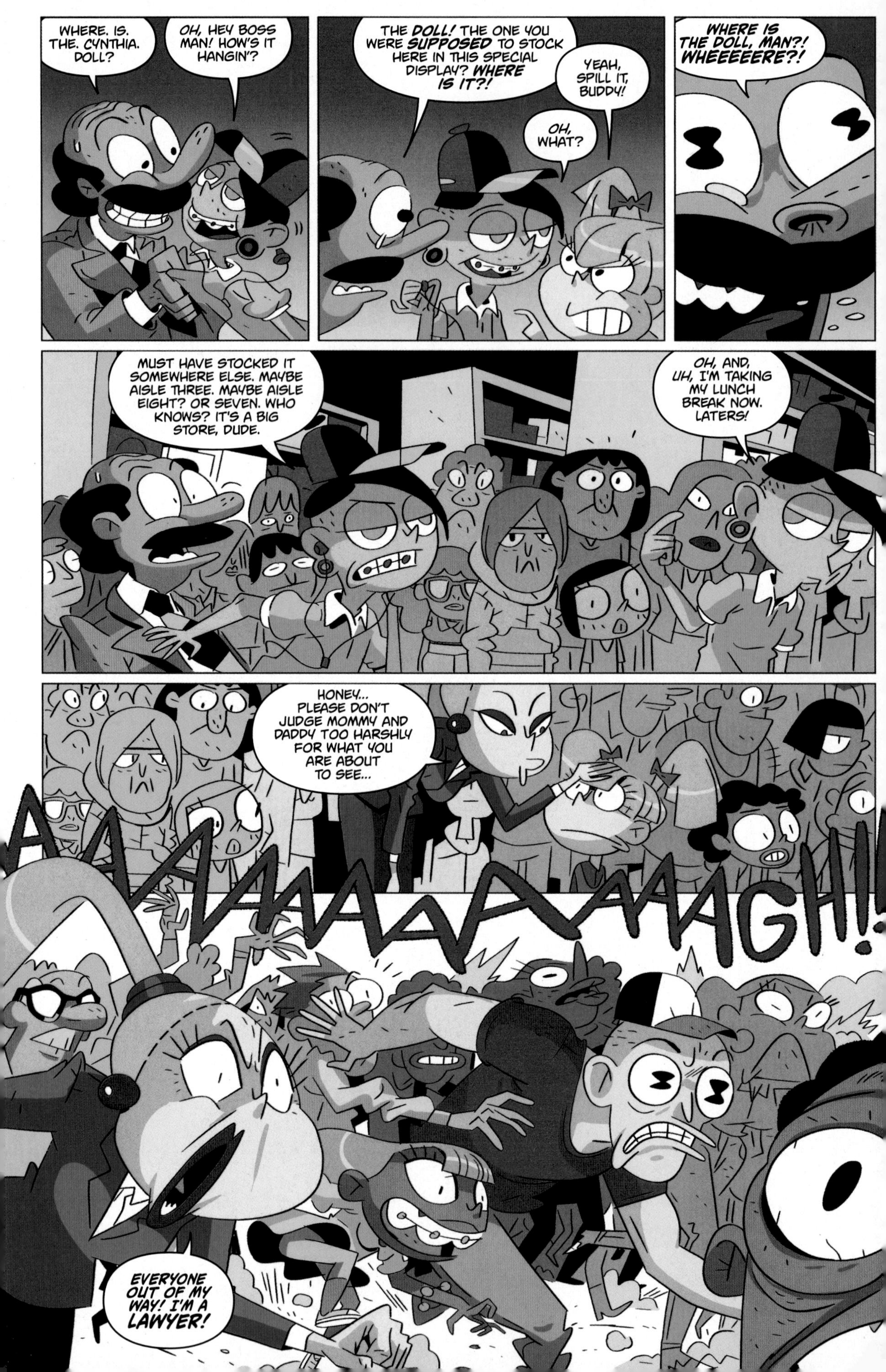
WHERE. IS. THE. CYNTHIA. DOLL?
OH, HEY BOSS MAN! HOW'S IT HANGIN'?
THE DOLL! THE ONE YOU WERE SUPPOSED TO STOCK HERE IN THIS SPECIAL DISPLAY? WHERE IS IT?!
YEAH, SPILL IT, BUDDY!
OH, WHAT?
WHERE IS THE DOLL, MAN?! WHEEEEERE?!
MUST HAVE STOCKED IT SOMEWHERE ELSE. MAYBE AISLE THREE. MAYBE AISLE EIGHT? OR SEVEN. WHO KNOWS? IT'S A BIG STORE, DUDE.
OH, AND, UH, I'M TAKING MY LUNCH BREAK NOW. LATERS!
HONEY... PLEASE DON'T JUDGE MOMMY AND DADDY TOO HARSHLY FOR WHAT YOU ARE ABOUT TO SEE...
AAAAAAAAAAAGH!!
EVERYONE OUT OF MY WAY! I'M A LAWYER!

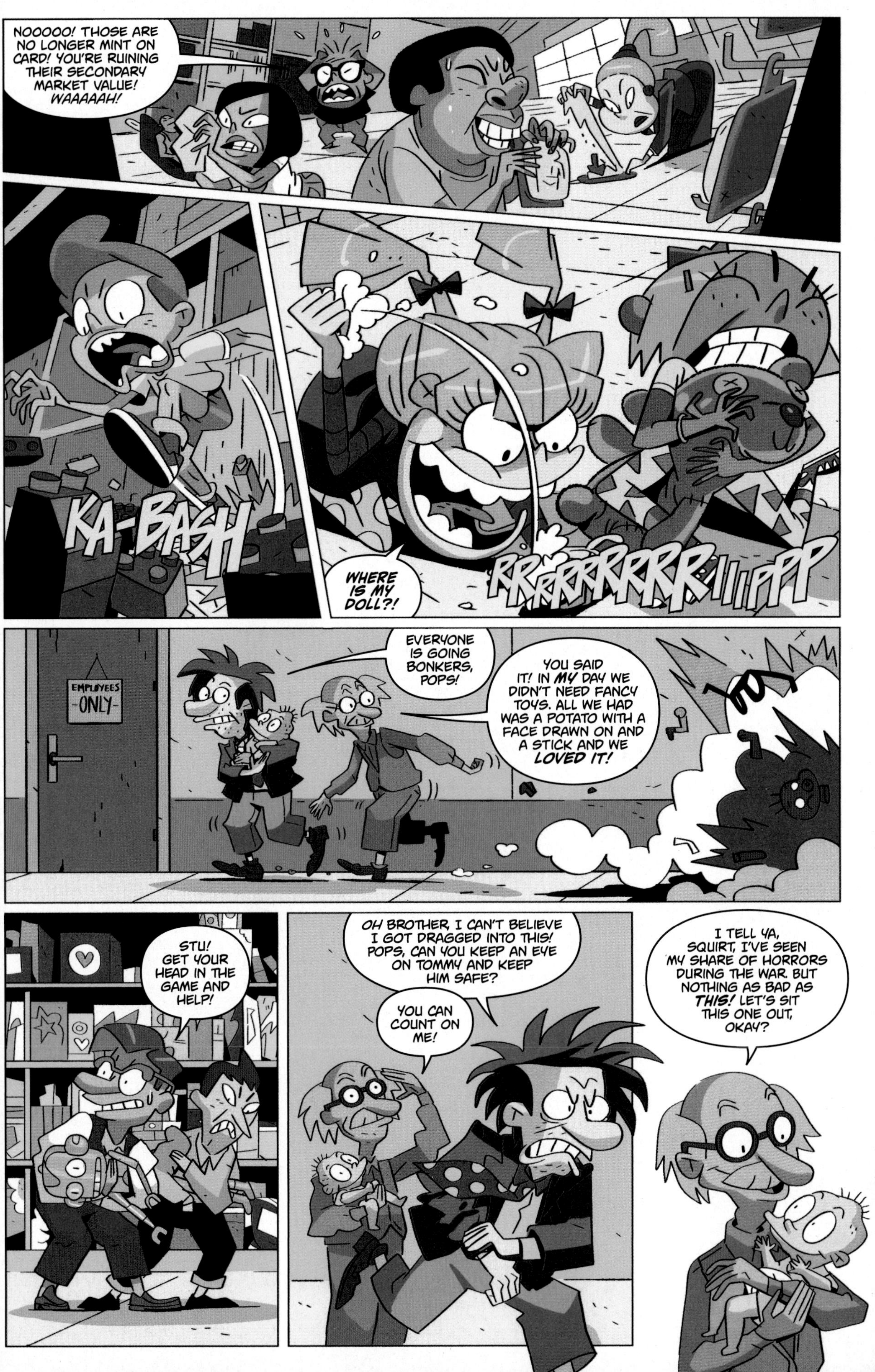
NOOOOO! THOSE ARE NO LONGER MINT ON CARD! YOU'RE RUINING THEIR SECONDARY MARKET VALUE! WAAAAAH!
KA-BASH
WHERE IS MY DOLL?!
RRRRRRRRRIIIPPP
EMPLOYEES -ONLY-
EVERYONE IS GOING BONKERS, POPS!
YOU SAID IT! IN MY DAY WE DIDN'T NEED FANCY TOYS. ALL WE HAD WAS A POTATO WITH A FACE DRAWN ON AND A STICK AND WE LOVED IT!
STU! GET YOUR HEAD IN THE GAME AND HELP!
OH BROTHER, I CAN'T BELIEVE I GOT DRAGGED INTO THIS! POPS, CAN YOU KEEP AN EYE ON TOMMY AND KEEP HIM SAFE?
YOU CAN COUNT ON ME!
I TELL YA, SQUIRT, I'VE SEEN MY SHARE OF HORRORS DURING THE WAR. BUT NOTHING AS BAD AS THIS! LET'S SIT THIS ONE OUT, OKAY?

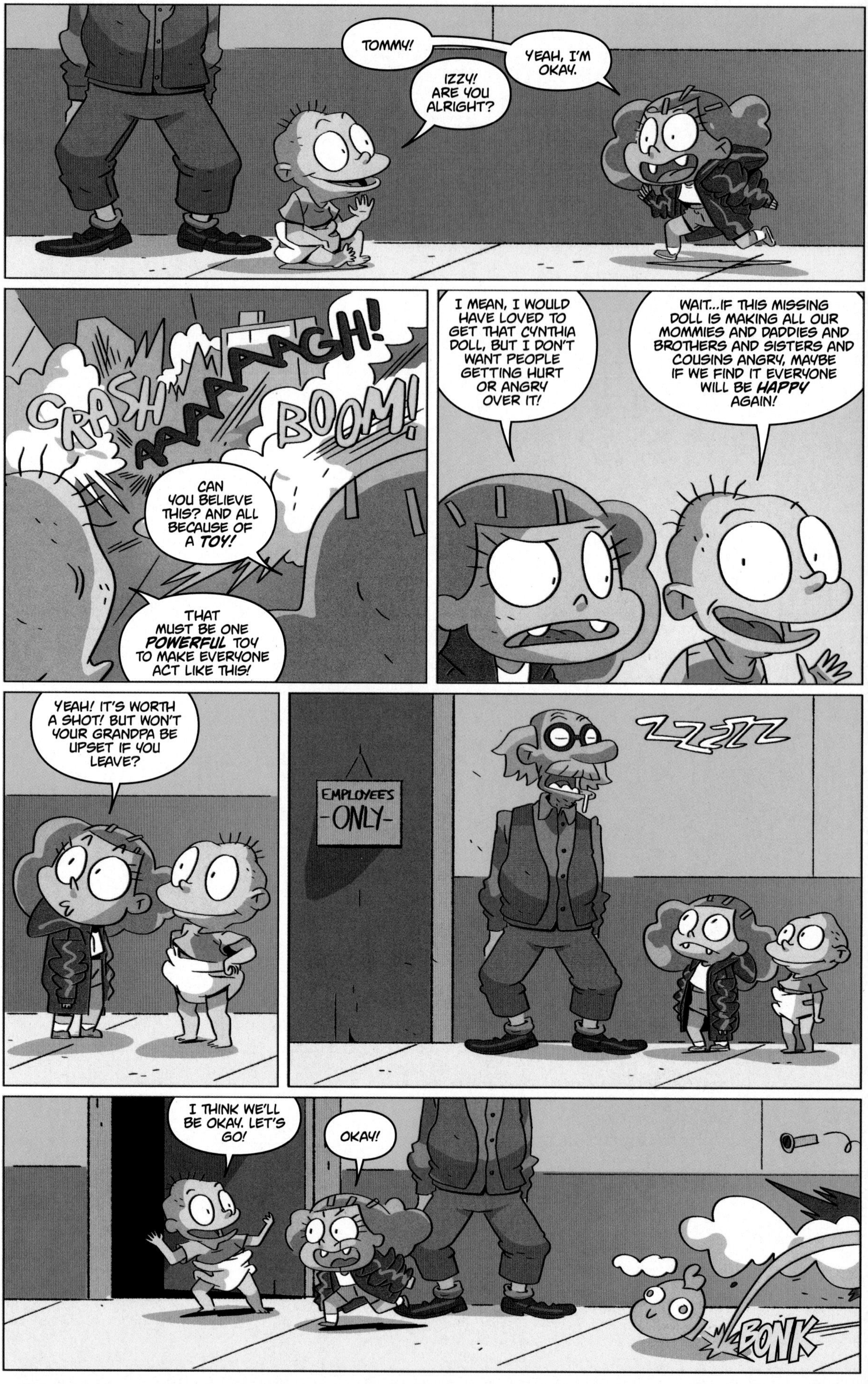
TOMMY!
IZZY! ARE YOU ALRIGHT?
YEAH, I'M OKAY.
CRASH
AAAAAAGH!
BOOM!
CAN YOU BELIEVE THIS? AND ALL BECAUSE OF A TOY!
THAT MUST BE ONE POWERFUL TOY TO MAKE EVERYONE ACT LIKE THIS!
I MEAN, I WOULD HAVE LOVED TO GET THAT CYNTHIA DOLL, BUT I DON'T WANT PEOPLE GETTING HURT OR ANGRY OVER IT!
WAIT...IF THIS MISSING DOLL IS MAKING ALL OUR MOMMIES AND DADDIES AND BROTHERS AND SISTERS AND COUSINS ANGRY, MAYBE IF WE FIND IT EVERYONE WILL BE HAPPY AGAIN!
YEAH! IT'S WORTH A SHOT! BUT WON'T YOUR GRANDPA BE UPSET IF YOU LEAVE?
EMPLOYEES -ONLY-
ZZZZZZ
I THINK WE'LL BE OKAY. LET'S GO!
OKAY!
BONK

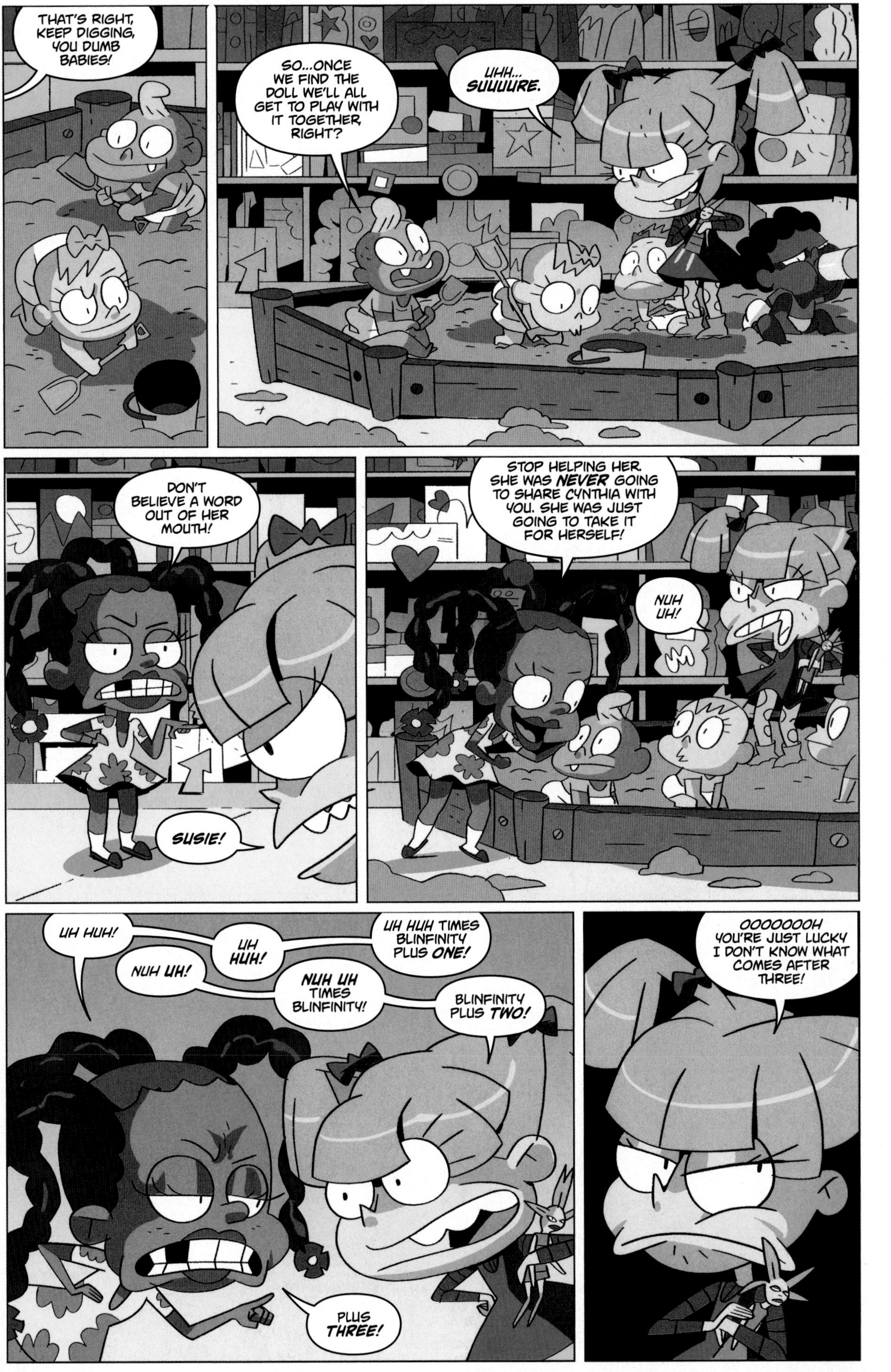
THAT'S RIGHT, KEEP DIGGING, YOU DUMB BABIES!
SO...ONCE WE FIND THE DOLL WE'LL ALL GET TO PLAY WITH IT TOGETHER, RIGHT?
UHH... SUUUURE.
DON'T BELIEVE A WORD OUT OF HER MOUTH!
SUSIE!
STOP HELPING HER. SHE WAS NEVER GOING TO SHARE CYNTHIA WITH YOU. SHE WAS JUST GOING TO TAKE IT FOR HERSELF!
NUH UH!
UH HUH!
NUH UH!
UH HUH!
NUH UH TIMES BLINFINITY!
UH HUH TIMES BLINFINITY PLUS ONE!
BLINFINITY PLUS TWO!
PLUS THREE!
OOOOOOOH YOU'RE JUST LUCKY I DON'T KNOW WHAT COMES AFTER THREE!

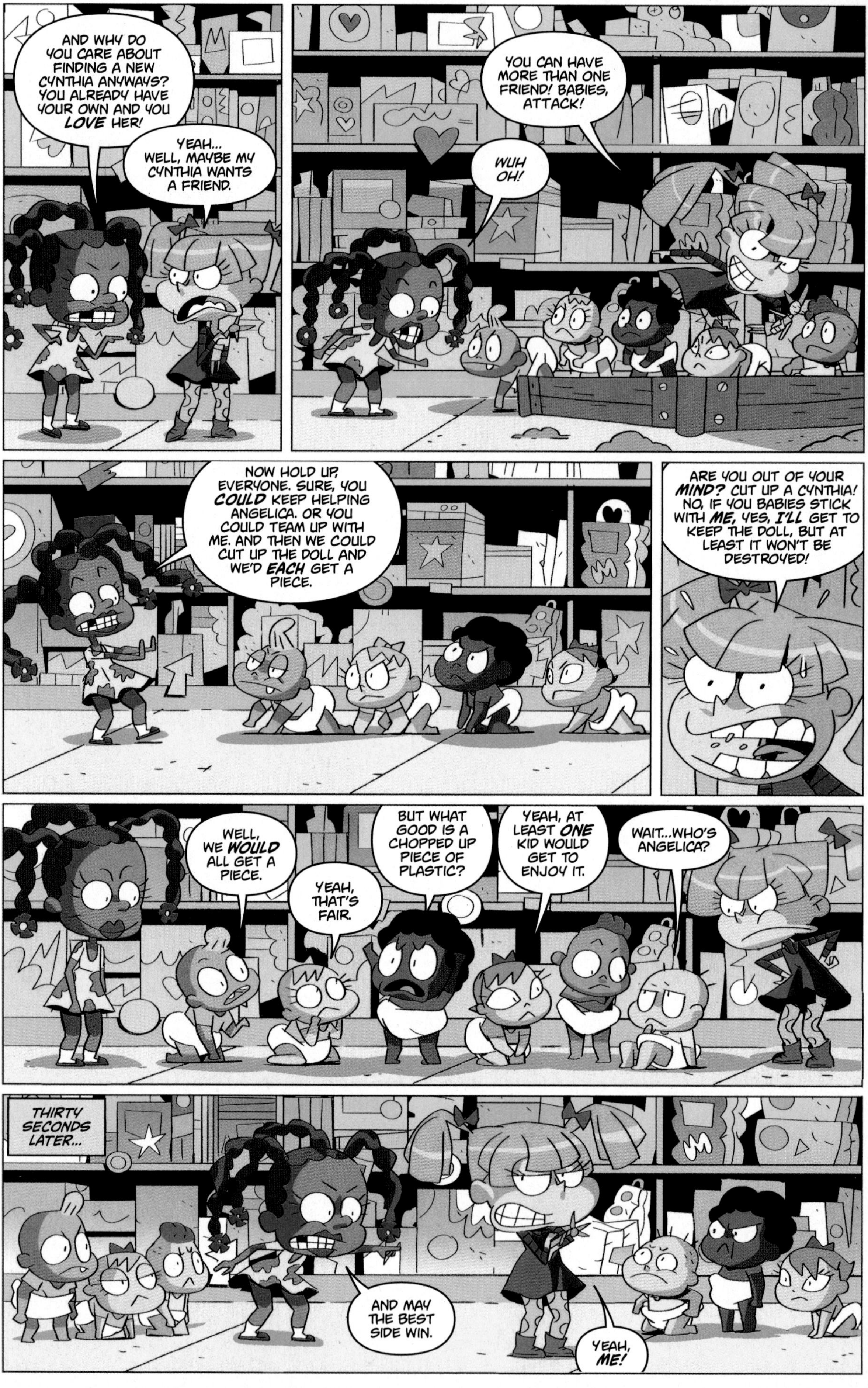

AND WHY DO YOU CARE ABOUT FINDING A NEW CYNTHIA ANYWAYS? YOU ALREADY HAVE YOUR OWN AND YOU LOVE HER!
YEAH... WELL, MAYBE MY CYNTHIA WANTS A FRIEND.
YOU CAN HAVE MORE THAN ONE FRIEND! BABIES, ATTACK!
WUH OH!
NOW HOLD UP, EVERYONE. SURE, YOU COULD KEEP HELPING ANGELICA. OR YOU COULD TEAM UP WITH ME. AND THEN WE COULD CUT UP THE DOLL AND WE'D EACH GET A PIECE.
ARE YOU OUT OF YOUR MIND? CUT UP A CYNTHIA! NO, IF YOU BABIES STICK WITH ME, YES, I'LL GET TO KEEP THE DOLL, BUT AT LEAST IT WON'T BE DESTROYED!
WELL, WE WOULD ALL GET A PIECE.
YEAH, THAT'S FAIR.
BUT WHAT GOOD IS A CHOPPED UP PIECE OF PLASTIC?
YEAH, AT LEAST ONE KID WOULD GET TO ENJOY IT.
WAIT...WHO'S ANGELICA?
THIRTY SECONDS LATER...
AND MAY THE BEST SIDE WIN.
YEAH, ME!

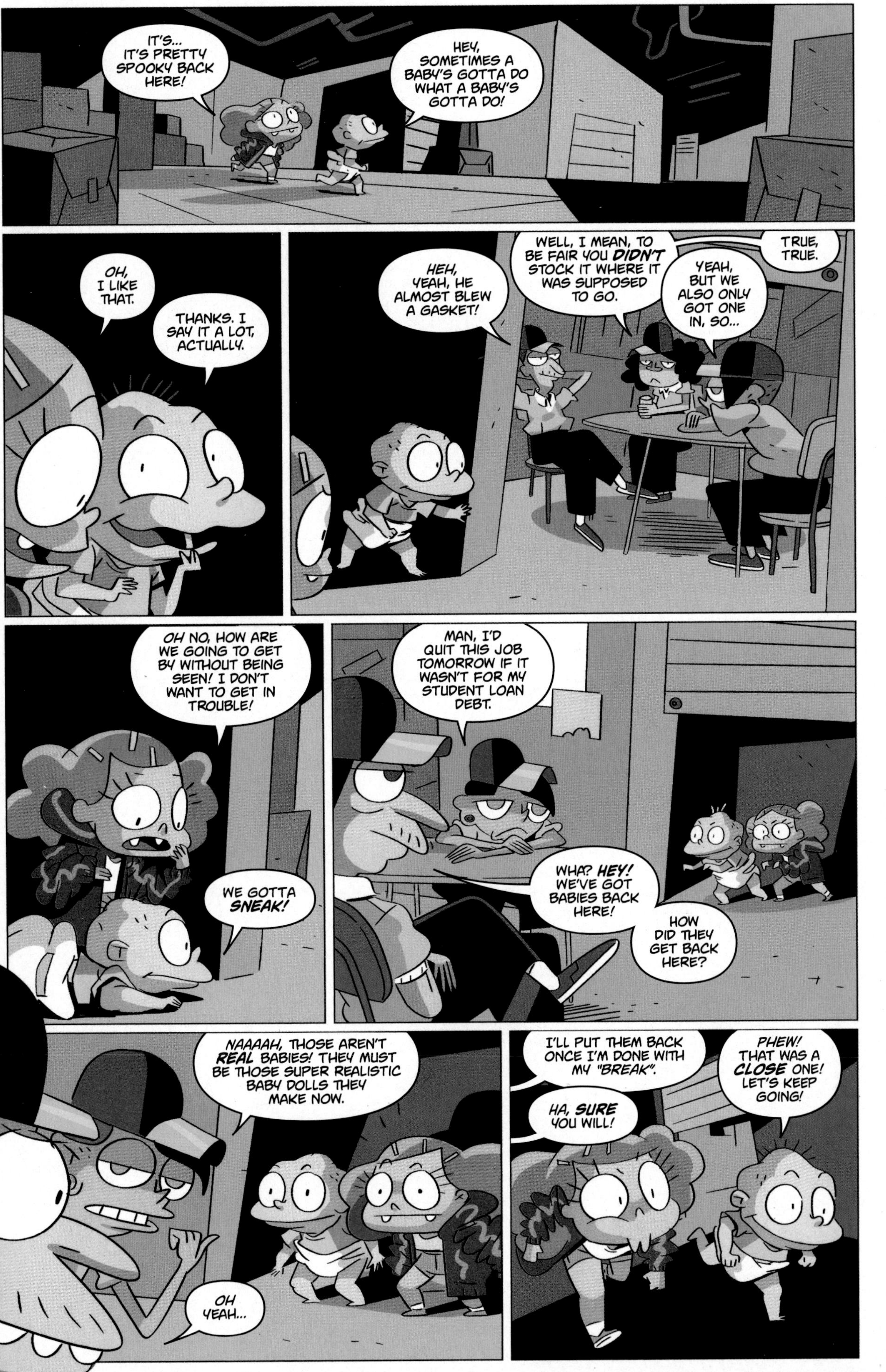
IT'S... IT'S PRETTY SPOOKY BACK HERE!
HEY, SOMETIMES A BABY'S GOTTA DO WHAT A BABY'S GOTTA DO!
OH, I LIKE THAT.
THANKS. I SAY IT A LOT, ACTUALLY.
HEH, YEAH, HE ALMOST BLEW A GASKET!
WELL, I MEAN, TO BE FAIR YOU DIDN'T STOCK IT WHERE IT WAS SUPPOSED TO GO.
TRUE, TRUE.
YEAH, BUT WE ALSO ONLY GOT ONE IN, SO...
OH NO, HOW ARE WE GOING TO GET BY WITHOUT BEING SEEN! I DON'T WANT TO GET IN TROUBLE!
WE GOTTA SNEAK!
MAN, I'D QUIT THIS JOB TOMORROW IF IT WASN'T FOR MY STUDENT LOAN DEBT.
WHA? HEY! WE'VE GOT BABIES BACK HERE!
HOW DID THEY GET BACK HERE?
NAAAAH, THOSE AREN'T REAL BABIES! THEY MUST BE THOSE SUPER REALISTIC BABY DOLLS THEY MAKE NOW.
OH YEAH...
I'LL PUT THEM BACK ONCE I'M DONE WITH MY "BREAK".
HA, SURE YOU WILL!
PHEW! THAT WAS A CLOSE ONE! LET'S KEEP GOING!

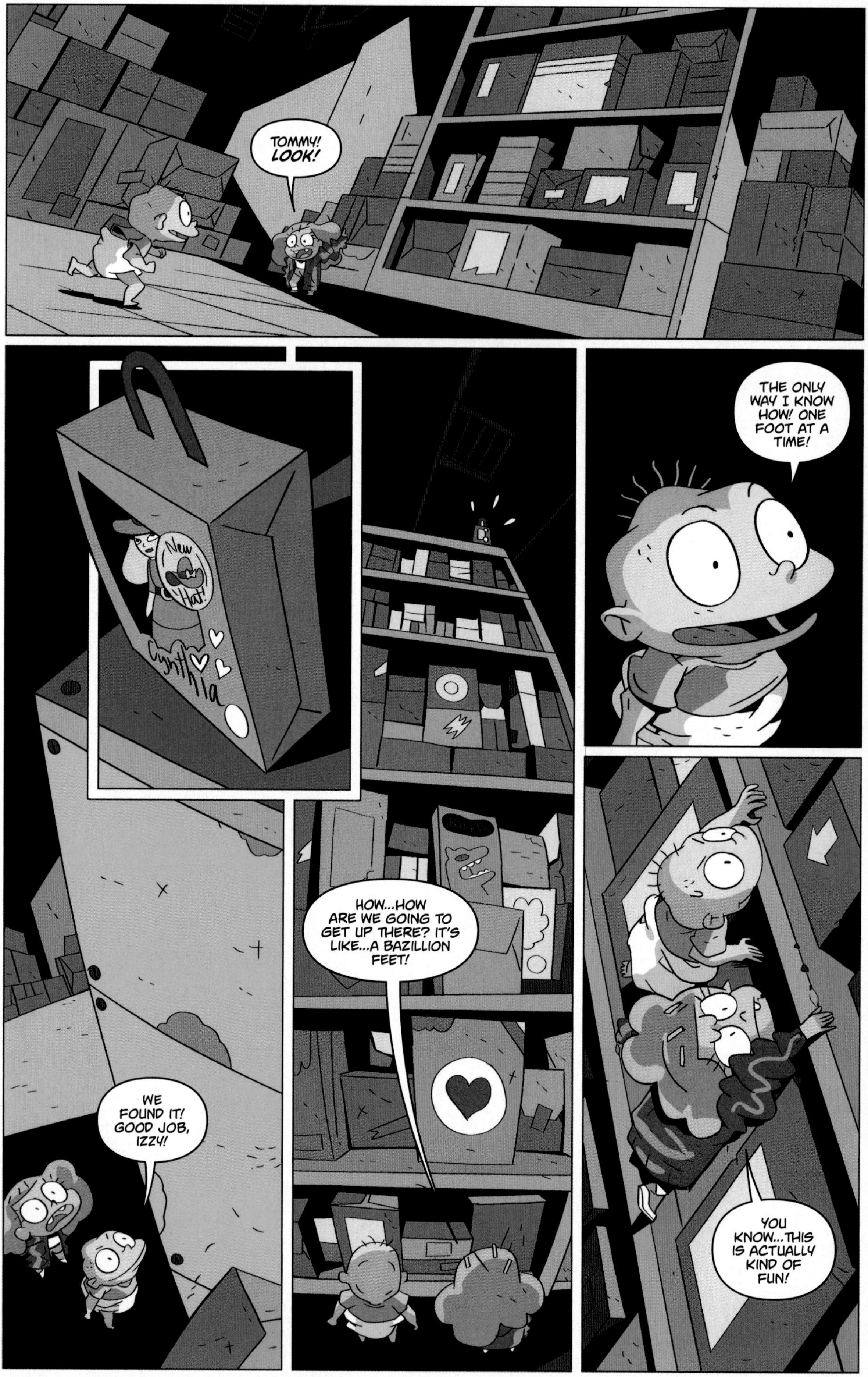
TOMMY! LOOK!
New Hat!
Cynthia
WE FOUND IT! GOOD JOB, IZZY!
HOW...HOW ARE WE GOING TO GET UP THERE? IT'S LIKE...A BAZILLION FEET!
THE ONLY WAY I KNOW HOW! ONE FOOT AT A TIME!
YOU KNOW...THIS IS ACTUALLY KIND OF FUN!

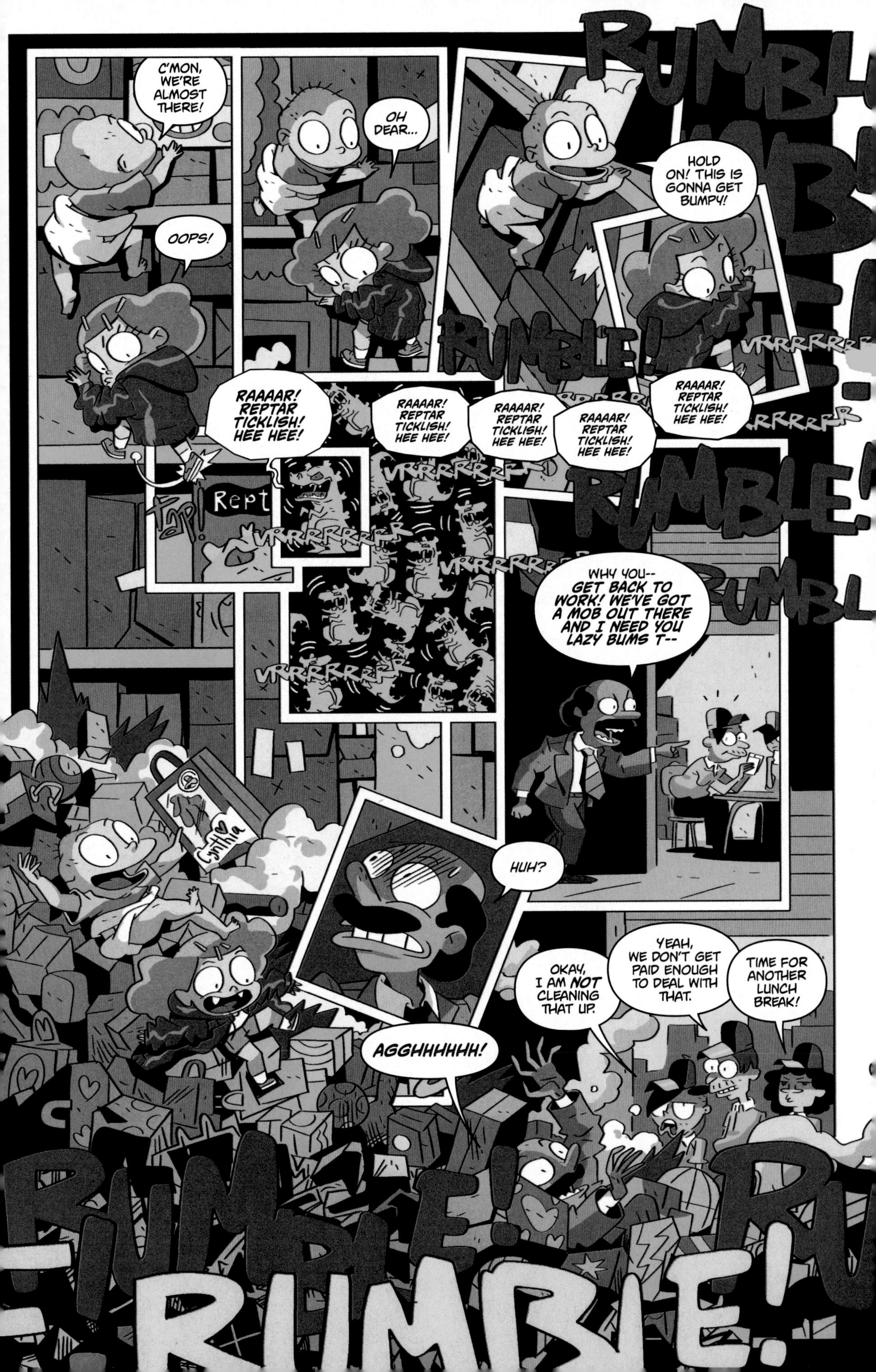
C'MON, WE'RE ALMOST THERE!
OOPS!
OH DEAR...
HOLD ON! THIS IS GONNA GET BUMPY!
RUMBLE
RUMBLE!
VRRRRRRR
RAAAAR! REPTAR TICKLISH! HEE HEE!
RAAAAR! REPTAR TICKLISH! HEE HEE!
RAAAAR! REPTAR TICKLISH! HEE HEE!
RAAAAR! REPTAR TICKLISH! HEE HEE!
RAAAAR! REPTAR TICKLISH! HEE HEE!
POP!
Rept
VRRRRRRR
VRRRRRRR
VRRRRRRR
RUMBLE!
RUMBL
WHY YOU-- GET BACK TO WORK! WE'VE GOT A MOB OUT THERE AND I NEED YOU LAZY BUMS T--
Cynthia
HUH?
OKAY, I AM NOT CLEANING THAT UP.
YEAH, WE DON'T GET PAID ENOUGH TO DEAL WITH THAT.
TIME FOR ANOTHER LUNCH BREAK!
AGGHHHHHH!
RUMBLE!
RUMBLE!

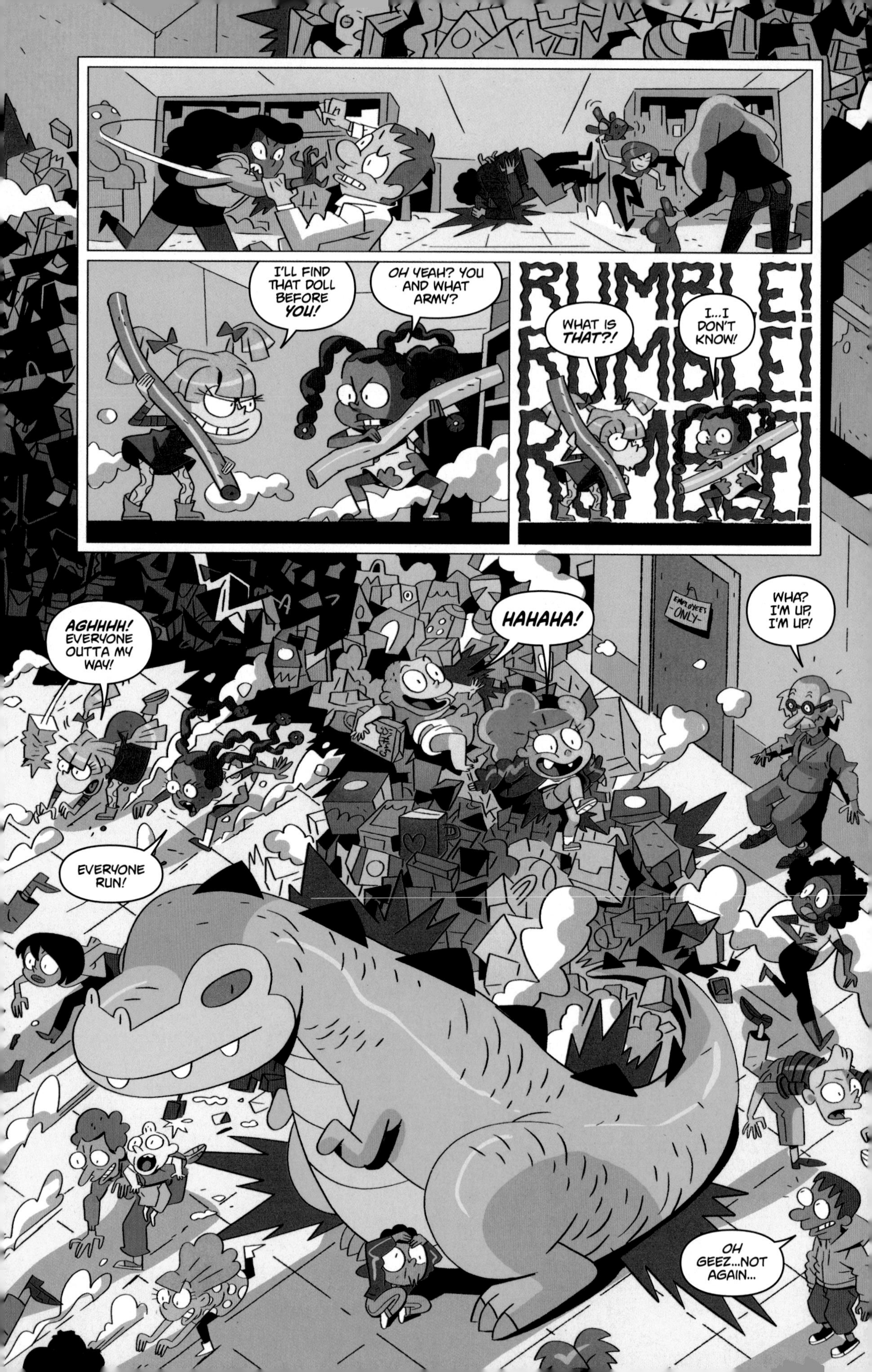
I'LL FIND THAT DOLL BEFORE *YOU!*
OH YEAH? YOU AND WHAT ARMY?
RUMBLE! RUMBLE! RUMBLE!
WHAT IS *THAT?!*
I...I DON'T KNOW!
AGHHHH! EVERYONE OUTTA MY WAY!
HAHAHA!
EMPLOYEES -ONLY-
WHA? I'M UP, I'M UP!
EVERYONE RUN!
OH GEEZ...NOT AGAIN...

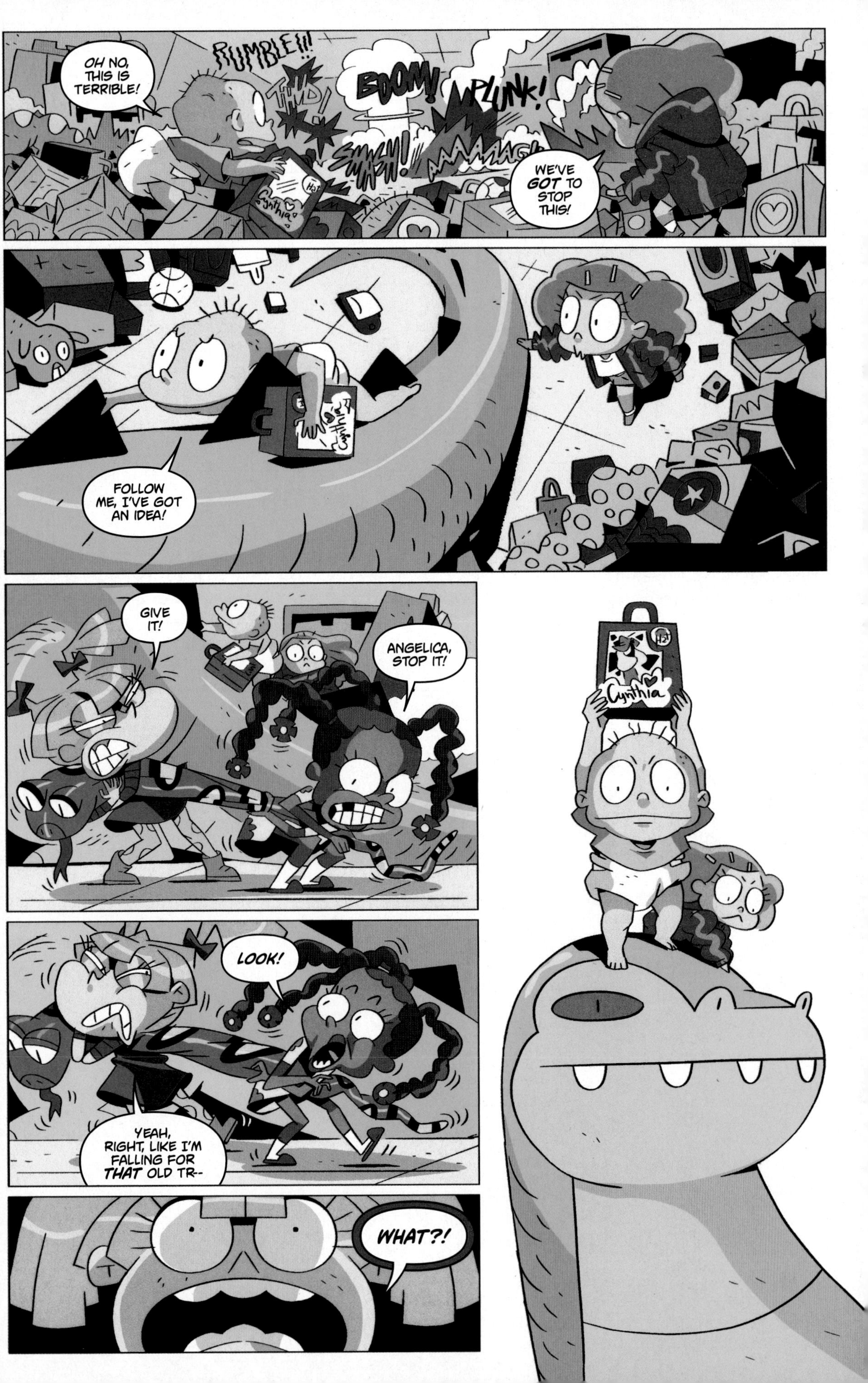

OH NO, THIS IS TERRIBLE!
RUMBLE!!!
THUD!
BOOM!
PLUNK!
SMASH!
AAAAAAGH!
WE'VE GOT TO STOP THIS!
FOLLOW ME, I'VE GOT AN IDEA!
GIVE IT!
ANGELICA, STOP IT!
LOOK!
YEAH, RIGHT, LIKE I'M FALLING FOR THAT OLD TR-
WHAT?!
Cynthia

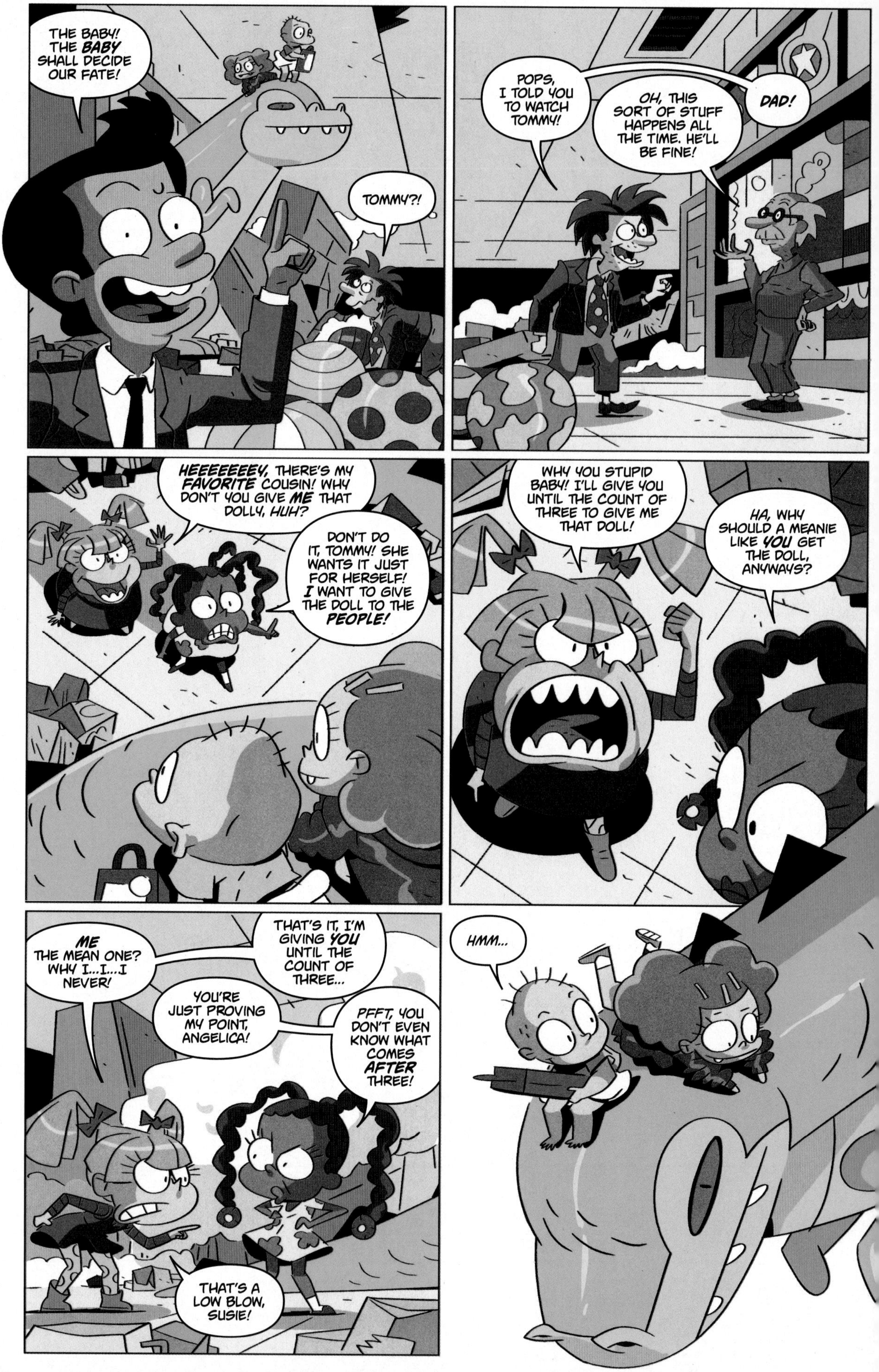
THE BABY! THE BABY SHALL DECIDE OUR FATE!
TOMMY?!
POPS, I TOLD YOU TO WATCH TOMMY!
OH, THIS SORT OF STUFF HAPPENS ALL THE TIME. HE'LL BE FINE!
DAD!
HEEEEEEEY, THERE'S MY FAVORITE COUSIN! WHY DON'T YOU GIVE ME THAT DOLLY, HUH?
DON'T DO IT, TOMMY! SHE WANTS IT JUST FOR HERSELF! I WANT TO GIVE THE DOLL TO THE PEOPLE!
WHY YOU STUPID BABY! I'LL GIVE YOU UNTIL THE COUNT OF THREE TO GIVE ME THAT DOLL!
HA, WHY SHOULD A MEANIE LIKE YOU GET THE DOLL, ANYWAYS?
ME THE MEAN ONE? WHY I...I...I NEVER!
THAT'S IT, I'M GIVING YOU UNTIL THE COUNT OF THREE...
YOU'RE JUST PROVING MY POINT, ANGELICA!
PFFT, YOU DON'T EVEN KNOW WHAT COMES AFTER THREE!
THAT'S A LOW BLOW, SUSIE!
HMM...

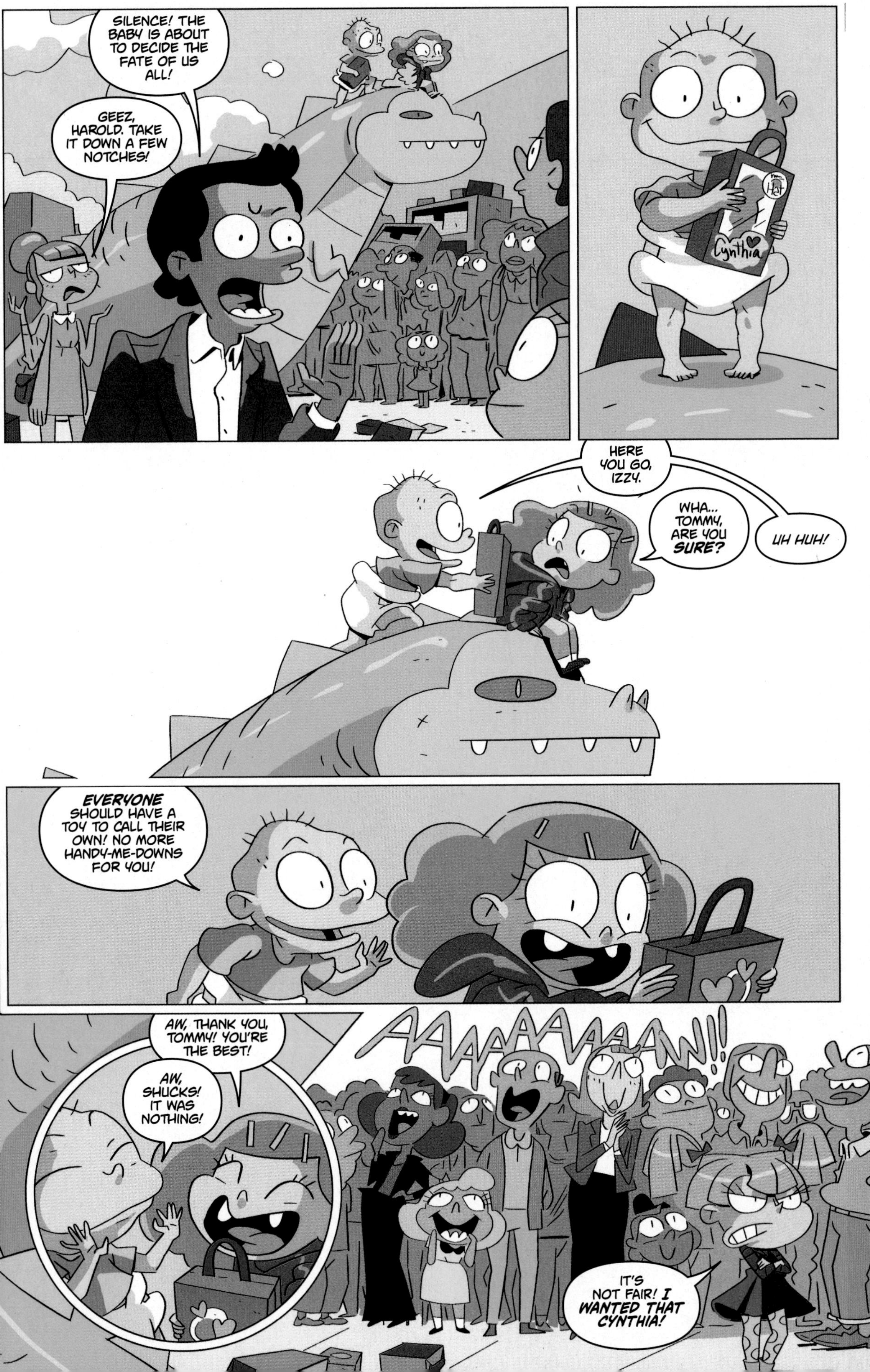
SILENCE! THE BABY IS ABOUT TO DECIDE THE FATE OF US ALL!
GEEZ, HAROLD. TAKE IT DOWN A FEW NOTCHES!
Hat
Cynthia
HERE YOU GO, IZZY.
WHA... TOMMY, ARE YOU SURE?
UH HUH!
EVERYONE SHOULD HAVE A TOY TO CALL THEIR OWN! NO MORE HANDY-ME-DOWNS FOR YOU!
AW, THANK YOU, TOMMY! YOU'RE THE BEST!
AW, SHUCKS! IT WAS NOTHING!
AAAAAAAAAW!!
IT'S NOT FAIR! I WANTED THAT CYNTHIA!

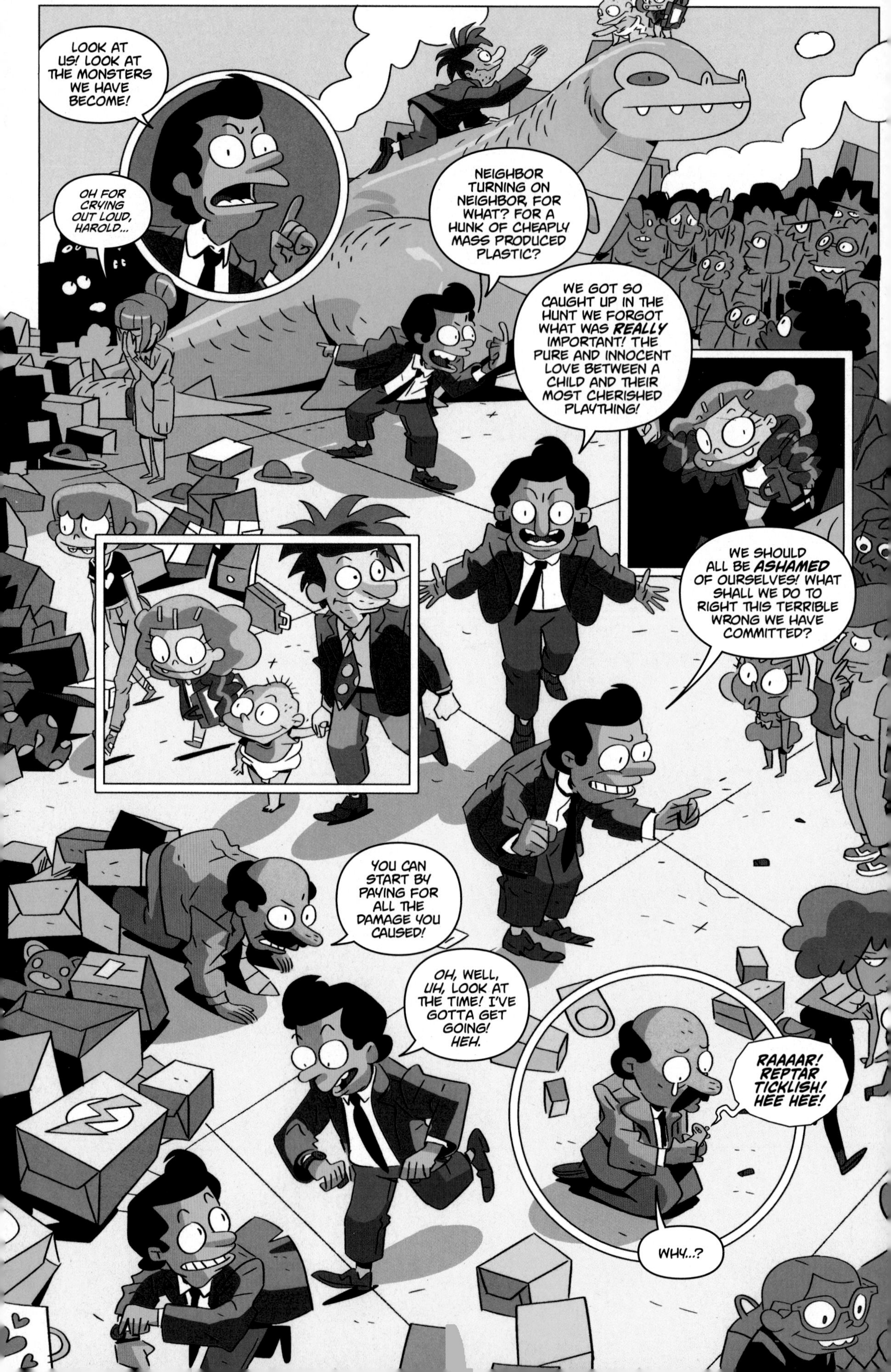
LOOK AT US! LOOK AT THE MONSTERS WE HAVE BECOME!
OH FOR CRYING OUT LOUD, HAROLD...
NEIGHBOR TURNING ON NEIGHBOR, FOR WHAT? FOR A HUNK OF CHEAPLY MASS PRODUCED PLASTIC?
WE GOT SO CAUGHT UP IN THE HUNT WE FORGOT WHAT WAS REALLY IMPORTANT! THE PURE AND INNOCENT LOVE BETWEEN A CHILD AND THEIR MOST CHERISHED PLAYTHING!
WE SHOULD ALL BE ASHAMED OF OURSELVES! WHAT SHALL WE DO TO RIGHT THIS TERRIBLE WRONG WE HAVE COMMITTED?
YOU CAN START BY PAYING FOR ALL THE DAMAGE YOU CAUSED!
OH, WELL, UH, LOOK AT THE TIME! I'VE GOTTA GET GOING! HEH.
RAAAAR! REPTAR TICKLISH! HEE HEE!
WHY...?

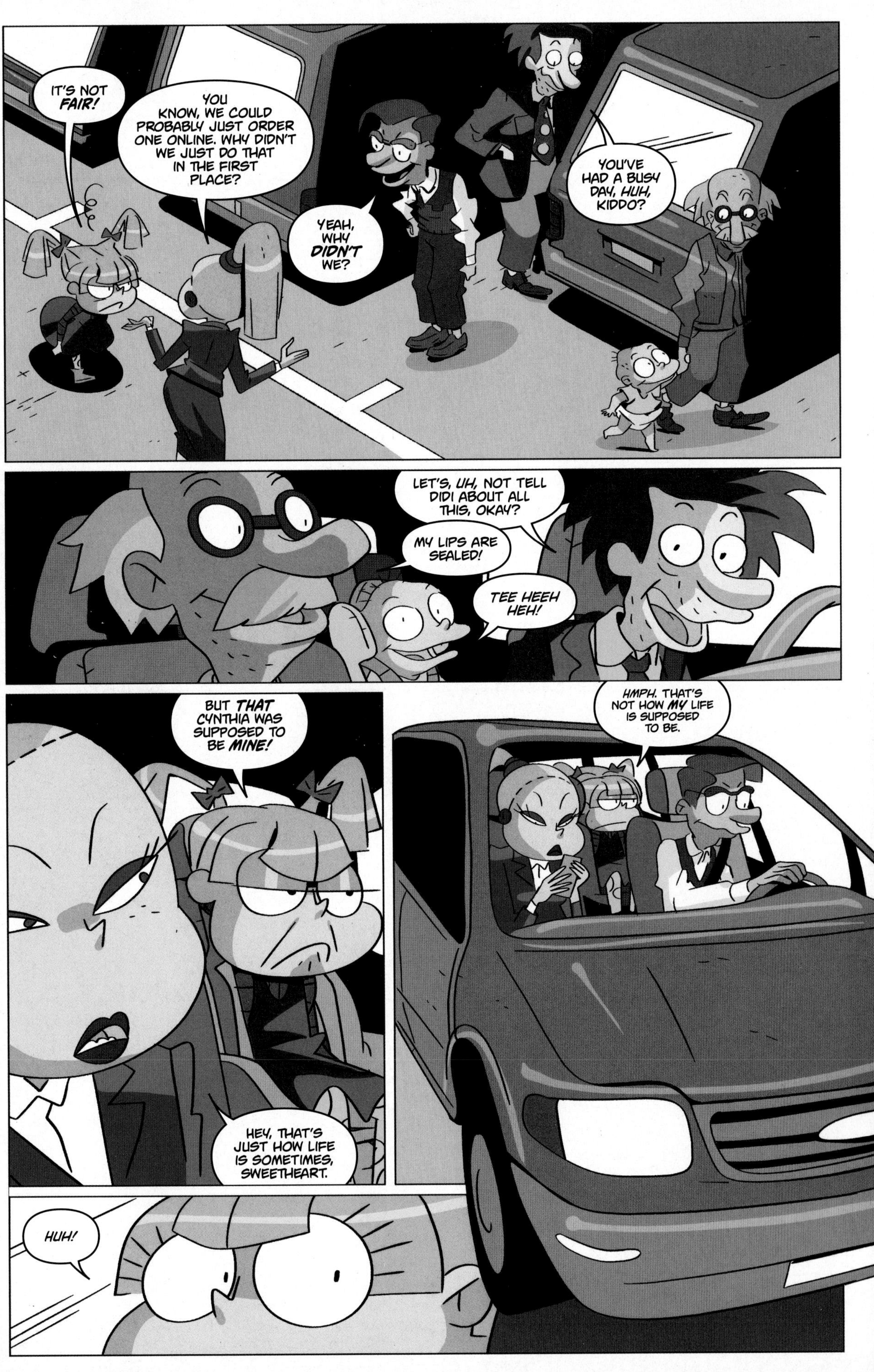
IT'S NOT *FAIR!*
YOU KNOW, WE COULD PROBABLY JUST ORDER ONE ONLINE. WHY DIDN'T WE JUST DO THAT IN THE FIRST PLACE?
YEAH, WHY *DIDN'T* WE?
YOU'VE HAD A BUSY DAY, *HUH,* KIDDO?
LET'S, *UH,* NOT TELL DIDI ABOUT ALL THIS, OKAY?
MY LIPS ARE SEALED!
TEE HEEH HEH!
BUT *THAT* CYNTHIA WAS SUPPOSED TO BE *MINE!*
HEY, THAT'S JUST HOW LIFE IS SOMETIMES, SWEETHEART.
HMPH. THAT'S NOT HOW *MY* LIFE IS SUPPOSED TO BE.
HUH!

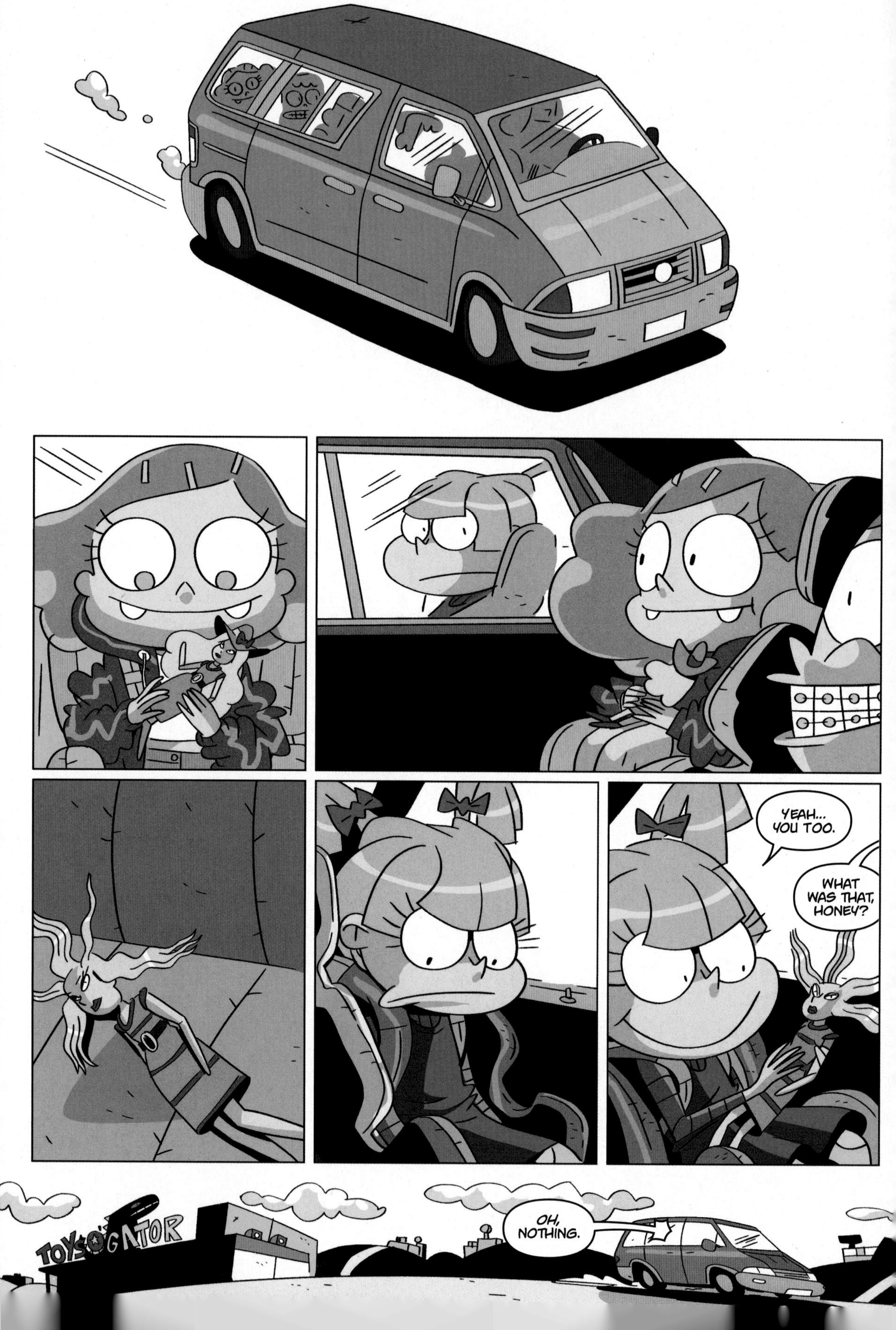
YEAH... YOU TOO.
WHAT WAS THAT, HONEY?
TOYS O' GATOR
OH, NOTHING.

I'M THE YOUNGEST OF SEVEN.
SO EVERYTHING I HAVE IS A
HANDY-ME-DOWN!

COVER
GALLERY

ISSUE ONE COVER BY **JORGE CORONA**

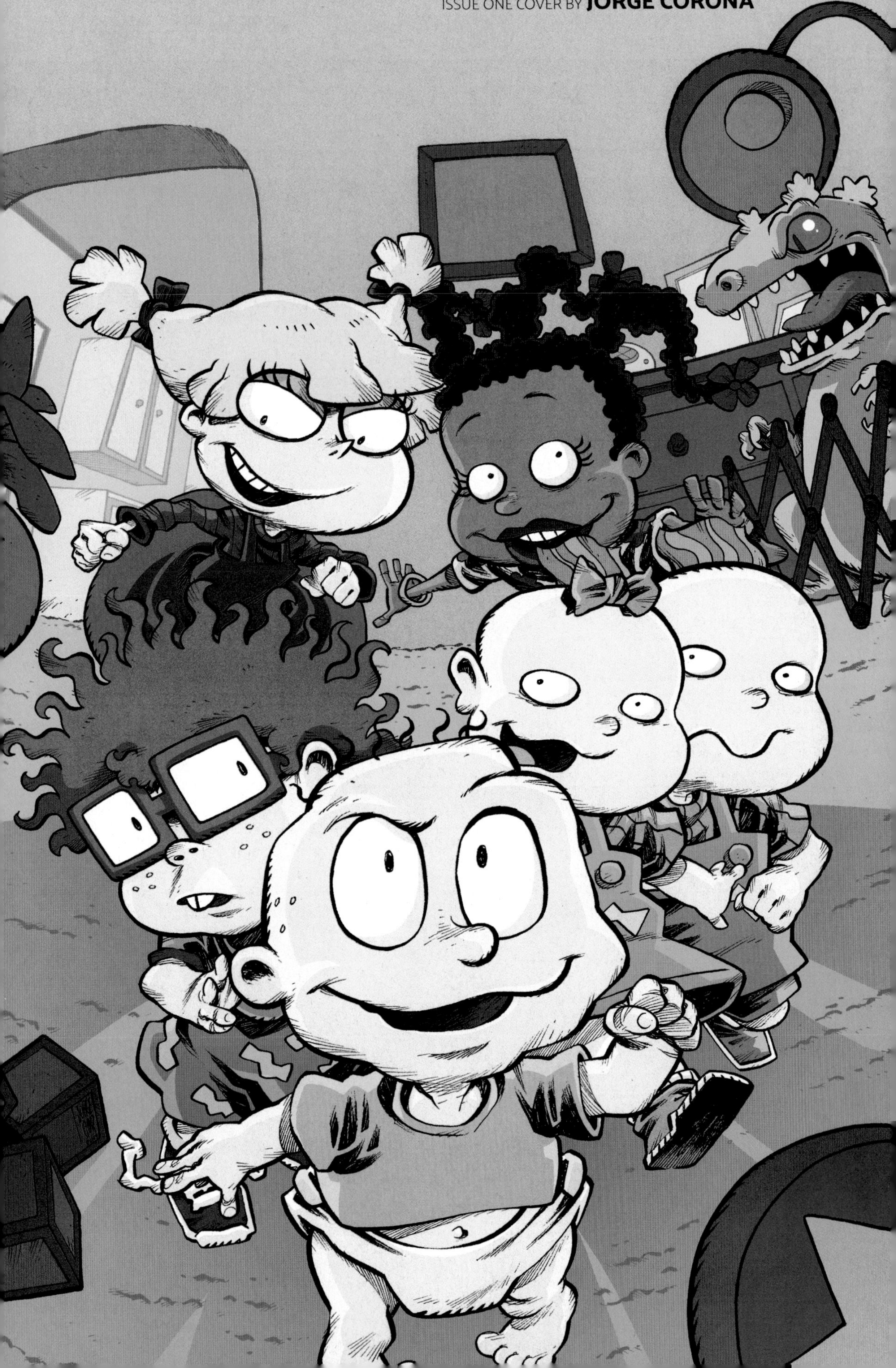

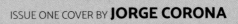

ISSUE TWO COVER BY **JORGE CORONA**

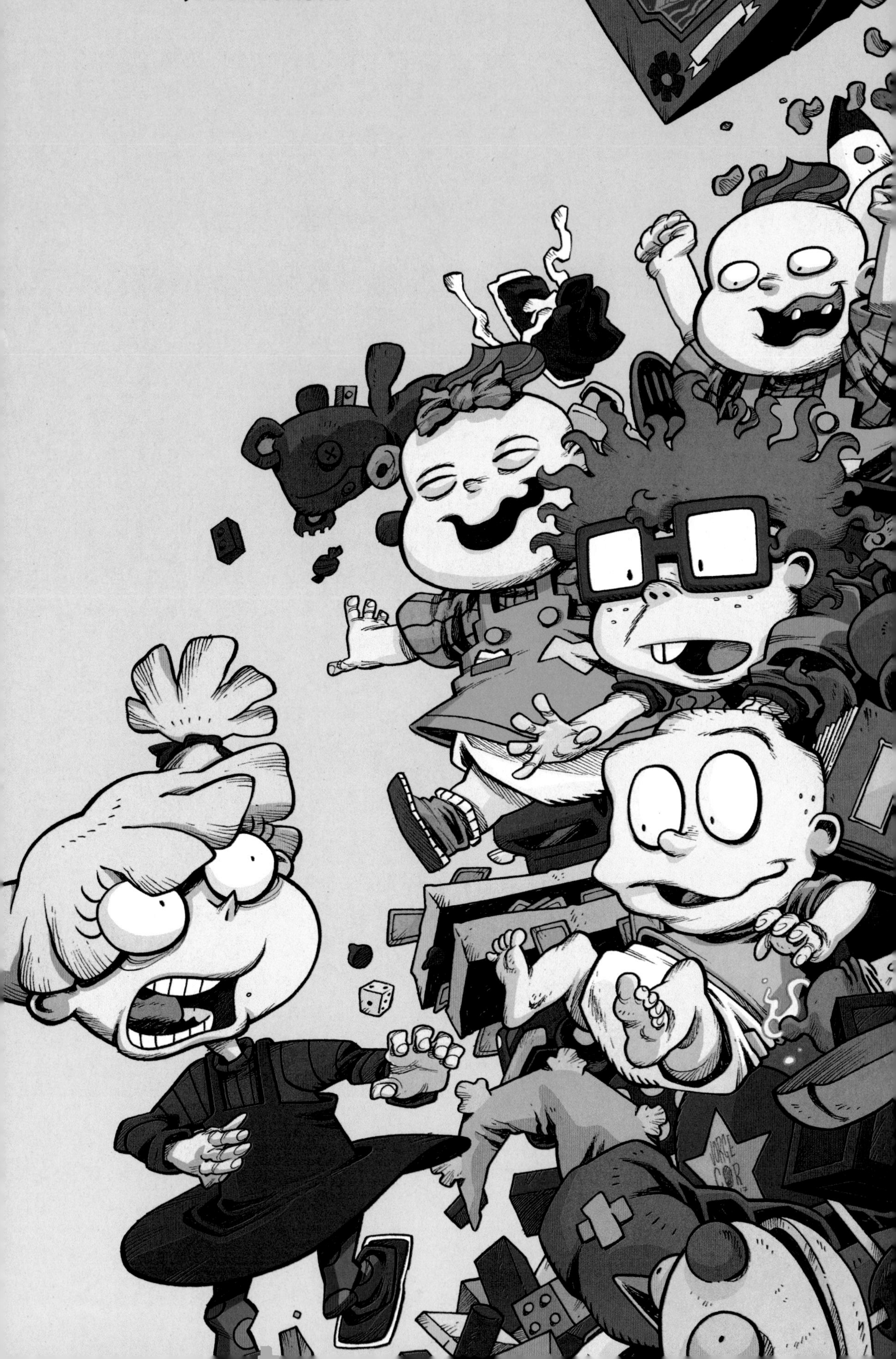

ISSUE THREE COVER BY **JORGE CORONA**

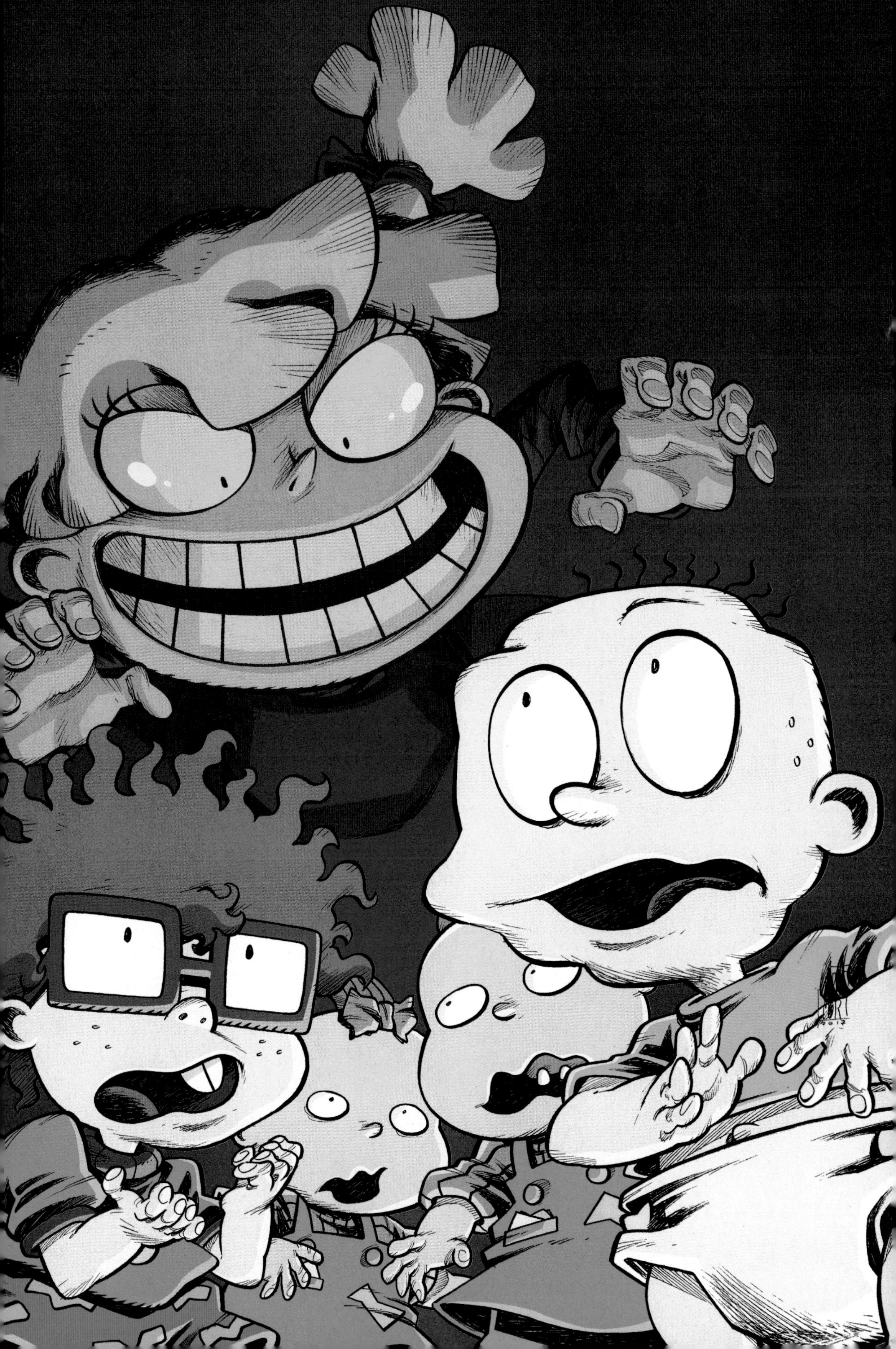

ISSUE FOUR COVER BY **JORGE CORONA**

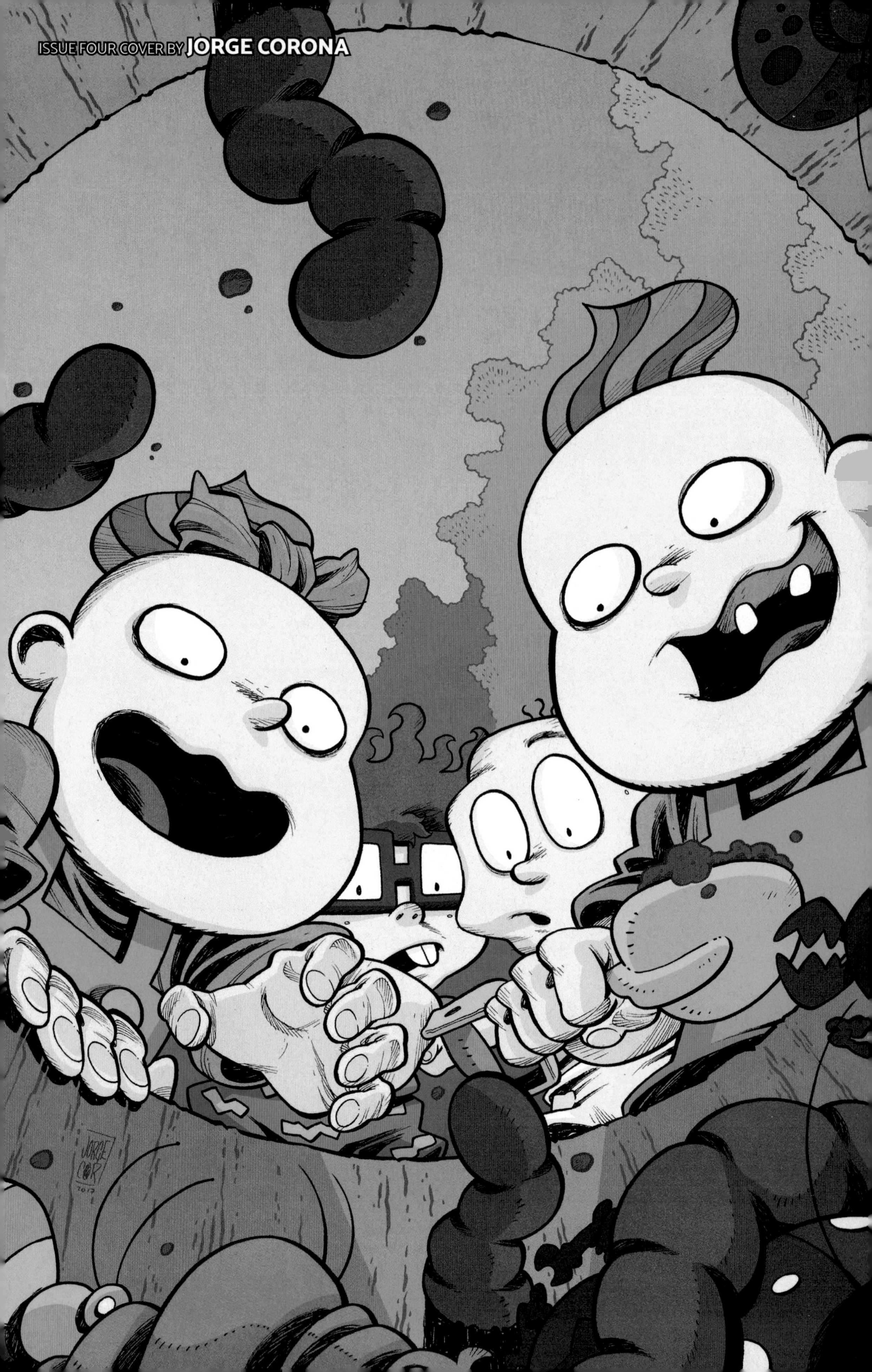

ISSUE ONE SUBSCRIPTION COVER BY **SHELLI PAROLINE** & **BRADEN LAMB**
WITH LUNCHBOX DESIGN BY **CAITLYN INGOLDSBY**

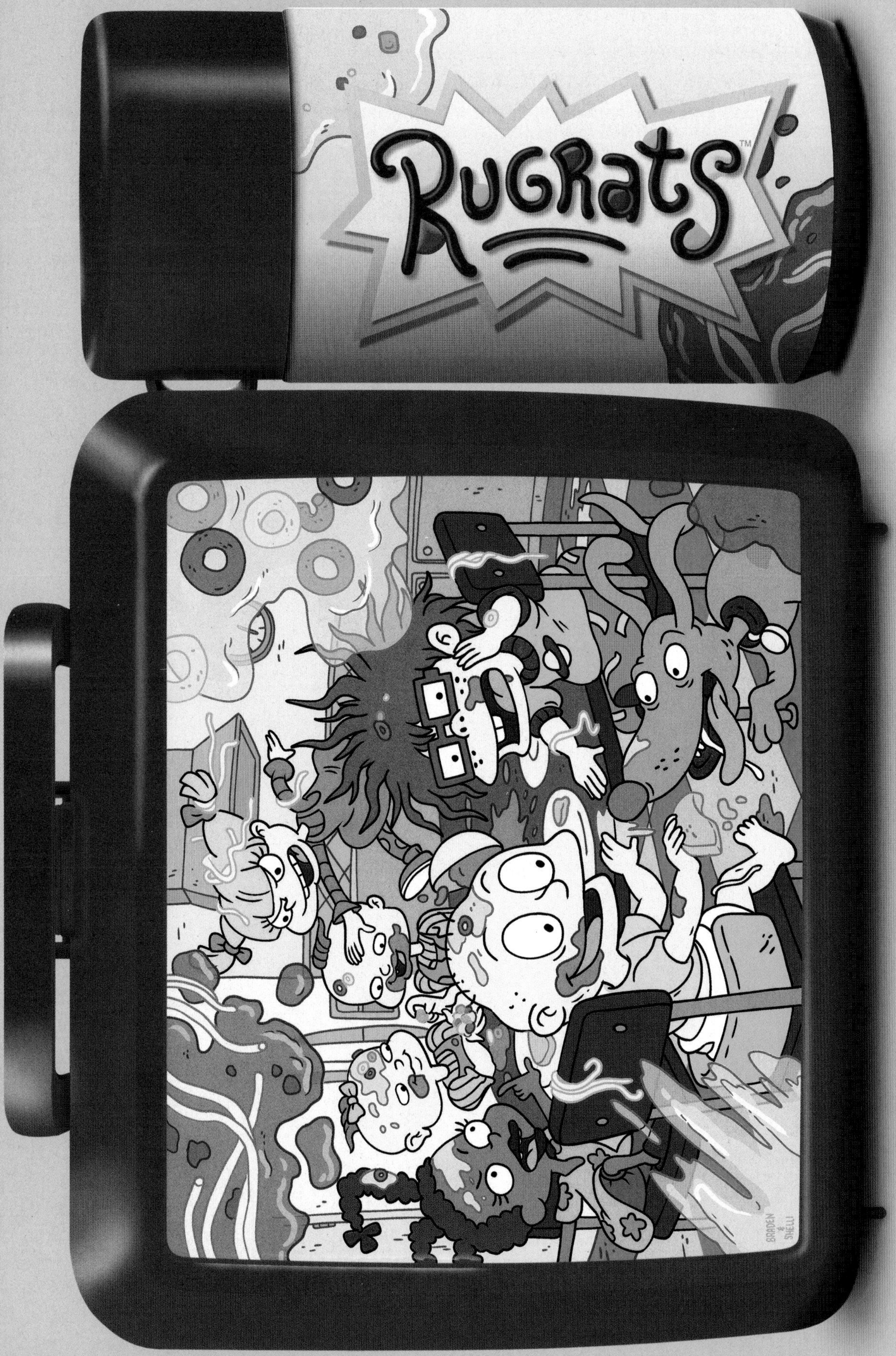
RUGRATS™
BRADEN & SHELLI

ISSUE TWO SUBSCRIPTION COVER BY **ZANDER CANNON**
WITH LUNCHBOX DESIGN BY **CAITLYN INGOLDSBY**

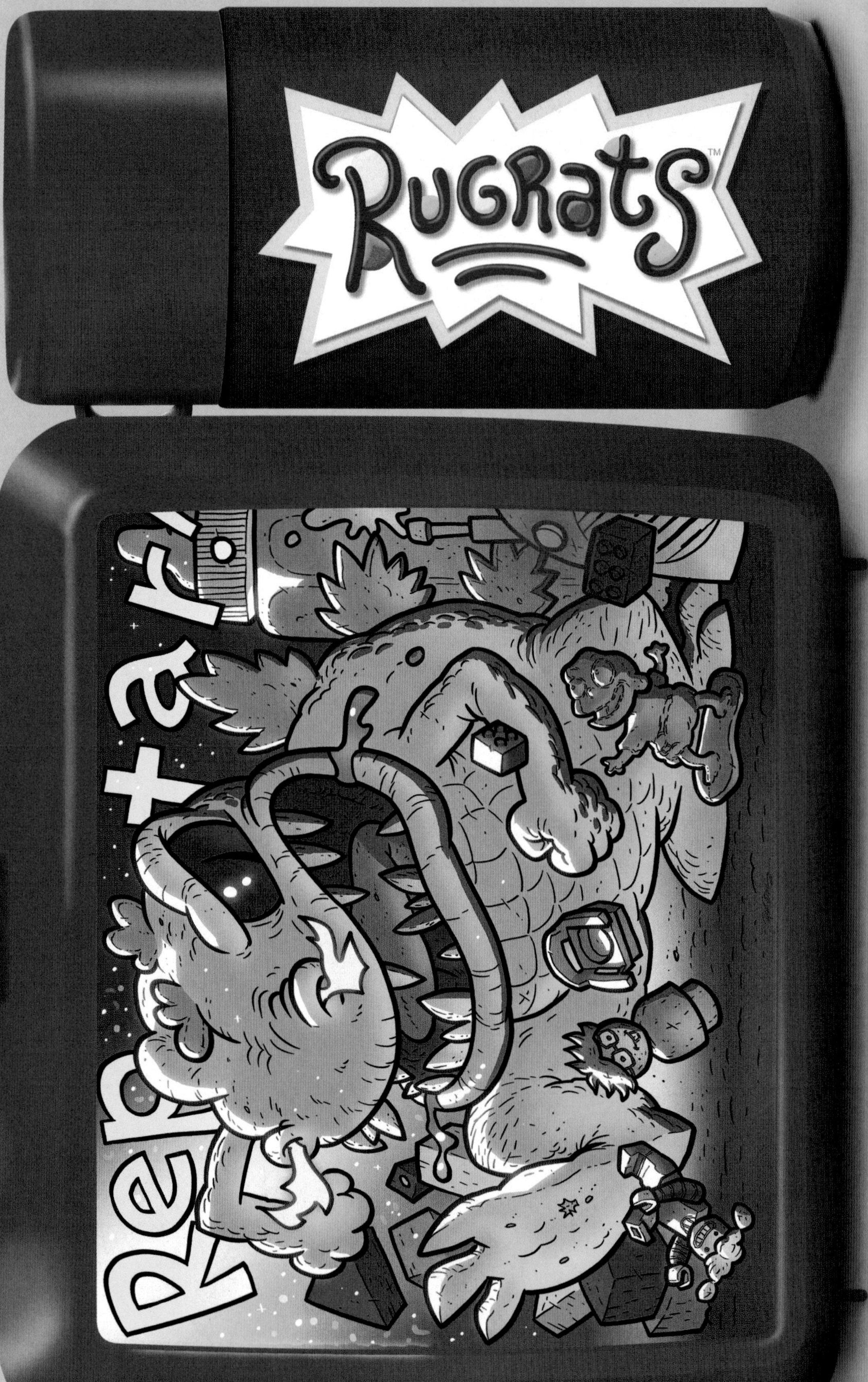
Rugrats™

ISSUE THREE SUBSCRIPTION COVER BY **CAITLYN ROSE BOYLE**
WITH LUNCHBOX DESIGN BY **CAITLYN INGOLDSBY**

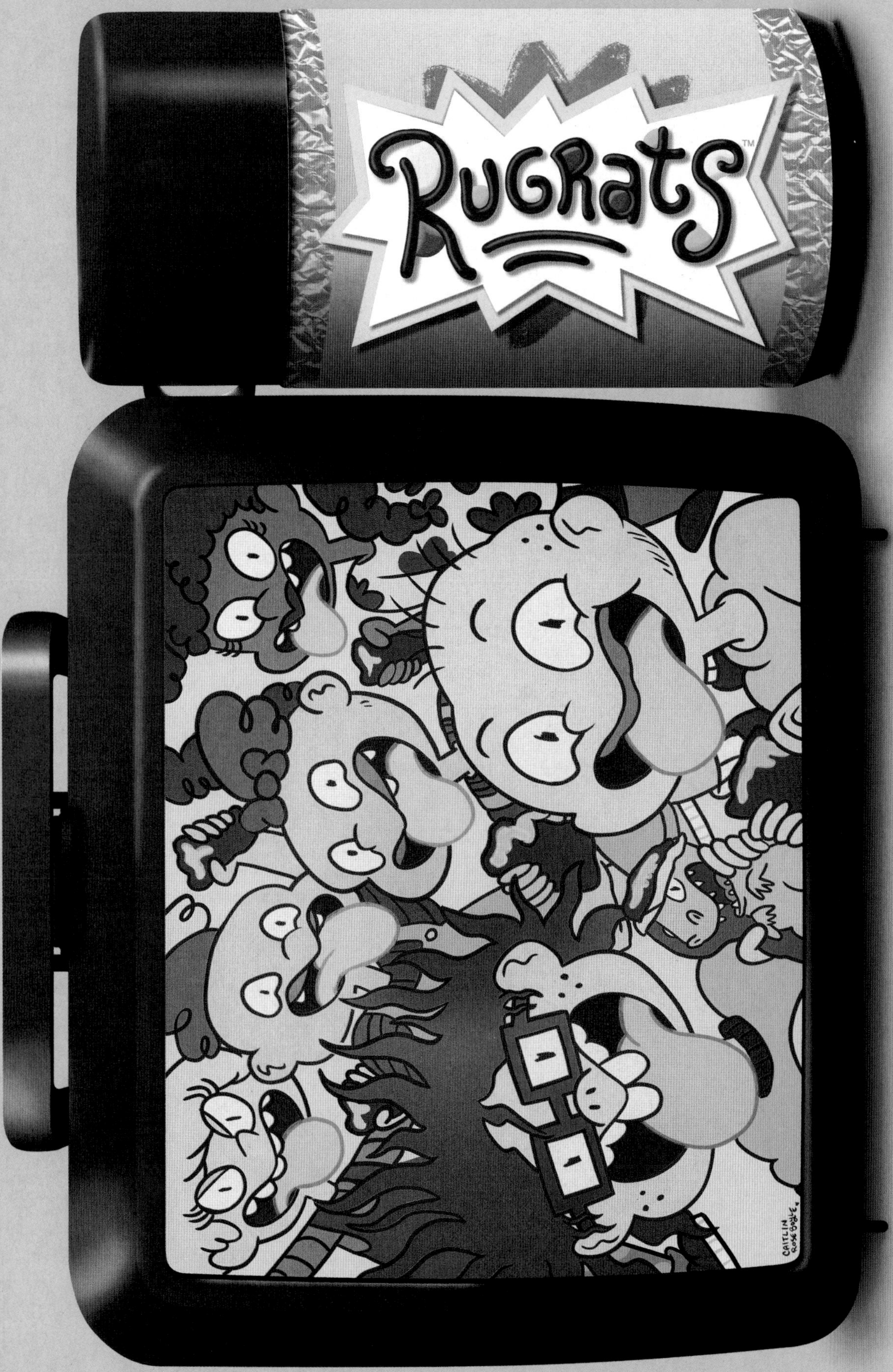
RUGRATS™
CAITLIN ROSE BOYLE

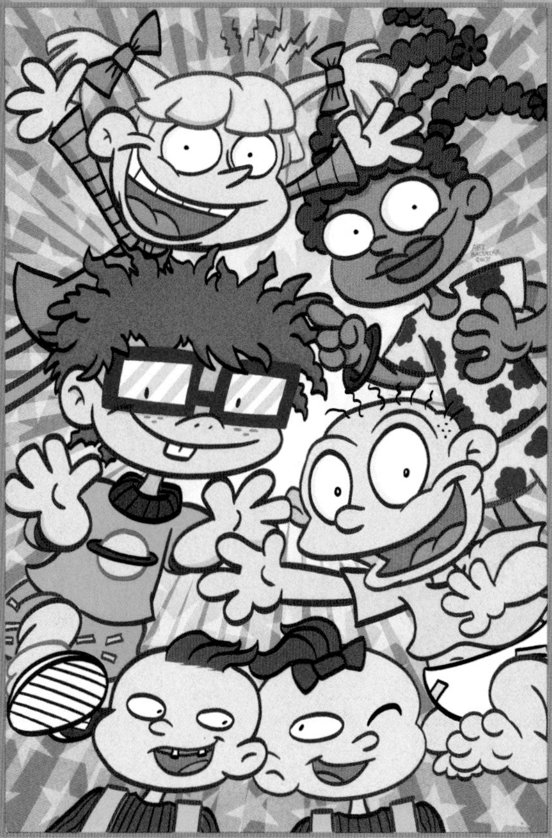

ISSUE ONE VARIANT COVER BY
ART BALTAZAR

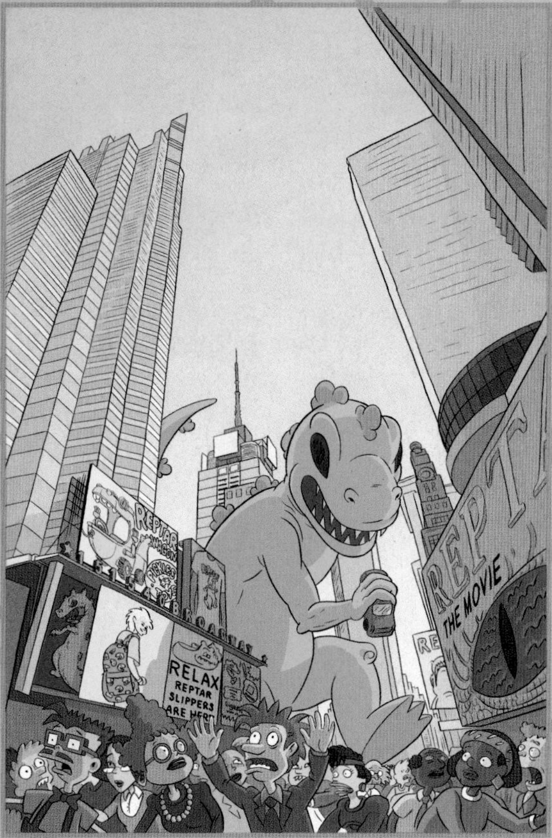
RELAX
REPTAR
SLIPPERS
ARE HERE!
REPTAR
THE MOVIE

ISSUE ONE NEW YORK COMIC CON EXCLUSIVE COVER BY
MALACHI WARD

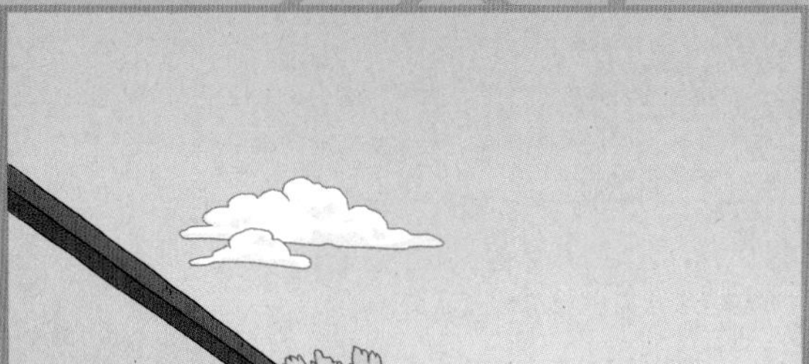

ISSUE ONE FRIED PIE EXCLUSIVE COVER BY
MEREDITH GRAN
WITH COLORS BY **ELEONORA BRUNI**

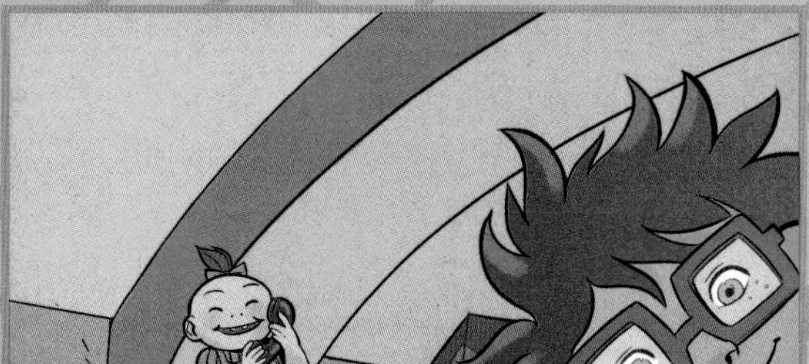
A

ISSUE ONE NEW YORK COMIC CON DIAMOND
RETAILER SUMMIT EXCLUSIVE COVER BY
NATACHA BUSTOS

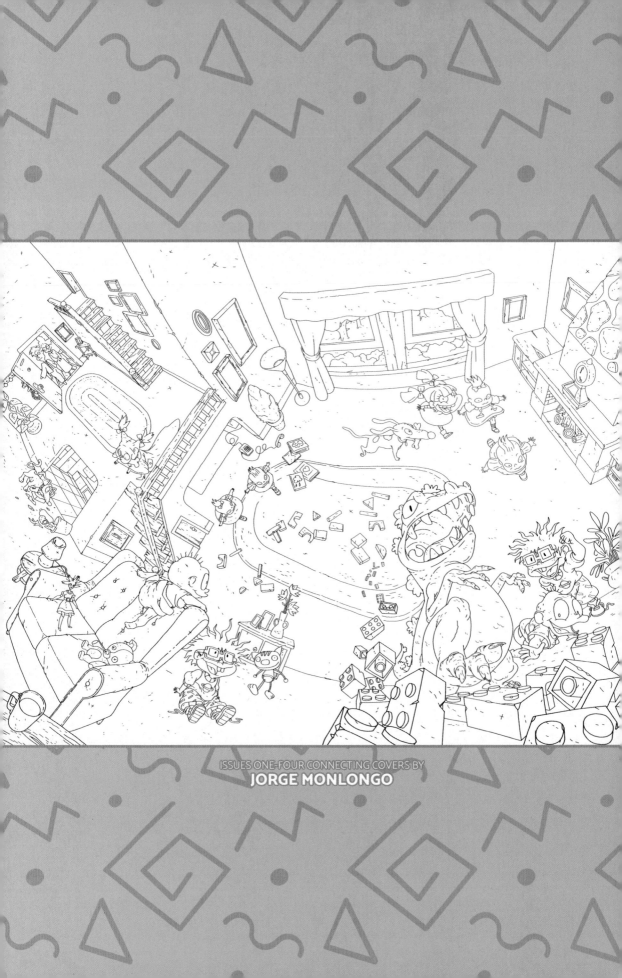

ISSUES ONE-FOUR CONNECTING COVERS BY
JORGE MONLONGO

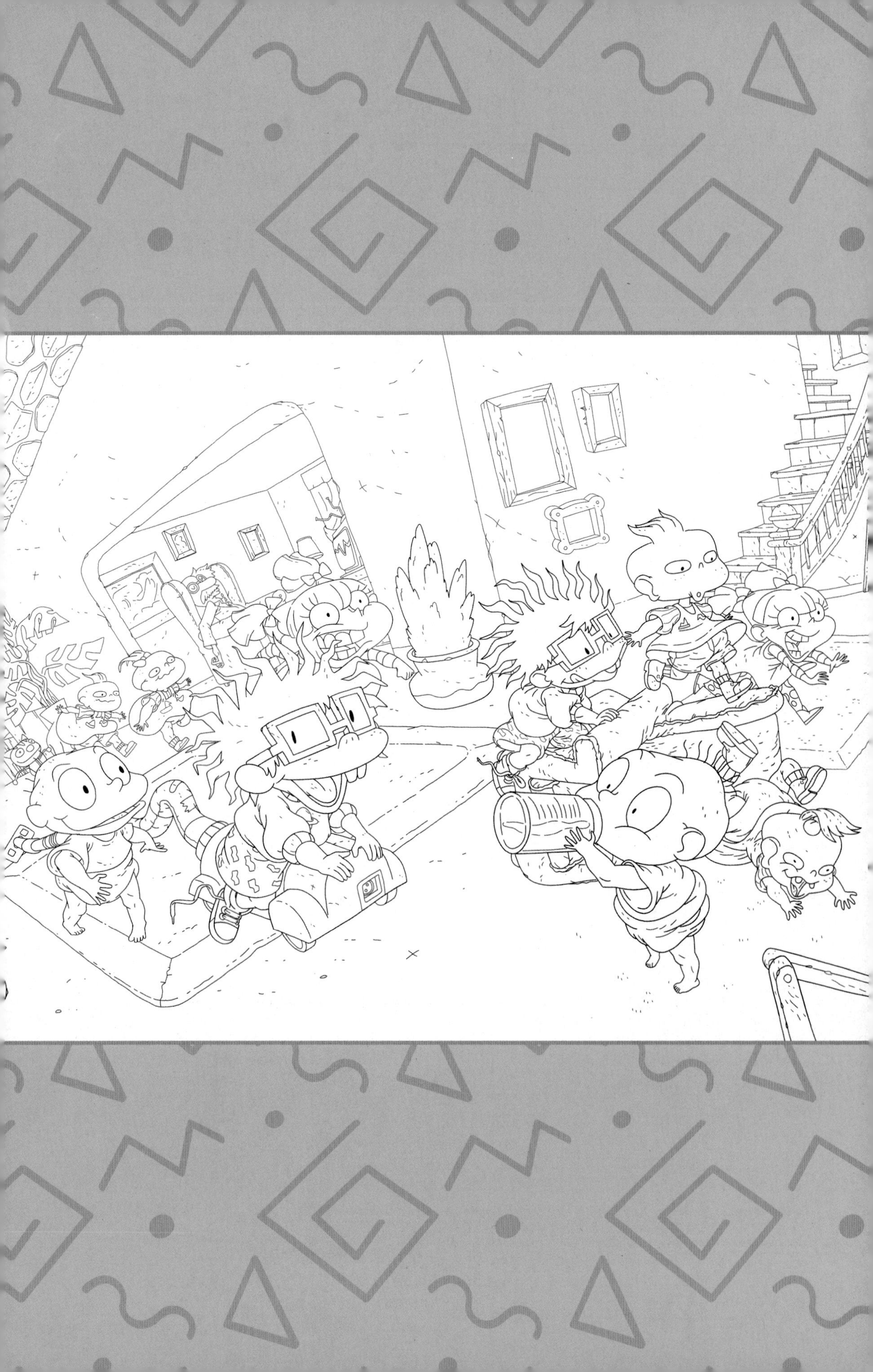

DISCOVER
EXPLOSIVE NEW WORLDS

ADVENTURE TIME

sam sykes · selina espiritu · sarah stern
BRAVE CHEF BRIANNA

KELLY THOMPSON BRIANNE DROUHARD M. VICTORIA ROBADO
MEGA PRINCESS

THE NOT-SO SECRET SOCIETY
DALEY · CRAFTS · CLARK · BRUNI

OVER THE GARDEN WALL

STEVEN UNIVERSE
VOLUME ONE

kaboom!™

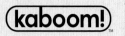

AVAILABLE AT YOUR LOCAL COMICS SHOP AND BOOKSTORE

To find a comics shop in your area, call 1-888-266-4226

WWW.**BOOM-STUDIOS**.COM

Adventure Time
Pendleton Ward and Others
Volume 1
ISBN: 978-1-60886-280-1 | $14.99 US
Volume 2
ISBN: 978-1-60886-323-5 | $14.99 US
Adventure Time: Islands
ISBN: 978-1-60886-972-5 | $9.99 US

The Amazing World of Gumball
Ben Bocquelet and Others
Volume 1
ISBN: 978-1-60886-488-1 | $14.99 US
Volume 2
ISBN: 978-1-60886-793-6 | $14.99 US

Brave Chef Brianna
Sam Sykes, Selina Espiritu
ISBN: 978-1-68415-050-2 | $14.99 US

Mega Princess
Kelly Thompson, Brianne Drouhard
ISBN: 978-1-68415-007-6 | $14.99 US

The Not-So Secret Society
Matthew Daley, Arlene Daley, Wook Jin Clark
ISBN: 978-1-60886-997-8 | $9.99 US

Over the Garden Wall
Patrick McHale, Jim Campbell and Others
Volume 1
ISBN: 978-1-60886-940-4 | $14.99 US
Volume 2
ISBN: 978-1-68415-006-9 | $14.99 US

Steven Universe
Rebecca Sugar and Others
Volume 1
ISBN: 978-1-60886-706-6 | $14.99 US
Volume 2
ISBN: 978-1-60886-796-7 | $14.99 US

Steven Universe & The Crystal Gems
ISBN: 978-1-60886-921-3 | $14.99 US

Steven Universe: Too Cool for School
ISBN: 978-1-60886-771-4 | $14.99 US